THE EXCLUSION PRINCIPLE

The Exclusion Principle

by

LEONA GOM

Leona Gom

*to Clara,
with much
love,
Leona*

SUMACH
PRESS

LIBRARY AND ARCHIVES CANADA CATALOGUING IN PUBLICATION

Gom, Leona, 1946-

The Exclusion Principle: a novel / by Leona Gom.

ISBN 978-1-894549-79-0

I. Title.

PS8563.O83E94 2009   C813'.54   C2009-900277-9

This is a work of fiction. The Joint Astronomy Centre and the James Clerk Maxwell Telescope in Hawaii are real, but the events depicted there are entirely fictitious. The Astronomy Department at UBC in Canada is in reality still a part of the Physics Department. Any resemblance to real people is wholly coincidental.

Edited by Jennifer Day
Design by Elizabeth Martin
Cover photo: STScI, NASA

Sumach Press acknowledges the support of the Canada Council for the Arts and the Ontario Arts Council for our publishing program. We acknowledge the financial support of the Government of Canada through the Book Publishing Industry Development Program (BPIDP) for our publishing activities.

ONTARIO ARTS COUNCIL
CONSEIL DES ARTS DE L'ONTARIO

Printed and bound in Canada

Published by

SUMACH PRESS
1415 Bathurst Street #202
Toronto Canada
M5R 3H8
info@sumachpress.com
www.sumachpress.com

Mixed Sources
Product group from well-managed
forests, controlled sources and
recycled wood or fiber
www.fsc.org Cert no. SW-COC-002358
© 1996 Forest Stewardship Council
FSC

ANCIENT FOREST ™
FRIENDLY

for Brad and Douglas,
with many thanks

The Exclusion Principle:

Proposed in 1925 by Wolfgang Pauli, it states that no two electrons in an atom can be in the same state or configuration at the same time. If one of these states is occupied by an electron of one-half spin, the other may be occupied only by an electron of opposite spin. This prevents matter from collapsing to an extremely dense state, keeps us, in other words, from imploding. The reason this is true and the physical limits of the principle are still unknown.

Later

*Astronomy compels the soul to look upwards and
leads us from this world to another.*

— PLATO, *The Republic*

AVEY

"Where do you want it?" Joan says.

I look up at her blankly, then see she's holding the morning's mail and eyeing my desk with its triage of curriculum revisions and un-marked assignments and hysterical reports on the problems with the Raman Spectrometer.

I clear a space at the side. She sets the mail in it, makes a point of tap-ping the edges of the bigger envelopes and a newsletter so the pile will be neat. Joan believes in neatness. That would be a good thing except that with her it precludes efficiency.

At the top of the pile of mail is a postcard. My heart gives an extra little ka-thump when I recognize the picture.

It's an aerial shot of the observatory atop Mauna Kea. There are more telescopes now than when I was there twelve years ago, but my eyes go immediately to the one on the left, the JCMT, not as revered as the two fat Keck domes, but still the best in its class. It's easy to identify, with its carousel enclosure and squarer shape. The roof and doors are open — the telescope is working, observing. Maybe there's even someone in-side cursing the plane flying overhead and stirring up dust.

If I turned and looked behind me at the bulletin board I'd see, tacked up in the top right-hand corner, another picture of the JCMT, one I took myself. I'd opened the roof panels, mostly just to see if I could do it. I like showing the picture to my students, explaining that the reason they can't see the actual telescope is that the world's largest piece of protective Gore-Tex is fastened in front of it. There's always someone who doesn't understand how submillimetre wavelengths can pass right through it.

"I'm going for lunch now," Joan says. "Anything you want before I go." It's not a question. She's still pissed because I wouldn't let her take off an hour early yesterday. She taps her mechanical pencil onto her left wrist so hard I can hear the lead inside rattling.

"No, I'm fine."

She walks to the door. The hair at the back of her neck is pulled tight as a fist. She's wearing a green dress in some fuzzy fabric, its hemline too high for someone in her fifties, and unfortunate green shoes which draw attention to the fact that her ankles have the same circumference as her knees.

"A student to see you," she says, not turning around.

Being department head should have meant no teaching, but I'm stuck with a section of Astronomy 102 this semester. The student is a cocky kid with a strangely convex face and hair dyed with blond streaks. Kevin something. He always sits at the back. What he holds out to me is the assignment I returned this morning.

"I'm wondering," he says, "if you could look at this again."

"And why is that?"

I don't take the pages he's holding out to me. I know what's on them. My eyes flick impatiently to the postcard, wanting to see what's on the other side. I could reach over and look at it right now, but it's not just the rudeness of such a move that prevents me from doing it; it's some creeping uneasiness that tells me I should wait until I'm alone.

"I'm thinking maybe I should get part marks for having most of the calculations correct, sir."

Sir. A good touch, but not good enough.

"Sorry. Frankly, C+ is generous. Your estimate for the neutrino flux isn't even in the ballpark."

He shifts his feet. "This is the only class where I'm not getting an A." Ah, that almost perfect symbiosis of whining and accusation.

"The assignment wasn't that hard. If you want an A you have to do A work."

"It just, you know, doesn't seem fair."

"Sorry," I say, pointedly pulling the pile of mail closer to me.

He says something else, some further mutter he both does and does not want me to hear about how unfair it all is. Now he'll go off and tell his friends what a mean bastard I am. That won't, unfortunately, be breaking news.

When he's gone I turn the postcard over.

Only one word is written on the message side.

Remember

What? Remember? I don't get it. There's no signature. I turn the card over again to the picture side, look at it more closely. Yeah, okay, there's the summit of Mauna Kea; there are the beautiful telescopes gleaming in the sun. Their combined power to gather light must be over fifty times that of the Hubble. Even now, after all these years away, it does something to me, that sight. My finger reaches out, touches the little white shape of the JCMT, the James Clerk Maxwell Telescope, the one that made my whole life here possible.

I look at the message on the postcard again, then at the address, in careful black print, giving my full title of Dr. Xavier Fleming, Chair, Dept. of Astronomy, UBC, Vancouver. The stamp is from the US. I peer at the postmark. It's smeared but I think it says Hilo, Hawaii.

Hilo. *Remember.*

A chill crawls up my neck, and I actually glance at the window to see if it has somehow crept open. The card could be from any of several people in Hilo. But I think I know now who sent it. A sliver of ice lodges itself in my gut. Nothing about this card is beautiful after all. I pull my hand away from it, push my chair back a little.

There's a small rumble outside. Thunder.

K A T E

Thunder. Thunderstorms are rare in Vancouver, especially this early in the year. The people in the office who laughed at me when I said I saw a flash of lightning a few seconds ago are giving me apologetic looks.

I'm checking the Multiples for a condo for the couple from Saskatoon when the mail comes, and I get up and stretch and wander over to the stand of small mailboxes into which the secretary is depositing our letters.

Most of the post, as usual, goes to Carol, and I wonder again, unkindly, if she has her personal mail delivered here to impress us with how important she is. Not that she needs to impress us: we are all aware she is the most successful realtor in the office. Jaws, some of them call her behind her back. I'm probably the only one who doesn't loathe her, and that's because I don't particularly mind if she poaches clients from me occasionally.

She joins me at the mailboxes. She's tall, with thick, black hair and bold features, and she has a huge chest. Even those of us who see it every day find it hard not to let our eyes be drawn there. It gives her an advantage when it comes to getting contracts signed: who can concentrate on the implications of subject clauses when those large, sweatered breasts also seem to be involved in the transaction? She doesn't make it easier for people who stare at them. I've heard her tell a man she was bioengineered to be a porn star. He nearly fainted with embarrassment.

"Finished your proofing yet?" she asks me.

I give her the laugh she expects, nod. She's not going to let me forget the typo in one of my listings in the *Real Estate Guide* last month. "Domed skylights" turned into "doomed skylights." The vendors were not as amused as Carol was. Fortunately she didn't notice the "floor-to-ceiling widows" that got by me the week after.

Carol pulls free her wad of mail, jammed so tightly into her pigeonhole it has crumpled at the edges, and literally trots back to her desk. No time to waste, no time to waste, her heels tap onto the tiles. She says something to the client who's just come in, and he laughs. The sound of it makes me whirl to stare at him. It's David's laugh. I know the man isn't David, can't be David, he looks nothing like David, but still, still. I close my eyes. *Stop it, stop it.* Once I actually chased after a man on the street because the back of his head looked like David's. Avey was with me so I had to admit to him what I'd been thinking, and of course it annoyed him. I suppose he tries to be sensitive about David, but he rarely succeeds.

There's only one piece of mail for me. A postcard. I catch my breath as I recognize the photo: the telescopes on Mauna Kea. I was only up there once, but as I stare at the picture I can feel the terrifying cold flood through me again, can actually feel goosebumps ripple up my arms.

I turn the card over. Beside my name and address, a single word is printed in red, in big block letters.

Remember

I have to take hold of the counter to steady myself.
I know who sent this.

Remember

There is no punctuation, and for some reason that alarms me the most, as though I am expected to supply it. *Remember?* or *Remember!* or just *Remember ....*

PART I

Hilo

One

A V E Y

Remember. Of course I do. It's as vivid to me as though it all happened yesterday, not twelve years ago, both the parts I like to think about and the parts I don't.

I was at U of A in Edmonton, sitting in the office I was sharing with Rob and the post-grad guy from China whose name I never did learn to pronounce, when the letter came. My whoop of joy must have echoed across the river all the way to Fort Saskatchewan. They'd accepted my proposal for four months working at the James Clerk Maxwell Telescope on Mauna Kea in Hawaii. The telescope would hardly be at my beck and call the whole time, of course, but I'd have access to as much data as I needed. Most astronomers were happy to get four *days* from TAG, the Telescope Allocation Group, but my grant was letting me live and work down there for four *months.*

I'd known my proposal was in the current hot zone — looking for planets outside our own solar system — but I also knew my credentials weren't as impressive as those of most of the candidates. I hadn't even finished my PhD yet. Obviously what earned my proposal that second look was saying I was continuing the work of Dr. Orlovski, the brilliant astronomer from Toronto who dropped dead in Hawaii just as he seemed to be getting close to finding the second extrasolar planet. He'd had the spectrographic results but couldn't verify them. I couldn't believe nobody else had had the idea to snap up his work. My supervisor said it seemed a bit opportunistic, and I said, "Thank you." He gave me a wry smile but signed my application. Of course he would. He'd share in the credit if I found anything.

And they'd accepted my proposal. Four months in Hawaii looking for the next extrasolar planet. I wasn't going to find the first one, but I was going to have a shot at the second.

The first extrasolar planet around a main-sequence star, in the 51 Pegasi system, had just been discovered a month earlier, in October, 1995, and just like that our little Earth and her companion planets were no longer alone in the universe. But the new planet was unlike anything we could have imagined. According to planet formation theories it shouldn't have been able to exist, a gas giant like Jupiter orbiting its sun in just four days, and so close it would have been roasting at 1900 Fahrenheit. No planet in our solar system is anywhere near that hot. It was baffling; it was weird; but it was there.

What excited me as much as anything, though, was not the discovery itself but who made it. We'd all expected it would be Marcy and Butler, the US pros, but it was Michel Mayor and Didier Queloz at the Geneva Observatory in Switzerland. Huh? we all said: who the hell are they?

They had to fight to get the credit, of course. *Nature* refused to publish their results without more proof. When they broke the news at a conference in Italy, newspaper headlines gave the credit to Italian astronomers. US articles gave the credit to Marcy and Butler. What a mess. Then when Ted Koppel interviewed some astronomers on "Nightline" the evening of the announcement, David Latham from the Harvard-Smithsonian claimed he'd found a second planet orbiting 51 Pegasi. Even I knew his spectrometer wasn't capable of anything near to the sort of precise measurements required, but it added to the excitement and confusion.

When Latham's claim couldn't be substantiated, the race was on again to find the second planet. And now there was a possibility, a very real possibility, that that discovery could be made by me. The Swiss weren't known to even be in the race, but they'd beaten all the other teams, some of them looking since the 1980s, to the prize. If they could find a planet, so could I. I could be the one to prove 51 Pegasi B wasn't a fluke.

The telescope I'd be using worked only at the millimetre and submillimetre range, which might have made it an unlikely choice, but Orlovski had installed his own special visiting instrument, a heterodyne receiver designed to have an amazing precision in measuring the Doppler shifts. I didn't have Orlovski's genius or his mechanical skills, but I understood what he'd done, and I knew how to continue his research. I even had a couple of ideas about how to improve the computer program he'd been using. Because the instrument was still technically in its test phase, I got to stay there until that was over. I would have to work my ass off, but I was ready for that. Being lazy wasn't one of my failings.

"Jesus, Kate," I kept saying when I got home, pacing around our one-bedroom apartment on the sixth floor of Garneau Towers a few blocks from campus. "I got the grant. I got the damned *grant!* I can't believe it. I'm going to be working at the best submillimetre radio telescope in the world. I could discover another planet. The second extrasolar planet! My name would be in the history books."

"I guess that would be rather thrilling." Kate was sitting at the kitchen table working on some real estate contract.

"Thrilling! It would be, it would be —" I threw my hands into the air; they felt ready to fly off into space without me. "Beyond thrilling. This is thrilling. Today is thrilling. Well, I won't need vocabulary. I'll be beyond vocabulary. I'll be a pure mathematical equation."

Kate laid down her pencil. She was sitting on her left hand, her elbow straight, which raised her left shoulder several inches. It was one of the few postures of hers I could read. It meant she was dubious.

"Look," I said. "This is the hot field now. Everyone's frantic to prove the Mayor-Queloz discovery isn't just some mistake. Whoever discovers the second planet will be almost as famous as the guys who discovered the first." I sat down across from her, leaned over and picked up her pencil and bounced the eraser end on the table, thump thump thump.

"But if everyone else is racing to make the discovery, too, is it really worth the gamble?"

"Of course it's worth it! I'd be scooping the Americans, I'd be scooping everyone. I'd be the first Canadian. I'd be the first North American. I'd be the first to use a submillimetre telescope. I'd be a first for all kinds of reasons. Every astronomy department I know would be begging me to work for them. No more of this whoring around after a sessional job here, a piddly TA there. It would make my career. I'd have the PhD sewn up, job offers coming out of my ears."

"But ... Oh, Avey, I don't know. We can't just drop everything and move to Hawaii —"

"Why not? Are you crazy? Hawaii! Who doesn't want to go to Hawaii?" I waved out the window. The air was thick with ice fog. Walking back from campus I'd felt as though I were breathing in shards of broken glass. The wind was vicious and straight from the Arctic and sliced right through my parka. When I'd crossed 111th Street a car skidded on black ice and nearly delivered me on its hood right into the lobby of the apartment building next door.

"I can't just walk out on my job," Kate said.

"Of course you can! Nobody's buying houses this time of year, anyway. This is more important. And didn't you say that one advantage of having a realtor's licence was its flexibility?"

"It's not that easy. I have a life here. I have Sandy to think about."

"She's nineteen. She's an adult. She hasn't lived with you for three years, for Christ's sake."

Kate poked her thumb at a fallen leaf from the grape ivy sitting on the corner of the table. The air was so dry it had sucked the life out of all but a dozen wizened leaves.

"I don't know. I don't know if I can pack up and go, just like that."

"It's just for four months. It's not forever. Kate, I have to do this. I *have* to. I've got a *grant*. I can't just say, oops, no thanks, to a grant. I'll never get a chance like this again. An opportunity like this comes along once in a blue moon."

I laughed, thinking of how just last week I'd told Kate that the popular definition of "blue moon" — two full moons in one month — was wrong, that it referred to a literal and much rarer event when the moon appeared blue because of unusual atmospheric distortion.

"This is my blue moon, Kate."

"Look at the moon through a piece of blue tissue paper and you can have one whenever you want."

I suppose she was trying to be funny, but it irritated me.

"Listen," I said, "I want you to come with me but if you won't I'll go without you."

I hadn't intended to say it quite like that. Kate winced and turned away. Her left shoulder went up another inch.

But she just drove me nuts sometimes, the way she didn't understand how important it was for me to get my career together. It was because she was older than I was, I suppose, by almost ten years, but it was also because she just didn't have much of a drive herself. If she sold three or four houses a year that was enough for her. Even I could have closed more deals than she did. But maybe it was her lack of ambition that attracted me to her in the first place. She was a change from the aggressive women in my classes, the ones fighting me for grades and scholarships, the ones I could never feel comfortable with.

And she was cute. Even in her late thirties, she was still cute, that kind of Hollywood ingenue cute. She had shaggily cut blond hair with a perky little cowlick at the crown, big green eyes, a petite nose, and a sexy mouth that seemed to have twice the nerves and muscles that mine did. My sister said nastily I liked Kate because she was shorter than I was, and maybe that was true, too, though I'd never admit it. I'm five foot six, and, yeah, all right, I don't like being towered over by women. Kate was five three and just right.

I first met her when she sold my parents their condo on Whyte Avenue, and it turned out that her daughter, Sandy, had been a student of my dad's in Grade 9 and that he'd played golf with Kate's husband about a month before the car accident that killed the man. Dad was always good at finding connections with people. Except with me. The only good thing he ever did for me was introduce me to his realtor.

"Look, I'm sorry," I said to Kate. "I know that sounded awful. But this is hugely important to me, all right?"

Kate didn't answer. I broke a banana off the bunch in the fruit bowl, peeled it back, took a bite. It was so hard I could have cracked a tooth. I wrapped the peel around the rest and put it back in the bowl.

"They're still too green," Kate said.

"In Hawaii they'll never be too green. We'll be able to pick them ripe off the trees."

I reached over and pulled at the wool scarf she sometimes wore indoors in winter because she said her neck got cold and stiff. She pulled away, put her hand on the scarf to stop me. "What are you doing?"

I kept tugging. "Let go. I'm not trying to *strangle* you, for Pete's sake."

The scarf crackled with so much static electricity it might have seemed, though, I was trying to electrocute her. But she let me pull it free. I balled it up, served it like a volleyball across the room. It uncurled, floated onto the floor.

"Your point being?"

"You wouldn't need that any more. It's summer there all the time. Your neck would never be cold."

Kate looked at the scarf on the floor, twisted the pencil in her fingers. The sociopaths in the apartment above us cranked up their stereo. Another leaf fell off the grape ivy.

She sighed. "All right. If it means that much to you."

"You won't be sorry. I promise you won't. Hawaii is paradise. It'll be great."

So we went. We put our stuff in storage and we went.

Remember. Jesus. Of course I remember.

KATE

Of course I remember. I hated the place.

When we arrived, exhausted from the trip — first a redeye to Honolulu and then a three-hour wait for a connecting flight — Avey phoned the owner of the house we would be renting and arranged to meet him there. All we knew about it was that it was a small two-bedroom on Kamana Street, about two miles from where Avey would be doing most of his work.

The first thing we noticed when we got there was the boarded-up front window. The taxi driver made us check the address before he helped us unload our luggage.

"Place looks abandoned," he said.

"Won't be now," Avey said. His voice sounded grim rather than reassuring.

We dragged our suitcases up the walk to the bottom step and sat down to wait for the landlord. The sweat was dripping off both of us. I was so thirsty that I began eyeing the water sitting in one of several rusty tuna tins dumped at the side of the house. I was in the middle of my period, and I wondered if the cramping was from that or from dehydration.

"Place could use a coat of paint all right," Avey said.

"At least."

The clapboard exterior had been painted green once, but most of the paint had flaked off, and in places the wood had rotted almost all the way through. The steps on which we sat didn't feel any sturdier. The wood railing had broken off some time ago. We could see bits of it decomposing in the overgrown shrubbery. The house itself was raised up on stilts, which I assumed was to help with circulation and to deter rodents, and I wondered if the stilts were also made of wood and if they were rotting, too, because the house had a distinct lean. A sour, fishy smell was coming from underneath. I told myself it was just the tuna tins. A large tank barnacled with rust sat at the side of the house, and I could see a pipe from the rain gutters leading toward it. I had a feeling this primitive catchment system might be our only water supply.

We were taking over the place from a French physicist whose grant had run out, and Avey had said we were lucky to get it. I wondered what "unlucky" would be. A column of small but fast-moving black ants was heading up the stairs beside me, disappearing under the house. On Avey's side the troop was moving the other way, carrying pieces of something white and gelatinous-looking. I hoped it wasn't the French physicist.

It was almost an hour before the landlord arrived to give us our keys. He was a tall, weighty Hawaiian wearing a red T-shirt with a rip under one arm extending down almost to the waist. His shorts rode perilously low on his hips, and to one of the belt loops was clipped a large ring holding over a dozen keys plus about the same number of ornaments of the kind that might decorate a charm bracelet. Charm, however, did not extend to the rest of him. He couldn't seem to bother making his eyes drop to meet ours and stared over our heads down the street as though something more interesting was happening there.

"You're here," he grunted. Then he simply held out his hand for the rent until Avey paid him, in cash, as required.

"Don't we sign a contract with you?" I ventured.

He shrugged.

"A rental agreement of some kind," I persisted. "You know."

"Last one didn't."

"Then ... a receipt at least."

"Last guy didn't need one."

"But ... it's customary. We need some, well, some security."

"Come on, Kate," Avey said. "I'm ready to drop. We can sort this out later."

I gave the man my best ingratiating smile. "Perhaps later, then," I said. "We can all sign something."

He shrugged, narrowed his eyes toward the end of the street. "Last one didn't," he said. Then, perhaps realizing that even for him that reply could use some enhancement, he added, "There wasn't any women."

"Let's go, Kate. Christ." Avey was starting up the steps.

I had no choice but to pick up my two suitcases, which seemed to have bloated since they left Edmonton, and follow him into the house.

The landlord had obviously seen no reason to clean the place for us, and if the French physicist had ever even swept the floor it was only to push the debris a little closer to the dirty walls. The furniture was sparse and rickety, most of it made from rough, ragged bamboo that seemed to have been hacked and whacked together by a drunk with a machete. The sour, fishy smell I'd noticed outside was everywhere.

In the kitchen the caked-on grease looked to be years old. Two of the burner coils were missing on the old stove, and it took a willing suspension of disbelief to imagine the opaque square on the oven door as a window. The fridge was blotched with rust, and a black sludge oozed out from the back. In the bathroom the toilet seat had a crack wide enough to have been colonized by a small spider, and the walls had a spackled look that I doubted had come with the paint. When I turned on the tap the water came out in a thin, asthmatic drizzle. I didn't care if it had just run off the roof or that it had a yellow tint; I used the glass sitting on the back of the toilet and drank and drank.

All we wanted was sleep. We pulled down the tattered blinds and fell onto the saggy, sheetless mattress. Avey was asleep in minutes, but the heat made it hard for me even to breathe. The mattress got slithery with my sweat. I had come from a freezing Edmonton winter to a climate in paradise, and all I could think was that I would give anything for a handful of snow. To make matters worse, the only windows that opened had louvres and no screens, and the house filled up suddenly with an attack of mosquitoes. It was as though they had been released by the hundreds just outside the window. I slammed the louvres shut, but already the bedroom was thick with them — in my ears, my nose, my eyes. Avey slept on, not feeling the bites. The house got hotter and hotter. I couldn't imagine ever getting used to this.

When we woke up early the next morning we found the room scuttling with cockroaches. They seemed to disappear into the walls when we moved, but knowing they were there was as bad as seeing them.

"It's beyond horrible," I moaned to Avey.

"I know, I know." He was lining the bottom of the mildewed dresser drawers with the pages of a report his supervisor had given him at the last minute and which he'd read on the plane.

"Are you sure you want to do that?" I asked.

"If I need the information I'll know where it is." He opened another drawer. Its knob had been replaced by a coil of wire.

I hadn't exactly meant that I was concerned about the report. I'd meant, are you sure we're going to stay here? But he began unpacking his underwear and shirts into the drawers, so I had my answer.

There was no closet, just a small, lopsided wardrobe with a dozen wire hangers. I hung up only a few of my clothes before deciding they would feel less traumatized left in the suitcases.

"God, Avey." I sat down on the mattress, slid my hands under my thighs. My skin was damp and sticky. "How can we live here?"

"There's nowhere else to go," Avey said. "You know that. The only way to get any accommodation at all is to inherit it from someone who's leaving." He scratched at a mosquito bite on his arm hard enough to make it bleed.

"Well — there must be apartments. A hotel, even."

"Look." He straightened. I could tell he was controlling his temper. "This is what we can afford. Period. Even a crappy hotel room is a hundred bucks a night."

"But — all these cockroaches —"

"It's a different climate here. Different problems, different standards. In the tropics people can't be as uptight about shutting out the outside."

"It's not a question of that. This place is a slum in any climate."

"What do you want me to say? Can't you just —" he waved his hand wildly at the air "— think of it as an adventure? This is Hawaii. There's bougainvillea growing wild outside the door. We're the envy of everyone we know."

"I hope they all come to visit."

"If you clean the place up it'll be better. And we won't have to spend all our time in it."

I didn't comment on the "you" instead of "we" doing the cleaning. "Of course, you'll be up at your office most of the time. But where am I supposed to spend *my* time? I don't have a visa. I can't get a job."

He sat down on the bed beside me. "Just ... give it a chance, will you? I have to start work tomorrow morning. I need you to, you know, help me out here. Give me a break. All right?"

And I thought: I could just walk out, take a cab back to the airport and leave him here with the dirt and the heat and the cockroaches.

But I couldn't do that to him.

"Okay."

"That's my girl."

"There *is* that bougainvillea just outside the door."

Two

*Our universe is a sorry little affair unless it has in
it something for every age to discover.*

— SENECA *(about 50 AD)*

AVEY

Kate was right, of course: it was a little house of horrors.

But the next morning as soon as I stepped outside I couldn't help feeling the thrill of where I was and what I was going to be doing here. I stood there in my shirt sleeves waiting for my ride and breathing in the sweetest air I'd ever breathed and thought about the wind chill factor in Edmonton yesterday.

The guy who picked me up in a lurching old Volkswagen was a skinny, young technician with chaotic red hair and an incomplete chin. He was wearing a baseball cap on backwards, a T-shirt saying "Neutrinos have mass," and a watch with so many buttons it probably included the time zones on Neptune. Perry, he said his name was, and he was from somewhere antipodean. His accent was a blend of Aussie, Irish and chewing gum. Apparently he was in charge of getting me settled. As we drove up the hill a few miles to the JAC, the Joint Astronomy Centre where I'd be working, he pointed out things in Hilo — the harbour, the downtown, a flowering tree, another flowering tree, another, okay, okay, I got it. All I really wanted to look at was Mauna Kea as it rose up on my right.

It's a marvel, of course. A dormant volcano, it's technically the tallest mountain in the world if you measure from the ocean floor, and it rises nearly three miles above the surface. It's the best place on earth for a telescope. There's the "best seats" advantage telescopes close to the equator have, of course, because more stars remain visible all year, but the Mauna Kea summit also has an exceptionally dry and clear atmosphere and more photometric nights than any other telescope site. For measurements of radio wavelengths, which is all I cared about, it's particularly great.

"Can't wait to get up there, can you?" Perry said.

"I dunno. I think I'll be grateful to do my work down here where it's warm."

"I thought you Canadians liked the cold."

"Who told you that? We just huddle in our igloos and wait for our two weeks of summer."

We pulled up to the JAC. It overlooked the Hilo campus of the University of Hawaii and was a modern-looking two-storey building with a distinctive and dominating red metal roof whose overhanging eaves jutted a couple of feet beyond the building itself. The place wasn't large; Perry said it held a few dozen offices at most, plus some workshops and mechanical areas and common rooms, but it had a spacious and quiet feel, maybe because it sat on at least an acre of well-kept grounds. There were palm trees in front. I didn't even have to go inside to know I would love it here.

I would be sharing my office, but that seemed like a minor inconvenience. When Perry opened the door to it the first thing I saw was the new computer, linked to the telescope on the mountain. It would be sending me data all night and sometimes all day, and something in all that information, I was convinced, was going to make me famous.

"So let me know if you need anything," Perry said.

"Thanks, thanks, I'm sure I'll be fine." I had eyes only for the computer. It was like meeting your partner in an arranged marriage and finding her better-looking than you'd hoped.

"There *is* an ocean view, you know," said Perry, gesturing at the east-facing window. I could hear the grin in his voice. He'd met obsessives like me before. "In case you ever have time to look."

I laughed, glanced out the window. He was right. There was an ocean view.

"Okay. I'll leave you to it, then," Perry said. "The key to the bike cable is in the desk drawer."

I didn't know who actually owned the bicycle he'd shown me outside, but apparently it was mine to use while I was here. I'd need to get into shape, but at least it would be better than walking, and there was no way I could afford a car.

The first thing I did when I unpacked the few files and notes I'd brought along in my backpack was tack up on the little corkboard beside the computer the picture I'd cut out of *Nature* before I left Vancouver. It was of the discovery data for 51 Pegasi B. It was beautiful. But it wasn't what you might expect to see. It wasn't some digitally enhanced blurry ball floating beside its alien sun. It wasn't even some pretty coloured picture of the spectrum showing the shift in the emission and absorption lines from the red end to the blue, showing the planet pulling at it, shifting its light to either shorter or longer wavelengths.

That was what was happening, all right, the Doppler effect, measuring a spectral shift so vanishingly small it was only plus or minus three metres per second. But what Mayor and Queloz actually saw on their computer screen was a series of dots, interpreted by their software program, the dots falling into this beautiful curve, snaking gracefully from left to right, rising to the top of the screen, falling to the bottom, rising again, over and over. Every dot on the screen was sitting right on the curve, no stragglers. It was perfect.

When I'd showed Kate the picture she said it looked like the pulse of a beating heart, the way you'd see it on a cardiac monitor. I suppose it sort of did. God knows, it was what my own heart was beating for: to see that curve, that rhythm, on my own computer screen. The dot at the top of the screen would tell me the star was moving towards us, the dot at the bottom that it was moving away, and the fact every dot fell on a perfect curve would tell me it was moving both toward and away. It would be perturbed, wobbling. And it would be wobbling because a planet was pulling at it.

My office mate had obviously been settled in for a while. The bookcase on his side of the office was filled, not tidily, to the ceiling with well-thumbed books and magazines, and I wondered how he had managed to transport them all here. Maybe he was a local. His desk, covered with printouts, was also littered with half a dozen Styrofoam cups containing shrivelled tea bags. On the wall was a big poster of the observatory, and he had stuck a green Post-it onto the James Clerk Maxwell Telescope, so I knew we must both be working at it and not at the United Kingdom telescope UKIRT, with whom we shared this centre. I stepped up to look at the note. It said, *Watch This Space.*

When I turned back to my desk I got a start, because a tall and bulky man, the kind my mother would have called "abdominous," was filling almost the whole doorway. He had the plump and rumpled look of a paperback fallen into the bath and dried in the sun. He grinned. His teeth were huge and the colour of weak tea: he must belong to the other half of this office. He was wearing a Toronto Blue Jays T-shirt and less-than-clean khaki cargo pants with something in one of the pockets that was square-edged and heavy enough to have broken through the side seam. I suppose I knew for sure at that point that I wouldn't need the necktie I had tossed into my backpack just in case.

"Bruno," he said, holding out his hand. "From Toronto."

"Avey," I said, shaking his hand, which had a rather sticky grip. "Bruno? Named for the martyred priest, are you?"

He laughed. "I was, actually."

"Really?" I'd been joking. Giordano Bruno, a former Catholic priest, was the original hero of astronomers: in 1600 he was burned at the stake for the heresy of insisting the billions of stars in the skies are suns like our own, orbited by planets like the Earth.

"My parents were both astronomers," he said. "That and the name imposed a certain, well, inevitability to my career."

"What's that phrase about your name being your destiny? Nomen omen?"

"Could well be," Bruno said. "Would you believe I was in grad school with a woman named Gagarin Armstrong?"

"Whoa! Great name. Better than the one that couple gave their daughter after the moon landing, when all the boys were being named Neil and Buzz. They called her —"

"Module!" Bruno exclaimed with me. "I remember." He scratched at his head, or rather at his hair, which was dark brown and so thick and woolly I couldn't imagine him even getting his fingers through it. "Ah, Module. I wonder where she is now."

"In the office across the hall, for all I know. How long have *you* been here?"

"A few weeks."

"Great. You'll be able to show me the ropes."

"Aren't a lot. Just those we use to tie ourselves to our computers and stare until we go blind." Perhaps as an illustration, he pushed his thick-lensed glasses further up his nose.

"Have you gone up to the telescope?"

"Just once. Cold as death up there." Bruno sat down at his desk, making whatever was in his cargo pocket, a Walkman, maybe, press more dangerously against the side seam with the broken stitches. He pulled a package of potato chips out of the top desk drawer and began eating. It made me realize I was ravenous. Crunch, crunch, crunch.

I sat down at my own desk. The chair was well padded but had the feel of having hosted many asses before mine. I found the height adjustment lever and cranked myself up a few inches.

"Jesus, I still can't believe I'm here," I said.

"It's a great place to work," Bruno said. "You'll like it."

"What are the other guys like?" I gestured at the walls behind which I imagined versions of myself gazing in narcotic rapture at computer screens.

"The usual collection. Nobody you'll hate. But Macpherson is from Ireland and you won't be able to understand a word he says. And Ivan across the hall looks like he's furious most of the time, but his heart's in the right place."

His heart's in the right place. It was a phrase that always made me wince.

The truth is that physiologically my heart *isn't* in the right place. I have dextrocardia, or, more accurately, dextrocardia with situs inversus, which means that my heart and my other internal organs are reversed. My heart bends to the right instead of the left. I'm a mirror image of normal anatomy. It's an unusual condition but hardly unique; it affects about one in five thousand people. My mother's grandfather had it, and it popped up again in me. There are no adverse health effects, unless I want to count things like the unwholesome delight of doctors who still treat me like a new toy, or things like the peckings of schoolyard bullies who found out about my condition but who in any case soon moved on to targets with more visible aberrations — the fat kid, the kid with the birthmark, the kid with the stutter.

And unless I count the jibes from my own father, who would introduce me as his "backwards boy." He blamed my mother's genetics, of course. By the time someone explained to me that it required recessive genes from both parents to produce my particular configuration it was ten years past the time for a useful rebuttal, and I didn't want to give him the satisfaction of knowing I remembered anything at all he'd said about me.

I avoid telling people about my little peculiarity. I didn't even tell Kate until after we were married. I suppose I've been afraid of people thinking it could explain all my other personality deviations.

"... the way God made his face." Bruno was still talking. I snapped my attention back. "Speaking of God, well, then there's Louisa." He paused. "Louisa is from Florida and she's doing some postdoc work here, but she's, well, she believes in ID."

"ID?" I was flipping through all the cosmological acronyms I could think of and drawing a blank.

"Intelligent Design. She's a creationist."

"Really? I remember my supervisor calling creation science an oxymoron. One of his first-years had just given him a new book about it where the author crunched the 'begats' in the Bible and came up with some time in 4004 B.C. as the exact date of creation."

Bruno made a face. "My favourite new book is one called *Noah's Ark: A Feasibility Study*. The author speculates, among other things, that because of the rain and cloud cover there would have been a problem with constant darkness but that it would have been alleviated inside the pitch-black ark by the glow of millions of fireflies."

"Rather ... poetic, actually."

"To be fair to Louisa, she does find this stuff a bit embarrassing. All the more reason for me to acquaint her with it."

It had been a long time since I'd talked to anyone about religion. My own beliefs amounted to some vague and unexplored notion that religion had evolved in our brains to stop us from killing ourselves when we figured out how pointless life was. If I did have what Sartre called a God-shaped hole in my consciousness, I'd filled it easily enough over the years with physics. But I guess there were those who looked up at the universe and lost their religion and those who looked up and had it confirmed. I didn't much care what other people believed, so long as they weren't trying to burn me at the stake or take my grant money away. Someone once called me "tolerant," but I think she meant that as a euphemism for "indifferent."

And suddenly I remembered something else about my dextrocardia, something my mother told me about only a few years ago. Apparently when she'd asked her old family priest, whom she'd told about my condition, to baptize me, he'd hesitated, then said, okay, he would, but did she know that, according to some interpretations, the Devil was also supposed to be reversed inside? I chuckled along with my mother at her little story, but, well, shit. The *Devil*.

"I don't mind fighting with Louisa," Bruno was saying, "but being the new boy you might want to be a bit more prudent."

"Right. Thanks. How did you know I wasn't some kind of fundamentalist myself?"

"Well, you seemed sane, for one thing. Plus you did use her Lord's name in vain. She frowns on that sort of thing."

Seemed sane. That was the nicest thing anyone had said to me in a long time. "Okay. Thanks for the heads-up. I'll keep my expletives deleted around her. So, what are *you* doing here? What's your project?"

"Extrasolar planets."

I stifled a moan. Bruno was going to be my competition. I'd been pretty sure most of the other projects here would have just involved star formation or interstellar dust emissions, something the submillimetre capacities of the JCMT were ideally suited for.

"I guess the Swiss discovery last month must have been a bit of a shock." I was stalling. That was stupid, obviously. He would have to find out I had the same project.

"Yeah, really. Who'd have thought they'd get there before Marcy and Butler? Or before me, for that matter?" He laughed. A bit of potato chip dropped onto his shirt.

"Well, it's a race for the second one now." I had to tell him. Oh, shit shit shit.

"I was pretty relieved when Latham's claim was discounted, I can tell you," Bruno said. "Nobody's going to care as much who finds the third or fourth or tenth planet. So, what are you here for?"

"I've got the same project, actually. Extrasolar planets."

"Really? Hey. Welcome aboard." If he was disappointed he was hiding it well.

"Funny they'd have approved two such projects for the same telescope," I said. "Different committees, maybe."

"Yeah, well, it's the big, hot subject now. And I suppose I had an unfair advantage. But to tell you the truth I didn't even want to apply. My field is chemistry. And I'm not one of those brilliant academic scholar types."

"So — am I missing something? What was your unfair advantage?"

"Aforementioned astronomer parents. And a sympathy vote. My dad had done some pretty good work on extrasolar planets, he was sure he was close to something in Pisces, he'd had one positive reading, and then he died of a heart attack. My mom really wanted me to continue his work."

My hands were clenching on the seat of my chair so hard I might be driving my nails right through it. I felt a little ill. "Orlovski," I said faintly. "You're Dr. Orlovski's son."

"Hey, right."

I swallowed. "You're not going to believe this. But I ..." Oh, shit shit shit shit. "I'd been following his work, he published everything, you know, and I was so impressed, just so impressed, and when he died I thought, well, it would be tragic to let his work just, like, languish, so I applied to continue it."

Bruno stared at me, his mouth dropping open a bit. "Jesus," he said.

"I'm sorry, man. If I'd had any idea anyone else, especially his son, was interested in continuing I'd have backed off. I swear. I just didn't want it all to go to waste. And if I'd found anything of course I'd have given him co-credit, I mean, how could I not?"

Bruno just kept staring at me. A little spittle had collected at the corner of his mouth.

Finally he swallowed, said, "That's amazing. I had no idea anybody else would care enough to pursue his work. That's so great."

That's so *great?* I laughed in relief. It was going to be okay. Bruno and I weren't going to have to hate each other. And what I'd said about his father, well, it was true, I guess, mostly true, a lot of it was true.

The secretary walked past down the hall. Perry had just introduced me to her, and already I'd forgotten her name.

"What's she called again?" I asked Bruno, nodding after her.

"Who? The sackatary?" He winced. "Oops. It's how she and the real Hawaiians get to say the word, but annoys her if we do it."

"'Real Hawaiians.' What's that mean?"

"Not sure, really. Probably that there's been no intermarriage with immigrant groups over the years. It's a pretty small number. But they have something here where if you have at least 50% Hawaiian blood you qualify for special status, special consideration. Something like that. It's called 'blood quantum.'"

"'Blood quantum.' Any relative of quantum mechanics?"

"Probably," he said. "I try not to understand either of them. Anyway, her name is Kani." KAHN-nee, he pronounced it.

She was coming back down the hall, and she stopped at our door. She was young, short, and plump, her skin seeming to fit her more tightly than most people's did. She had disconcertingly large brown eyes and a thick black braid. A white scar at her hairline looked as though it had been pinned there like a barrette. I gave her my best smile.

"A fax for you," she said to Bruno. "From your mother."

I gave a bit of a chuckle — I mean, a fax at work from your mother. Was that wrong, to think I should give some kind of amused response? Apparently it was. Kani gave me the kind of look that said as much.

"Thanks," Bruno said.

I watched Kani walk away. It probably would have looked as though I was ogling her ass, when really I was thinking that I should remember to ask her for the office's fax number so that I could send it to my supervisor at U of A. It would be an excuse to remind him of who I was, where I was. He was one of those guys who lost interest in things as soon as he wasn't looking directly at them.

Bruno skimmed the first page, then handed it to me, began reading the second. I had no idea why he wanted me to look at a letter from his mother, but I glanced down at it.

In case you haven't seen this ... was handwritten, by the mother, I assumed, across the top of the page, which I saw now was a photocopy of part of an article in *Nature*. Then I remembered Bruno had said *both* his parents were astronomers. Oh: so it wasn't exactly a fax from a mother, then. It felt as though he and the secretary had been using the word in an unfair way. Women having the same careers as we did meant we had to doublethink everything.

The article was about how astronomers at the Canadian Institute for Theoretical Astrophysics were trying to explain the weirdly short and precarious orbital period of the new planet at 51 Pegasi, to figure out how the planet, a gas giant with nearly the mass of Jupiter, could be there at all, twenty times closer to its sun than the Earth is to its sun. And apparently the only explanation the scientists could live with and save their basic planet formation theories was that it likely had been created elsewhere.

So the planet had migrated to its current location.

Damn. If 51 Pegasi B hadn't formed there, if it was a freak, what were the odds of finding another one?

Bruno finished reading the second page, but he didn't hand it to me. I could see it was mostly handwriting.

"What does she think about this?" I asked. As though it were any of my business.

"She says that if it's some kind of freak we might not find another one."

"Shit."

"Ah, well," Bruno said. "It's about the journey, not the destination, right?"

"Yeah, right." It didn't occur to me that he might have been serious. I handed back the page I'd read. I didn't want to think about it. "I'm starving," I said. "Anyplace around here I can get some of those chips?"

Bruno smiled, as though I had paid him a compliment. "I have an emergency stash in the staff lounge," he said.

As I walked down the hall with Bruno I wondered guiltily how Kate was managing with the cockroaches. Good lord, but there'd been a lot of them. I remembered some graffiti someone had found on a tenement building in New York: *Whatever the missing mass of the universe is, I hope it's not in cockroaches.*

KATE

Cockroaches. They seemed not to like the daylight, so I could almost tell myself they were not as bad as they'd seemed. I took advantage of their absence to make a start at cleaning the house. Everything was covered with a thick, oily, velvety dust.

Under the sink I found a surprising diversity of cleaning products, most of them unopened, and by late afternoon I had managed to get the living room, at least, into somewhat better shape. I'd even managed to reduce the frills of green mould on the walls near the ceiling to a less toxic-looking grey. The kitchen was a greater archaeological challenge. I scraped away layer after layer of caked-on grease, my fingernails getting ragged and stained. The colour of the countertop kept changing the further down I went. Finally the smell of ammonia made me dizzy enough to quit for the day.

Behind the house I found a battered bicycle, and, though the chain was stiff with rust and the handlebars wobbly, I was able to ride it down to the small store the taxi driver had told us yesterday was the closest, about five blocks away.

It had been a completely cloudless day when I set off, but when I reached the store I was suddenly drenched with a rain that came out of nowhere. In the store the old man behind the counter gave me an amused look as I tried ineffectually to brush the rain from myself.

"It comes up fast," he said. He had thick, crinkly white hair and Japanese features that probably had several other genetic influences. His accent sounded Scandinavian.

"Apparently," I said.

"*Hilo i ka ua kinakinai, ka ua mao 'ole.*"

"Pardon?"

"Old Hawaiian saying. It means, 'Hilo of the constant rain, where it never clears up.'"

"Oh, dear."

"You get used to it. You just change your attitude."

He went back to watching his soccer game on TV as I filled a basket with some canned beans, bread, peanut butter and a few vegetables that seemed encouragingly fresh. When he rang them up, I winced at the price. We were supposed to be living on Avey's meagre grant money.

This was over twice what I would have paid in Edmonton.

"You get used to that, too," he said, seeing my expression. There was an edge to his voice now.

"It's just ... the different money," I said. "I'm Canadian."

"Can-*ad*-ians. You think you have a separate country. Hawaii did once, too."

"Oh. I suppose so." I smiled gamely, trying to cajole back his amiability.

But he only grunted. "Yeah."

"So ... is your store open in the evenings?" I picked up the two plastic bags. One of them had a Wal-Mart logo.

He shrugged, said, "Sometimes," and turned back to the TV.

I sighed. Obviously, not wincing at the price of things was another of the changes in attitude I would have to learn.

Outside, the rain had slowed to a drizzle. As I was trying to hang the grocery bags onto the bicycle handlebars, a woman with a boy of about eight entered the store, and I heard her tell him, "Teachers can be smarter than they look."

Teachers can be smarter than they look: such eavesdroplets, as I called them, were a habit I had gotten into as a child with my mother. When we were out together, which didn't happen often because she was always so busy with work, she would expect me to remember one thing I overheard, and when we got home I had to report my selection. I still remember some of them. "Nothing is more important than ice cream." "Never late than better." "It costs more because it's expensive." "Get a life, he told me, but I've got a life, that's the problem." Sometimes later my mother, giving me a wink, would repeat these, unexpectedly and without explanation, to our friends, who would look bewildered. I thought they were envying what was a private joke between mother and daughter, but as I grew older and more critical of my parents I thought people had probably been annoyed, just as I would think that these weren't special memories we shared but only something we had stolen from strangers.

Still, as I stood outside the store, hot and sweaty and tired, with my inadequate bags of groceries that refused to hang in any reasonable way from the handlebars, I could feel tears welling up, because all I wanted was to see her, an ocean and half a continent away.

I suppose I should have been embarrassed. I was a grown woman, after all, with a grown child of her own, and I was starting to cry outside a grocery store because I missed my mother.

I thought suddenly of David, too. But I knew if I let myself grasp that rope of memory then I would not pull myself up into anything but complete despair. I had to not think about David, not today.

I gave up on being able to ride the bike back to the house with the bags suspended from the handlebars, so I pushed it along instead. It was windy now, and the rain picked up again. I trudged on, telling myself it was just a warm tropical rain, refreshing even, telling myself that Avey was right, that we were the envy of our friends and that surely I would start, too, to think there was something about our life here that was enviable. I made myself look up at the banyan trees and smell the richly scented plumeria whose blossoms kept falling at my feet.

A block from our house I passed the pair of old red carpet slippers I had noticed earlier. They were still sitting on the grassy strip between the sidewalk and the curb, and I told myself: see, already there are things that you recognize here, that look familiar.

But the house offered no comfort of the familiar. If anything, it had gotten worse in my absence. One of the front steps seemed to have rotted right through while I was gone. I leaned the bicycle against the steps, where it promptly fell over. I watched the rear wheel turning, ticking, more and more slowly, a clock running down. When it stopped I bent to pick up the spilled groceries, discovering at that point that the beautiful red bougainvillea crowding around the house came with thorns set on "eviscerate."

Inside, the rain sounded loud as pebbles on the tin roof, and as I unpacked my groceries the slow plink, plink, plink I heard in the second bedroom confirmed my suspicions about the bucket that had been left sitting on the bed.

I found the number we had for the landlord and told the woman who answered the phone about the leak.

She snorted. "Of course it leaks. It's windy."

"But ... could someone come to fix it?"

"Fix what? The wind?" She laughed.

"The leak."

"It doesn't leak when there's no wind." She hung up.

When Avey came home, late, I made myself swallow my accumulated complaints, because he seemed so delighted with how things had gone at work. The site was gorgeous; his co-workers were helpful and friendly; his computer worked better than he had imagined; he had been able to get his program running; the hours had flown; he could hardly wait until the first downloads from the observatory came in.

"So what did *you* do all day?" he asked.

"Oh, just lay around, had a nap, read a book."

"Good, good, I knew you'd like it here. Isn't it great? Isn't this climate bloody wonderful?"

"Yes," I said, wiping a drop of sweat from my chin, "wonderful."

"I know this house is grotty. But it's *Hawaii*. Did you ever even dream you could live in Hawaii?"

The next two weeks I did what I could to make the place more habitable, though the cockroaches seemed impervious to the sprays, and I suspected a mouse was sharing our house, as well. That did not make me excessively squeamish, or squirmish, as Sandy had called it when she was little, but I knew I was never going to grow fond of the house. I did grow fond of the little green gecko on the living room wall. It would stay absolutely still for hours, then vanish, then appear on another part of the wall. The whole time I was there I never actually saw it move. It became a little game for me: where's the gecko?

I made a point every day of leaving the house for several hours, either walking or bicycling, and I discovered both a cheaper grocery store and a library. I hadn't appreciated the importance of either before. In the late afternoons, if the mosquitoes allowed, I sat out in the shade in the overgrown back yard and wrote long letters. Dear Sandy, Dear Mom and Dad, Dear Ingrid. I tried to be amusing, tried to describe the new trees and flowers and birds around me, and by the end of the letter I had usually cheered myself up. I still preferred not to be here, but I was no longer miserable. This was Hawaii, after all, and I'd heard that in Edmonton a blizzard had closed down the city for three days.

Avey left early for work every day, even the weekends, and came home after dark, exhausted but happy. In the five years we'd been married I'd never seen him that happy. He seemed oblivious not only to the wretched house but to my casual standards of tidiness. Back home if I had left my dirty plates and coffee cups sitting around or my clothes tossed onto the backs of chairs they would not have gone unmentioned. But here he seemed not even to see them. I alternated between thinking this an improvement and an annoyance. Once an affable ginger cat came for a visit just before Avey came home, and when he saw it the first expression on his face was bewilderment: I could almost hear him thinking, *Do we have a cat?*

One day, because a problem with the computer system had caused everything to shut down, he came home earlier than usual, and after we had something to eat he suggested we go for a walk, just a few blocks, to work off a cramp in his calf. Of course I agreed. Avey liked walking, actually, though usually not "going for a walk," which implied too much lack of purpose, of destination.

At the end of the block I showed him the carpet slippers still sitting at the curb, and we made each other laugh with silly speculations about how they'd gotten there. They didn't seem to be the sort of thing people wore here, which was a kind of sandal called "thongs" in Canada and "flip-flops" in the US and "slippahs" here. Every porch seemed to hold several pairs.

The evening was so pleasant and free of mosquitoes, the other pedestrians so numerous and unthreatening, that we walked farther than we intended and wound up in Wailoa Park near the waterfront. It was a flat and open place, with pretty curving rainbow bridges looping over the ponds and with trees I had come to recognize but, except for the palms and banyans, not yet name. Across the narrow Wailoa River we could see the statue of Kamehameha, the chief who, not without the usual brutalities, had united all the islands.

We sat down on a bench, kicked off our sandals and sank our toes in the thick-bladed grass that covered the grounds. Parakeets called to each other in the trees above us. A faint smell of eucalyptus drifted in on the breeze.

"This park wouldn't be here except for the tsunamis," Avey said.

"I know." Homes of Japanese sugar workers had once stood here, until the two gigantic tsunamis half a century ago. Hundreds were killed. I couldn't help glancing past Kamehameha at the open ocean, hear that slow beat and retreat of the waves on the sand.

"But I'll bet you don't know that we probably wouldn't be here, either, except for the tsunamis," Avey said.

"How do you figure that?"

"After the 1960 one wiped out Hilo, the Big Island's economy was devastated, right, so the Chamber of Commerce started looking around for other moneymaking opportunities. They lucked into finding an astronomer who went along with the crazy idea of building an observatory on top of Mauna Kea. It was a pretty daring project. There wasn't even a road up to the summit."

"Always surprising, the things that cause other things."

The sun had set, and it was quickly growing dark. I thought about the three stages of twilight. First there was "civil twilight," when things on earth could still be readily seen. Then came "nautical twilight," when general outlines were still distinguishable; sailors could see the horizon to navigate by star altitudes. Then there was "astronomical twilight," when more and more stars could be seen, but it was still too light for astronomers to do major observing. Only when the sun slipped to eighteen degrees below the horizon was twilight over, and official "astronomical darkness" began. At home in summer twilight could last for hours, but here it seemed we plunged through the three stages in a few minutes, right from day into night.

I kept waiting for Avey to say we had to get back, but he only sat there, looking up at the sky. We could see the incredible, thick splash of the Milky Way. It was hard to believe we were in a city, but the whole island had a strong lighting ordinance to ensure the darkest skies possible for the astronomers. "Skyglow" was the astronomers' name for the light pollution that affected just about the whole planet, and even here in Hawaii I knew we were seeing far fewer stars than Galileo would have seen in the seventeenth century. Still, it was dazzling, more than I could have seen in the night sky in a Canadian city, where the "glare bombs," the outdoor light fixtures particularly loathed by astronomers, cast most of their light sideways or upward.

"It's so ... much," I said inadequately. "I guess on the mountain the sky would look even more amazing."

"On a moonless night there the stars actually cast shadows on the landscape. But you'd still notice some interference and distortion from the atmosphere."

"Rather sad, the stars sending their light all those millions of years and millions of miles, only to have it get crumpled up by our own atmosphere."

"You make it sound like a personal letter the mailman drops in the slush on your doorstep."

I laughed. "Well, maybe it's just their hydro bill."

Avey pointed to the north. "There's my star system." He pointed lower. "And there, just through those branches, you can see a fuzzy splotch that's not a single huge star or even binary stars or even clusters, but a whole other galaxy. Andromeda."

I looked at where he was pointing, a small hazy patch of light. Another galaxy. Billions of stars in that small dash of light.

"From far enough away," I say, "I guess there are no individuals. No trees, just a forest of light."

"Huh. Very poetic."

"Maybe a galaxy is like this great collective, everything part of a whole. Isn't that what we all crave?"

Avey snorted. "We don't crave it. We're scared to death of it. Our scariest fiction has us taken over by the hive mind, the pod people, the Borg. It's individualism we crave. That's why communism never had a chance."

"Maybe communism never had a chance because it tried to do without religion, which is communal."

"It's not communal. It's hierarchical. But you have a point. I guess you're not as dumb as you look."

I gave him a punch on the arm. But I was pleased: Avey did not readily make jokes about my intelligence, even though I knew he had told people my IQ was higher than his. I'm not sure that it is. It's probably something my father told him. We try to avoid the subject.

"Have you thought of a name for your planet if you find it?"

"Oh, something like HD114762A. There aren't any official rules in place for naming planets so I can call it 'Kate' if you like."

"That would be nice." I looked back up. "Is the star visible to the naked eye?"

"Doubt it."

"But with a telescope it is?"

"I'm using a radio telescope, Kate. I don't much look up at the stars. I look at a computer."

"But when you do look up, like now, you obviously understand what you see in a more complex way than the rest of us do."

"There are hundreds of billions of stars in our galaxy. There are over three hundred billion galaxies. Every second a billion neutrinos are passing through our bodies. Every second we hurtle through space another 375 miles. It's overwhelming. I don't think about it in any particularly complex way. I keep my head down and hang on."

I laughed, tightened my fingers on the bench.

"We aren't even really sitting here on this bench," Avey said. "We're sitting on an angstrom of electrons being repelled by the bench's electrons."

"I'm sitting on an angstrom?"

"Yup," he said. "There's a measurable distance between our bums and the bench."

"So I can't hang on tighter even if I wanted to."

"Nope. The bench is too repulsed by you."

We sat looking at the sky. I began to notice some stars blinking on at one horizon and blinking off at the other as the earth rotated.

"It's all going away, you know," Avey said after a while.

"What is?"

"The universe. Moving. Expanding. Packing up and saying adios. The dark energy out there is an accelerator, an antigravity, and the effect is only increasing. We can see maybe 100 billion galaxies now with our telescopes, but one by one they'll move out of range. Even the stars in our own galaxy might be driven apart."

"I thought the dark matter was counteracting this," I said.

"It's not enough, apparently. Nobody understands how it works, but they *are* sure about the expansion. It's the Big Goodbye, the cosmic diaspora."

"I thought the Andromeda galaxy was on a collision course with us, though, not moving away."

Avey nodded, waved at the sky. "You're right, you're right. Andromeda didn't get the memo. It's falling toward us. We're actually in a binary galaxy system with it and still have a mutual gravitational attraction, which is why it defies the cosmic expansion laws. So, in three billion years, we'll collide head-on."

"I wonder who'll be here to see it."

"Well, our sun will still have a few billion years of life left. But nobody knows what cosmic expansion will do before that. Maybe it will simply overwhelm the electromagnetic force and tear everything to shreds: suns, planets, us. It's a scenario they call 'The Big Rip.'"

I sat there for a while thinking about that. Avey must have thought he'd really alarmed me because he added, "It's not something we need to lie awake worrying about."

I smiled, patted his arm. He lifted it, put it around my shoulders. I could feel his fingers lightly drumming on my biceps.

It was nice, being here. I would remember this time later, this happy moment, sitting here with Avey on our angstroms, thinking our large thoughts about the universe, the smell of eucalyptus in the air, the warm night air floating around us, our feet in the thick-bladed grass.

I would remember this time later, this happy moment: was there ever a sadder sentence?

"Anyway," Avey said, "I don't waste my time thinking about all that stuff. That's for philosophers, mystics, the mushy humanists. For me it was always about the science. The physics."

"But as a child you must have looked up sometimes and felt that pure awe. And I thought you said your uncle gave you a telescope when you were young."

"Yeah, I had a telescope. It was probably the most valuable thing I ever owned. Then my father came home drunk one night and tripped over it and broke it."

His father. "Oh. It couldn't be repaired?"

"I suppose it could have been. Though after he smashed it against the wall there wasn't a lot left." I could feel his whole body clenching, the way it always did when he spoke of his father. He pulled his arm away from around my shoulders. "Well, who knows, maybe that was why I went into astronomy. Because I thought he'd hate it." He gave a bitter laugh.

"Or you could think of the incident as something that helped to establish an interest, a direction." I don't know why I felt I had to soften that memory.

"Or maybe I couldn't." He got up. "Let's go," he said. He started walking away before I even got to my feet.

On the way back I tried to find more neutral things to say, something to bring back that affable and conversational mood he had been in earlier. But he was closed in on himself now, responding, if at all, with low-voiced mutters I grew tired of asking him to repeat. He walked so fast that I finally had to stop to catch my breath. He was half a block ahead of me before he realized I wasn't struggling along beside him, and even then he didn't stop, just slowed his pace, kicking at pebbles and leaves on the sidewalk, until I caught up.

We were only a few blocks from the house when for some reason he began talking about a problem with sidereal time, but when I asked him to explain it he said impatiently, "How can you have gotten through school without knowing the difference between a synodic day and a sidereal day? A sidereal day uses the stars as a reference and it's four minutes less than a day based on the sun."

"And why is that?"

"In one sidereal day the Earth completes one rotation on its axis. But because the earth moves in its orbit about the sun, the sidereal day is about four minutes shorter than the solar day. Any given star will rise four minutes earlier each night. The night sky at, say, 3:00 a.m. tonight will look the same as it will at about 10:30 p.m. in a hundred days. The night sky a hundred days ago at 3:00 a.m. looked the same as it will tonight at 10:30 p.m."

His math was wrong. It would be the same at 8:20 p.m., not 10:30. But I didn't correct him. My parents would have shuddered: for them this was the loathesome sin of playing dumb for a man's ego. But I remember my mother more than once adroitly changing the subject when she could tell she and Avey were headed to an argument she was likely to win. How was that different? Was it a question of timing? Why was mine an abdication of self-esteem and hers a social skill?

In any case, my motive that night was simply to cut the irritation from Avey's voice, so I said, "Ah. You'd make a good teacher."

He grunted. But I could tell that at last I had said something that pleased him. I was ashamed, though, because I was thinking the opposite. I was afraid he would not be a good teacher at all.

We got back to the house, which looked so desolate from the outside with its boarded-up window it might have been slated for demolition the next day. We trudged up the steps, trying not to hear the scurryings underneath.

"I was thinking," I said, "that maybe I could call the agency back home, see if by some chance I could do some caretaking work at a condo here we helped sell. Just, you know, something to get me out of this house. If they paid me in Canadian dollars I might not be breaking any laws."

"So call them," Avey said impatiently, opening the door, which required such an adroit combination of lift and push and turn that a lock was redundant. "God knows we need the money. What are you waiting for?"

"I guess I could check it out."

"Why didn't you do it before now? This *attitude* you have about money. And work."

My attitude to money and work: well, yes. He wasn't the first person to find it problematic.

My parents were the proverbial workaholics, my father a doctor and my mother a senior executive for a mining company, and what it taught me was that I did not want that kind of life. They came home exhausted every night, rarely capable of enjoying anything but work. When they would say, *yes, we love you*, but be always absent, I saw this at first as some paradox; but by the time I started school I thought I had resolved the paradox: my parents were lying about loving me. I persisted with this aggrieved notion far longer than I should have, but it is satisfying to have an explanation, however increasingly inapt it becomes, especially when you can make someone feel guilty. Of course, making your parents feel guilty only leads to making yourself feel guilty.

I was bright enough as a child to be labelled "gifted," but I could see that, first, being gifted would simply put me on a fast-track to a life like theirs and, second, it would annoy them considerably if I showed no interest in that destination. For both those reasons I aimed at underachievement, and it became, I suppose, a habit.

"But isn't there anything that really excites you?" my father would say, exasperated. "Anything that inspires you, that makes you so curious you want to jump out of bed in the morning just to get at it?" I thought about it, but only insofar as I told myself I had better be wary of any such passions, had better nip in the bud any incipient enthusiasms that would grow me into the same kind of person he was.

It was around this same time that my mother had snapped at me, "Are you what feminists have fought for?"

"Are *you?*"

It shook us both, that brief exchange. I still play it in my head, thinking of what I should have said instead, because I understood immediately how much I had hurt her. I knew too little about feminism then to consider hers an equal insult.

As Avey headed off to bed and I started scrubbing the pot I'd left to soak, it occurred to me that perhaps I'd chosen my course in life for the same reason Avey might have chosen his: because at least one of our parents would have hated it. The idea was a little frightening.

If I had learned to be lazy, however, I had also learned to be, at least with everyone but my parents, agreeable. The price I paid for such agreeableness was to hold no opinion so dear I could not lose an argument about it. "You're right," I would say disarmingly, rewarded by that glitter, however brief, of triumph in the eye of whomever I was talking to. Only one friend ever called me on this. She said I was manipulative. It wasn't quite the right word, but I saw her point. "You're right," I said. We both laughed.

I was also cute. It is not immodest to admit that, since it was the first adjective people thought to apply to me.

Cute, lazy, agreeable. It was probably the way most of my friends would have characterized me.

I married David, who ran his own accountancy firm, right after high school, which I didn't quite bother to complete. That I had no interest in university was of course a huge disappointment for my parents, but at least they did not blame David for this. In fact they quite approved of him; he was rather like they were, smart and energetic and in love with his work. And in love with me, of course, as I was with him. He was utterly confident that our lives would turn out exactly as he expected them to. I've never known anyone so able to access every drop of happiness in the moment. In every memory I have of him he's smiling. When he wanted to grow a moustache I begged him not to — I wanted to see all of that smile, every small turn and muscle and nuance of it.

"A handsome couple," people called us. When Sandy was born David was happy to have me stay home with her while he worked. It was an old-fashioned relationship, I suppose. Sandy adored her father and grew up to excel in everything academic. It occurred to me once that perhaps one of her motivations was not just to please her father but to make a choice deliberately opposite to mine, as I had done with my parents. I didn't care much either way; I was an example of how it didn't pay to have ambitions for your children.

David's death was devastating for me. My mother said, not unkindly, "It's the first bad thing that's ever happened to you."

She was right, I suppose. I had no defenses against such loss, against that terrible understanding that every day for the rest of my life David would not be in it. For two years I sank into a dullness and blankness that made people think I was on ill-advised medications. They would practically have to shake me to get me even to see them. My sadness was like a heavy, hooded cloak I was afraid I would never be able to remove.

Sandy, I thought, was dealing with David's loss better than I was, but of course later I understood that her growing anger with me was also a kind of mourning. She had been encouraged by her English teacher to write about her feelings, and she began leaving her poems conspicuously around the house. In them there were always an insensitive mother and an angry daughter. I pretended I hadn't read them, but this seemed only to annoy her more, so I made myself comment on them in some neutral way. I remember one of the lines: "My mother likes to suffer, likes to walk barefoot on the broken glass of grief."

What did I feel, reading that? Numbness, emptiness. Not the dismay and hurt I feel even now thinking of it.

I told Sandy that this was probably good writing for someone her age.

"I don't care, I don't care," she shrieked. "That wasn't why I wrote it! I hate you like this, I *hate* you!"

"I'm sorry," I said. That still wasn't what she wanted to hear, but it was all I had. *Sorry*, derived from *sorrow*.

I couldn't blame her then for saying she wanted to move out. I said, "Whatever you want."

That same evening she moved in with my parents, where she stayed for almost half a year. They were as loving and supportive of her as they knew how to be, and I was surprised when Sandy asked to move back in with me. My father told me it was probably because the three of them together produced too much testosterone for one house.

My mother, without telling me, signed me up for a realtor's course, and that did rather startle me back into life. David had left me with few financial resources, so there was a practical side to my mother's intervention, though we both knew that she and my father had more money than they knew how to spend and that it took an effort on their part not to lapse back into their guilty habits of giving me money to compensate for not giving me their time.

In any case, I found the real estate work, at least as much as I wanted to do of it, pleasant enough and relatively easy, perhaps because I felt no need to be particularly successful. Escalating one's income simply required an escalation of expenses. I wasn't being disingenuous when I told people I simply didn't see the point. Of course, in the real estate business one has to be careful not to admit one finds money, well, boring.

Perhaps I was drawn to Avey because he had enough ambition for both of us.

My parents liked that ambition and were grateful I had found someone, were sure he would be good for me, to me. And they liked his academic promise, the idea of a son-in-law who might become a professor. But I knew they found him a bit exhausting, a bit too abrasive, and more than once I would meet their eyes and see there a forbidden and never-spoken thought: he's not David. I don't think Avey ever deciphered these traitorous glances. He admired my parents, said he wished they had been his. He suspected *me* of missing David, but he didn't suspect my parents.

But Avey made me look forward to life again, made me feel sexy and interesting, made me enjoy improbable things like hockey games and visits to the planetarium. He had a caustic sense of humour and a cut-to-the-chase conversation I had never experienced before. On our second date he told me he liked my hair, and when I thanked him for the compliment he said it wasn't a compliment, which implied flattery instead of the truth. I was quite enchanted: such honesty! I thought how trustworthy such a man would be, how transparent, how incapable of deceptions. Maybe that was all it took to win me, his paying me a compliment that was not a compliment.

So we married. *Yes, I do love him,* I assured my friends, a little annoyed with them for needing to make me say it. But the way I loved him was different from the way I'd loved David. My love for Avey added components of loneliness and need and loss and evaluation. *Added:* no, these are surely subtractions to love, at least as it is conceived of in romance. Oh, I don't know. I try not to think about it. I am rather good at not thinking of things that make me uncomfortable.

Which is probably why I do not often think of Hale.

Three

"Every great scientific truth goes through three stages. First, people say it conflicts with the Bible. Next they say it has been discovered before. Lastly they say they always believed it."

— LOUIS AGASSIZ (1807-1873)

A V E Y

Bruno decided to have a party before Christmas, before people flew off to all the global corners they came from.

"You'll come, won't you?" he said. "My arse is turning permanently into the shape of this chair. Let's do something standing up."

I was peering through a magnifying glass at a printout of the spectrum. I can't remember why. The computer did a far more sophisticated analysis of any spectra produced at the telescope than the human eye could ever do.

"Huh?" I squinted up at him.

"You're going blind, man."

I rubbed my eyes. Maybe I *was* going blind. It seemed harder than it used to be to keep anything in focus.

"You're right," I said. "And when I close my eyes all I see is a black field with white dots."

I wasn't exactly joking. I was describing what the afterimage of my computer screen looked like. I'd see it at night, too, when I'd be trying to fall asleep. It took me a while to realize I wasn't visualizing the night sky.

I'd been at it over a month now. Even though I knew it could take years to find anything, I'd been optimistic that Dr. Orlovski's research would have cut out a lot of that fumbling in the dark, would have given me a star system to focus on with more than a random chance of success. But damned if I had seen anything at all. I was beginning to wonder if he'd fudged his results. Meanwhile, there were God only knew how many other rabid planet hunters closing in on the prize.

"You work too hard," Bruno said. He pulled his tea bag out of his cup and set it on top of two others inside an improvised and leaking saucer of tinfoil.

I yawned, to stop myself from saying something about how he didn't work hard *enough*. Yesterday he spent most of the morning just reading aloud to me silly definitions from Ambrose Bierce's *The Devil's Dictionary*. For the rest of my life I will probably have to remember his definition of a telescope: to the eye like the telephone is to the ear, an invention of the devil enabling distant objects to plague us with a multitude of needless details.

I should have been relieved that Bruno wasn't as obsessed as I was, but his lackadaisical attitude was irritating. He came in late and left early, and he hadn't bothered to run any checks of his program. As far as I could see he'd made no changes at all. I'd found at least one glitch that could affect our readings.

We could have arranged to actually work together, to share and cross-reference our data, but neither of us had suggested that. I could have told him about the program glitch I'd found but I didn't.

I remembered my first-year Physics prof explaining Pauli's Exclusion Principle by saying it was rather like people fighting for the same seat on the bus. Maybe Bruno and I were the electrons that couldn't occupy the same office unless we had opposite spin. It was what kept everything from imploding. Lord help us if we got the same spin at the same time.

Wolfgang Pauli, though: there's someone I wouldn't have wanted to fight for a seat on the bus. He wasn't Mr. Congeniality. About a paper submitted by a colleague, Pauli said, "This isn't right. This isn't even wrong." Ouch. Perfect, but ouch.

"Yeah, well," I said to Bruno, "somebody's got to find that damned second planet. It might as well be us." At the last second I'd had the finesse to say "us" instead of "me."

"Ah, who knows if in ten years they'll even consider it the second anymore."

"Huh?"

"Oh, you know. Maybe 51 Pegasi B will have been disproved by then. Remember van de Kamp's claim in the sixties of two planets around Barnard's star? It took a decade to fully discredit that."

"Okay, so we might be first, not second. I could live with that."

"But maybe they'll decide the first was really something earlier," Bruno persisted. "How about that 'solid matter' orbiting a main-sequence star in Vega that one of our satellites observed? Wasn't that a planet? Or they could still give the credit to Wolszczan and Frail."

"Yeah, they could." A few years ago Wolszczan and Frail had found three planets orbiting a pulsar, a neutron star, in Virgo. National Public Radio even had a competition for naming them. The leading candidates were Larry, Curly and Moe.

"Or they'll decide brown dwarfs are really planets after all."

"Shut up, man. You're making me crazy." He was, actually. There was a real possibility that, in the ongoing and nasty debate over whether brown dwarfs, stars with too little mass to ignite, could be considered planets, the planet proponents would win. And the first verifiable brown dwarf was discovered by Caltech just a few months ago.

"Frankly, I think my martyred namesake Giordano Bruno should get the credit. He believed with absolute conviction that planets were out there. According to his church's own a priori argument, God exists because otherwise we wouldn't have the idea of God, right? So the extrasolar planets exist because otherwise how could Bruno have imagined anything so outlandish, so impossible?"

"You'll have to tell Louisa that."

"Oh, she'd agree. She's ecumenical enough to think God didn't stop with us — he made everything we could possibly find out there."

"That would solve the problem of who gets the credit."

We laughed. I leaned back, stretched my arms up over my head. My shoulder muscles felt as though they were calcifying.

"Anyway," I said, "did I hear you right? A party?"

"If you can tear yourself away from here long enough," Bruno said.

"Okay. Rip."

"This Saturday. We'll pretend the stars are just pretty little dots in the sky."

"Who's coming?"

"Oh, I suppose most of the people from JAC you know. Perry. Macpherson. The Markowskis. John. Hilde and Dieter. And some of the Keck people my father knew are coming down from Waimea."

"Ah. The Keckos." Bruno and I made fun of them because we envied them, with their NASA connections, their überscope confidence. The second Keck telescope was just getting finished, so they would be twice as king-of-the-hill as before, would have the *two* biggest telescopes in the world.

Well, they had the budgets for it, the endowments, the big bucks. That's what you got by naming yourself for an oil executive. William M. Keck, founder of the Superior Oil Company. Now founder of the Superior Telescope. Maybe our telescope should have been named for a Bronfman or a British lord.

Still, James Clerk Maxwell: that's class. Astronomy is fond of him because of his study of Saturn's rings, but his biggest accomplishment was his four brilliant equations unifying electricity and magnetism in a single force. I'd say it was the greatest achievement of 19th-century physics.

The man is up there with Newton and Einstein, but Kate hadn't even heard of him. All she said was that it was too bad one of his names didn't begin with a vowel so that we wouldn't have to say Jay Cee Em Tee every time. She said it reminded her of the time a new bank clerk, looking at our transfer statement from a trust company, kept asking Kate how she pronounced her last name. "Fleming," she repeated, puzzled, until the clerk pointed to the word after that: "JTWROS." We had to explain that it meant Joint Tenants With Right Of Survivorship. I'd called Kate "Mrs. Jtwros" for a while.

Bruno took a gulp of tea. "Yeah. The Kecknocrats. They're just the usual geeks. Like us."

I didn't appreciate the word but I let it pass. "Shall I bring something?"

"Just your lovely wife."

I smiled, trying to look as though I appreciated the "lovely," as though it wasn't something I'd heard about Kate a hundred times before. I was glad he'd asked me to bring Kate, though. I was feeling guilty at how little time I was spending with her. She was out doing things on her own now and had, somewhat to my surprise, gotten some little property management job for a Canadian conglomerate, but I knew she must be resenting this workaholic frenzy I was in. A couple of times I'd gotten so engrossed I didn't get home until midnight, so tired and with my leg muscles knotted up so badly I almost crashed my bike going down the hill. When we had sex she could probably feel that I wasn't really into it the way I used to be. Find a planet, stroke, find a planet, stroke.

"Great," I said to Bruno. "I'll bring the wife." I had meant to give "the wife" the ironic emphasis he might have expected, but the words came uninflected out of my mouth. The wife. Kate had better not ever hear that.

I hunched my chair back to my desk and adjusted my computer monitor up a little to give my head a different angle at which to get stiff. When I began pawing around in my desk drawer looking for the Tiger Balm I sometimes rubbed on my neck, I came across the page my thesis supervisor had typed up for me just before I came here. It was a quotation from Leo Szilard, the physicist who developed the linear accelerator and electron microscope, and it said, *You don't have to be much cleverer than other people, you just have to be one day earlier.*

*

Bruno lived on the northwest side of Hilo. It was hard to tell directions here exactly, but I wasn't about to start imitating Bruno and use the Hawaiian directional words, *mauka* and *makai*, which simply meant "toward the mountain," usually uphill, and "toward the ocean," usually downhill. The words made sense, but I wasn't going to stay here long enough to start thinking like a native.

We could have gotten a ride but Kate wanted to walk, to look at the poinsettia shrubs that seemed overnight to have turned their milky green leaves into the large starred blossoms we had only seen in pots in Edmonton. It was a surprise to find such a sense of season here.

Kate had been reading about some of the other trees on the island, and she pointed, pleased, to things she could identify.

"That's a candlenut tree," she said, spotting one in an overgrown yard. "It's the official state tree of Hawaii. See the big clusters of white flowers? And there's a pink tecoma." She pulled me to a stop under a giant canopied tree with sickle-shaped leaves. "This is a koa. Koas are everywhere. People grow them for the beautiful red wood. I like its flowers, those little fuzzy yellow balls. And here's plumeria, of course." She picked up some of the waxy pink blossoms that lay everywhere on the streets and passed them to me to smell.

"Mmm," I said. I resisted saying something about how I knew she'd get to like it better here. The truth was that for the first two weeks I thought there was a good chance she would pack up and leave.

We walked along Kilauea Avenue past Wailoa Park and through the downtown. I'd never actually come downtown before. There didn't seem to be anything over two storeys, just a lot of vintage false-front buildings leaning into one another, awnings everywhere to keep out the rain. It had that "place that time forgot" feeling to it. Some of the buildings had been restored, but to me it just seemed like a clash of architectures, stone or wood buildings side by side with ones of concrete and brick, art deco and California-looking terra cotta and Buddhist temples and local styles all jumbled together. Nobody seemed to have distinguished between what might be genuine heritage buildings worth saving and what weren't. The new paint jobs looked like bad makeup on old women. Everything smelled of dust and old wood.

Kate seemed to find it all delightful. "Things are on such a human scale here," she said.

"Would it hurt to put up a nice high-rise?"

She gave me a look.

We crossed the little arched bridge over the Wailuku River and headed up Pu'ueo Street. We were only a block from Bruno's when we were set upon by a gang of mosquitoes, and we ran, flailing, beating them away from our faces. When we reached the house a breeze from the ocean whirled them abruptly away, and we were able to catch our breaths and stroll up the walk.

The house was huge, built mostly of redwood, with a wraparound lanai and lots of windows. Inside, I knew, it was just as impressive: the living room had an open beam ceiling with vented skylights, and the furniture was new and expensive. Half the house had a second floor with a spectacular view across Hilo Bay. It was hardly surprising that the first time I saw the place I was envious as hell. Bruno's father had bought it when he did his research here. I'd had to swallow back some sarcastic comment last week when Bruno said dolorously that it was hard to be the son of a famous father. Yeah, right.

Kate whimpered when she saw the place.

"Don't get any ideas," I said. "He mentioned a girlfriend." He hadn't, actually, and I've no idea why I felt I had to say that to Kate. As though she would walk out on me for a big fat Torontonian in a big fat house in Hilo. It was just my old knee-jerk insecurity, when I thought I was seeing in people's faces that look of "what's a gorgeous woman like you doing with this homely little prick?" And Kate had this easy charm about her, too, could get people to trust her just like that. At her job back home she could have sold the High Level Bridge to the mayor of Edmonton. It actually annoyed me sometimes, how comfortable she seemed with people, because if I studied for ten years I could never be like that, yet here she was, having apparently neither learned it nor earned it, just been born with it, that confidence that the very air would part before her like an adoring crowd as she walked.

She looked effortlessly beautiful tonight. Her pale skin had taken on a nice pinkness from the sun, with maybe an additional flush from our gallop away from the mosquitoes. She was just wearing shorts, but she had on a new top made of some shimmery, beaded stuff, and if you looked at it for longer than a few seconds you could tell she wasn't wearing a bra, a habit she'd gotten into here and which I thought was okay in private but dubious in public. She'd used a curling iron on her hair, which didn't really need it; the humidity here gave it enough body to walk about on its own. She'd clipped in some butterfly-shaped barrettes, too, and maybe the look was a little young for her, but I supposed women like Kate got to keep their little-girl accessorizing longer than most.

In any case, she got a lot of looks when we came in. A skinny, blond guy I recognized from one of the UKIRT offices slowly trickled his gaze down her like a confectioner glazing a cake. I could say I felt proud of her, but I had no right to that word. I could take no credit for anything about her, except her being here.

Besides, "proud" is one of those proprietary words I hate, maybe ever since I heard my father use it to one of his buddies when he heard

I got accepted into graduate school, and I thought, you bastard, you did nothing to get me here, nothing. There wasn't one minute of my university education that wasn't paid for with my own sweat: construction jobs every summer where the blackflies made the mosquitoes here seem barely peckish, part-time work wherever I could scrounge it during the term, student loans I'll still be paying off when I'm eighty.

I think Kate didn't really believe how poor my childhood was. We didn't *look* poor. My father was a teacher, after all; we seemed well-dressed and genteel and cultured; we lived in a clean middle-class house full of books and classical music. What could anyone really know of the misery behind those nice stuccoed walls, of what went on while Bach was playing, of how my father's salary went to booze and junkets to Vegas?

But I've tried hard not to feel bitter about my childhood. Unless I'd had an exceptionally shitty day I didn't let myself use it as any kind of excuse. Sometimes I think it's people with happier childhoods who do that: life never measures up to their expectations.

My eyes bounced around the room. There were about fifty people here, few of them out of their thirties. Most of them I recognized from the JAC. I hadn't expected Bruno to invite only astronomers and PhD students since the majority of workers there were support staff of some kind — technicians, engineers, machinists, computer programmers, telescope operators — but I was surprised to see some maintenance and clerical staff, too. Okay, so that was snobby of me.

Kate got talking right away to the wife of one of the programmers, something about the Kamehamehas and Hawaiian history, boring boring, so I wandered off to do the required schmoozing, though I was better at it when Kate was with me. She always knew how to segue from supportively spousal to independently interesting.

ABBA's "Dancing Queen" had been playing when we came in, but now someone put on a techno music so loud that whatever cochlear hair cells I hadn't fried from that Stones' concert in the 90s were starting to sizzle.

Perry came over and said, "Show me yours."

"What?"

"I said, how are you?"

"Fine, fine," I screamed. "Quite the place, eh?"

"Yeah, I know, yesterday."

Mercifully, someone turned the music down then, and the shrieking conversations also lowered themselves after a few seconds. The word "altimeter" hung comically in the air the way words did at such times.

I headed upstairs, cornering, as much as one can corner someone on the stairs, Dr. Schultz from the University of Calgary, trying to think of something to say that would make him remember me the next time U of C had a position open. Maybe I could tell him how the variable I'd started using was helping with my data reduction routine. Schultz got a lot of respect, I knew that, but he preferred to spend more time up on the mountain than in the office, so I didn't see much of him at the JAC. He had a lean and awkward appearance, and when he walked his head jutted forward, as though his body was always labouring to keep up with his thoughts. He let his incredibly frizzled black hair grow longer than he should have, perhaps because it had the effect of making people look at it instead of at his face when he had to talk to them. His eyes would never look directly at you. A man uncomfortable around people. I suppose it could be an asset in our business. I wondered how long Schultz had been at the party. Introverts, I'd read, were supposed to be able to endure only about an hour of socializing before they got too twitchy and desperate to be alone. I was often feeling that way after five minutes, though I'm usually not overly eager to be alone with my enchanting self, either. Maybe I'm that fine line between introvert and misanthrope.

"Nice to get away from work for a change, isn't it?" I said, immediately thinking it was exactly the opposite of what I should have said.

"Yes, yes," he answered, his eyes scuttling around the room below us. His voice was so heavily accented with German that he seemed to be saying "ja, ja" with a slight sibilance at the end.

"Are you staying here for Christmas?" That was better. I could, if necessary, say I would be.

"Yes, yes. I do not think I will miss the snow."

"Well, you can always find some up on the mountain, I guess."

He laughed as though I had been especially witty and then held up the two wine glasses he was carrying and said, "Must replenish." He eased his way down a step, and I knew I'd lost him. Damn it.

I went up to the second floor sitting room with its floor-to-ceiling windows overlooking the bay. The ocean rose and fell, rose and fell, onto the beach. I thought about tidal friction, how it was slowing us all down, how eventually the planet would be rotating only once a month, then once a year, then not at all. In a billion years the tides would be still. Meanwhile, here they were, like us, possessed by that bizarre and loopy energy, rising and falling, rising and falling.

The sun had just set behind us, in its abrupt tropical way, plop, and the water was already losing its glow, turning dark. Off to the east I could see Coconut Island and the breakwater and a smaller cove called Radio Bay. Bruno liked that: Radio Bay, though the name probably had nothing to do with radio telescopes.

A breeze strolled in and out across the lanai, and the smell of plumeria sweetened the air. The temperature was that of a perfect summer evening, and I had to remind myself this was the middle of winter, that at home it was forty below zero. A dangerous thing, letting Canadians travel south in winter. I'd never spent a winter outside of Edmonton, and I knew I would never want to spend one there again.

What would it be like to grow up in a climate like this, to have no winter, to never once think you could freeze to death just waiting for the bus? It would have to affect your personality.

"Lovely evening, isn't it?"

Louisa was standing beside me, looking out at the bay. She was wearing a long dress, low-cut, with huge purple flowers on it. I'd never seen her in a dress before. She didn't look half bad. The thick, black hair that she usually anchored into a tight ponytail at the nape of her neck was still there, but she'd pulled some strands free and they curled into loose ringlets around her face. She had a somewhat beakish nose, but her other features were pleasant enough: big, brown, deep-set eyes just starting to crinkle at the corners, skin so smooth I had the absurd urge to reach up to feel if it was some kind of synthetic.

Watch the wine, I told myself. Louisa wasn't someone I wanted to flirt with, not after Bruno's warning about her religious proclivities. I was surprised he'd invited her. I'd heard more than one nasty argument they'd had, and his vehemence surprised me. But I suppose being named for someone burned at the stake by the church gave him a certain touchiness about the issue. Louisa had never lost her composure: watching the two of them you'd have thought Bruno the less rational one.

"Sure is," I said. "One of God's better days."

Good grief: saying that was even worse than stroking her skin.
She stiffened. "Don't mock," she said quietly.

"I wasn't. Really. It was just an observation."

But I could tell she was still on her guard. Even if she didn't know
anything about my religious beliefs, she knew I was Bruno's office mate.
I'd kept my mouth shut around her, though, kept those expletives
deleted. Louisa wasn't someone I could imagine myself ever coming
to for a favour, and her recommendation might do more damage than
good, but you never knew.

"I'm sorry," she said, not exactly sounding it. "I get sick of people
trying to make me feel like a superstitious idiot."

"Yeah, well." How to respond? I looked out at the water, hoping my
expression suggested something meditative. "I guess in our business it's
just our job to be questioning everything all the time."

"So maybe we should be questioning why the whole anthropic
principle scares us so much."

Ah, the anthropic principle. A perfectly interesting scientific proposal warped by creationists into something like Aristotle saying the
reason there is rain is that plants and animals need it. Apparently
the laws of physics are so incredibly fine-tuned for the existence of
intelligent life, for marvelous us, that, well, only God could have done
it. Myself, I like the anthropic principle version that says we're living
in a fake universe, in a virtual reality simulation. But what was the
point of arguing with Louisa? She'd have counter-arguments ready for
everything. I wouldn't be able to shake her beliefs. I didn't even want
to. I wasn't like Bruno.

"*Everything* in the universe scares *me*," I said, trying for the jocular.
"Black holes scare me. Dark energy scares me. Quantum mechanics
scares me."

"Quantum mechanics doesn't scare me. It's a way of seeing how
God can act without violating the laws of physics. Without needing
miracles as an explanation. And understanding that electrons can be
simultaneously waves and particles is even a way of understanding
how Jesus can be both fully divine and fully human. It depends on
which face He turns to you. Quantum mechanics takes a lot of the ...
well, the strangeness out of Christianity."

"Strangeness?"

"Well, yes. It's the nature of faith to accept the strangeness, but it's nice to see it meshes with the science."

"Ah."

"You think it's all nonsense. I know."

"No, really, I ..." Behind Louisa's head I could see the string of Christmas lights Bruno had draped across a tree branch that had meandered onto his lanai. The lights were blinking on and off. Fireflies on Noah's ark.

"It's all right. I know this makes people uncomfortable."

I shifted my feet, worked on my meditative look. "I guess no matter where we're coming from or how far we go it still comes down to Paul Tillich's question: 'Why is there something, when there could have been nothing?'"

Tillich. Brilliant.

She gave me a smile. It must have been the first one I'd seen on her. It made me feel pretty good. She was standing so close to me that I could see her contact lenses lift, then slide back down over her irises, when she blinked.

I don't know what Louisa and I would have said to each other then because Bruno came up at that point, thinking perhaps I needed rescuing. He clapped me on the back. "Come downstairs and meet one of the Kecknophiles. She's every bit as obnoxious as I'd hoped," he said cheerfully.

As I followed him down the stairs I noticed the people below me turn their eyes to the door, where Kani Waiohu, our secretary, was entering. It wasn't Kani they were looking at, though, as it never was when she arrived anywhere with her brother.

People looked at Hale because he was almost unbelievably handsome.

KATE

Handsome. That was an understatement.

When he walked in I was talking to Karen, the wife of one of the British computer programmers with whom I had gone for walks in the Lili'uokalani Gardens. She was a programmer, too, but unable to work here, so she was glad to find someone to spend time with. She was more chattery than I'd have liked, but energetic and witty, and I let myself be pulled along in her glittery white slipstream and was usually not sorry. She had a gift for linguistic mimicry that made her able to echo perfectly and at unexpected times the accent of every one of the dozen or so nationalities I had heard here when they spoke English. "We Brits get to do that," she'd said. "It's part of the original copyright agreement." She was tall and very thin, with joints that seemed disproportionately big. Her face was rectangular and dominated by a large and expressive mouth to which she drew additional attention with glossy lipsticks. She tried to keep her dark hair, streaked with red, curled across one cheek to hide a sickle-shaped scar.

She had been interrogating me about the work I had started doing for the Edmonton lawyers who had bought a condo complex just outside of Hilo, but she stopped in the middle of her question and nodded at the door.

"Isn't he gorgeous?" she whispered.

"Yes. Wow."

"He did some modelling once. Someone showed me a calendar where he was the picture for July. Nothing lewd, just with his shirt off, wearing a lei."

"Who is he?"

"Brother of Kani Waiohu — you've met her. He works at the JAC, too. Maintenance, I think, and the groundskeeping and gardening, though there's not much of that."

He walked over to the bar. Something about him, maybe just the easy curve of the lips, reminded me of David.

He was in his mid-twenties, perhaps, wearing a loose, white shirt, white slacks, and white shoes without socks, all of it contrasting with the thick black hair and large brown eyes and chestnut skin of the native Hawaiian. His small nose gave his face a somewhat feminine beauty, masculinized, perhaps, by heavy brows that lifted up a small bit at the outer edges. His hair was shoulder-length and pulled back over one ear, a style that might have seemed mannered except that it also conveyed a casualness, a sense that he had just reached up and brushed it out of his eyes. Everything about him, in fact, suggested that: an elegant, languid gesture just completed, as though he had just become conscious somehow, perfect and new and brushing the past from his eyes.

"What's his name?" I knew I should stop looking at him. But I wasn't the only one.

"Hale." She pronounced it in two syllables, accenting the first, softening the vowels. "I'll introduce you if you want." There was something amused and faintly insinuative in her voice.

"That's all right," I said. "I'll worship from afar."

"We all do, my dear. He's a man undeniably made to be looked at."

"What's he like? Does he have the arrogance his appearance entitles him to?"

"He's reasonably amiable, Joe says."

A teenager came past with a tray of cheese and crackers, and I piled some onto the napkin I had been holding under my drink.

"Yum," I said. "Gouda." When I looked up the beautiful Hale was, to my relief, no longer in sight.

Karen plucked some slivers of cheddar from the tray before the server moved away. "Okay, so now tell me," she said, "are you sure there isn't any way this company you work for can get me hired, too?"

Perhaps we should have continued to talk about the beautiful Hale. I wished I hadn't told Karen about my new work at all. For one thing, I wasn't completely sure it was legal, even though it was for a Canadian company and I was just replacing a local woman glad of a reason to go on holiday for a few months.

"Really, Karen, you'd hate it. It's caretaking, that's all. Chambermaid work. Scrubbing toilets. Laundry. Cleaning up other people's dirt and listening to their complaints."

The truth was something quite different. The truth was that people were expected to clean the condo before they left in order to get their deposit back, and most of them left the place spotless. Usually all I had to do was go in to check, phone in my report to Edmonton, and perhaps restock a little dish detergent or occasional light bulb. Rarely did any of the tourists call me with problems, which I was authorized to have fixed by calling someone from a list the company had supplied. The complex was just down from the Bayfront Highway and had only ten units, all in the luxury class, secluded and quiet, with extravagant views across Hilo Bay; and since there were usually a few unrented I was able, even encouraged, to stay there as much as I wanted.

It was no exaggeration to say that I would have paid to do the job, instead of collecting almost a thousand dollars a month from the company for it. I hoped none of the lawyers would ever come to see me in the squalid house in which I lived or they might have concluded the same thing.

"Well," Karen said, "let me know if you hear of any other work I can do. I don't care how menial. I'm going mad doing nothing. Joe has forgotten how to talk to anybody out loud anymore. He's started to send me email from work rather than speak to me in person."

"At least you *have* email," I said.

"I think if I went to the office and flung Hale onto the floor in front of him and we made mad passionate et cetera Joe would just squint down at us from his computer and say to be careful not to bump the surge protector."

And then her eyes widened and her face suddenly went red, and when I turned to follow her gaze I saw Hale standing at my shoulder.

"Hello," he said. "*Aloha ahiahi.*" His voice was low but not noticeably ironic, though he must have heard what Karen had said. "Karen, right? From England?"

"Yes." Karen's face was still pink. I had never seen her so discomfited.

"Your husband introduced us once. In the staff lounge. You'd brought him ... some '*ohelo papas.* Strawberries."

"I'm surprised you remember."

"I remember all the women who might throw me to the floor and do ... interesting things to me."

"Oh, dear." But now that Karen should have been most embarrassed she simply laughed and said with a fluid smile, "Ah, then you must require a large memory indeed." She had taken on, for some reason, an Irish accent. Hale's voice, on the other hand, had surprised me for its English preciseness, its slightly British inflection. I had heard the Hawaiian saying: When in doubt talk pidgin, when in trouble talk Hawaiian. Perhaps Hale felt neither in doubt nor in trouble and was as good a mimic as Karen, with an accent and vocabulary for the occasion.

"And you are?" He turned to me.

"Kate. I'm Avey's wife. Canadians. We've been here a month."

"Avey? Dr. Fleming?"

Doctor Fleming? Avey did not have his doctorate. Was Hale just making an assumption or had Avey been using that title? My mind was blank for a response. Finally I just said, "His real name is Xavier but everyone calls him Avey."

"Yes. He shares an office with ... Bruno." He had an odd way of pausing between some words, just slightly, not quite enough to be a speech impediment, but as though he were applying to the whole sentence the glottal stops I had noticed in Hawaiian words.

People had started dancing, spilling out into the back garden, which was full of purple and white bougainvillea and shaded by a huge and dense mango tree. Even from here I could see the fruit on it.

Karen took Hale's arm and said, "Come on, boyo. Let's dance." She sounded as though she had been born and raised in Belfast. As she well might have been, I realized: she was quite drunk and the accent might simply be a lapse into the old and familiar.

Hale touched my arm. "See you again, I hope," he said.

I could feel a tingle where he had touched me, a tiny vibration going from there up and down my arm, as though I had received an injection. I watched him walk away, and I knew I was feeling something I would rather not have. But, oh, it was all very simple, very primitive, nothing to be ashamed of, I could feel it and not act on it, of course I could, I had been attracted to men I wasn't married to before and it was bothersome but not overwhelming, not enough to make me want to betray my husband, and perhaps it would have been unnatural not to feel attraction to someone like Hale.

Still, it was disquieting. That rush of hormones, that sly ambush on the rational brain. That reminder of David.

I looked around for Avey. I saw him standing at the bottom of the stairs, talking earnestly to a man whose eyes were flicking away in that manner I knew meant, sadly, that he would rather be elsewhere. I wished Avey wouldn't try to make every conversation into an opportunity. Perhaps unconsciously, he put a foot onto the bottom stair, and I knew he was about to pull himself up onto it because that would bring him above the height of the man he talking to. I felt my heart twist for him. He could never believe that people did not care if he was a bit short, that he could actually have used it to his advantage to appear nonthreatening to people who, like some of his colleagues I had met over the years, lived eye-level with paranoia.

I murmured a friendly refusal to someone asking me to dance and headed across the room to Avey. He was more good-looking than he gave himself credit for, with thickly lashed dark eyes under rather charmingly untidy eyebrows, a mouth that turned interestingly asymmetrical when he smiled, a strong chin, and thick auburn hair I envied because he could style it by just running a hand through it; but he grew irritable if I said I liked his appearance. He told me once that a good placard on a short stick could never get as much attention as a poorer one on a taller stick.

"Hi." I extended my smile to the man beside him. He was only slightly taller than Avey, with a flushed face and greying hair with such deep, crisp waves they looked like what my grandmother would have called marcelled. I could tell both men were glad of my interruption.

"Kate," Avey said, "Dr. Cardin."

"No relation to the designer, I'm afraid," said the man, with an urbanity that suggested he had said this often to women.

"Just as well," I said. "It's hard to dress in enough clothes in the tropics to be fashionable."

He laughed. "Absolutely." He gestured down at his own attire: sandals without socks, khaki Bermuda shorts, a white French-cuffed shirt that perhaps he could dismiss as unfashionable but not as inexpensive.

"It doesn't seem to take long for people to adjust," I said. "I haven't seen a man in a suit and tie since I got here."

"Not surprising. After we've been here for a while we do become sartorially challenged. Perhaps we should amend Wilde to say, beware any job that requires the wearing of *old* clothes."

I laughed. So did Avey, more heartily than necessary.

"Wilde," I said. "I would have guessed Thoreau." I knew it was Thoreau.

"Thoreau? Possible, I suppose." He raised an eyebrow at me. "One doesn't expect astronomers to read the transcendentalists."

"Oh, I'm no astronomer. My husband's the astronomer. I'm a high school dropout."

"Really? A literate one, though."

A woman in a short red dress with a reckless neckline and earrings with glittering stones so big they could have developed their own solar systems came up to us then and pulled Dr. Cardin away to dance. He cast back at us an overdone look that implied he was desolated to leave.

"Jesus, Kate," Avey whispered. "Why did you have to tell him you were a high school dropout? It's not something to say to people we want to impress."

"You're wrong," I said, watching Dr. Cardin and the young woman. "There are men who would be impressed by how well-educated your wife is and men who wouldn't be. Your Dr. Cardin wouldn't be. I probably shouldn't even have chanced the Thoreau. Although that kind of casual repartee isn't as threatening as a real education."

"Good grief, Kate. This isn't 1955. You're allowed to have a *brain*."

"Brains are overrated." I laughed. I'd drunk too much. "Come on," I said. "Let's dance." I pulled him toward the garden.

When we reached the sliding doors I could see Karen and Hale outside, standing by the brilliantly blooming poinsettia bushes. He was pointing up at the mango tree, at a cluster of reddening fruit. When he looked down his glance swept across to me. And I felt it again, that small jolt, that tingle that went down my arms and seemed to pool in my fingertips, like what my yoga instructor would have called bad chi, and I had to shake my hands to dispel it.

F o u r

"Although the universe is under no obligation to make sense, students in pursuit of the PhD are."
— ROBERT P. KIRSHNER, *Harvard astronomer, 1991*

A V E Y

I woke up soggy with sweat. Kate lay beside me, her breathing just audible, wearing only her pajama top and tangled in the single sheet we used as a blanket.

I'd been in the office, and I'd seen something, a flickering across the screen, like a faint, unexpected heartbeat on a flatlined cardiogram, and then Dr. Schultz had come in and I was pointing to it excitedly and Dr. Schultz laughed and said, "Oh, that, that's nothing new. If that is the best you can do you had better go home." And then some of the others came in and were all laughing at me, even Bruno, and I could see then that the computer was really just some kind of toy, playing a tinkly nursery rhyme.

I got up, stumbled to the toilet, trying not to hear the scuttling sounds in the dim corners. The bathroom had the slightly apricot scent of cup of gold flowers, from a vase Kate had set on the windowsill to counteract the mildewy smell coming from the shower walls. She had taken to buying local flowers from a woman at the market, and though I'd groused at her for the expense I had to admit they made being in the bathroom less of an olfactory ordeal. It was typical of Kate, though: she'd buy flowers to cover up a smell instead of trying to scrub away the smell itself.

I sat down on the toilet, cradling my head in my hands the way I'd cradle a toothache, trying stupidly both to shake the nightmare from my brain and to remember it. Those faces, laughing at me. I shuddered. And suddenly I could see another face there, one that made its nasty way into too many of my dreams. My father's. Looking over Bruno's shoulder, laughing harder than any of them.

"You sit there, boy, until you get it right." Smack, the ruler comes down an inch from my fingers. I jerk my hand away, the pencil skittering across the kitchen table.

"You hear me? You hear me?" He takes another gulp of rum.

"He's doing his best, Gordon." My mother across the table from me, shelling the peas.

Smack, the ruler says. Smack, smack.

Oh, Jesus. I breathed in deeply, smelling the cup of gold, the mildew, the urine, all of it. I put my head down onto my knees. Why couldn't I just grow up?

The room was getting lighter. The twilight of morning was as abbreviated here as the twilight of evening. *Don't let the sun catch you crying.* Yeah, right. I remembered that song from once when Kate and I stayed overnight at her parents' place, and in the morning her father sang it in the shower, and when he came out in his robe he bumped into Kate's mother and, still singing, danced her into the kitchen, all of us laughing, except my laugh had the murky undertow of thinking: what would it have been like to grow up in such a household, with such a father?

I knew I'd never get back to sleep, so I got dressed, left a note for Kate, and unchained the bicycle from the front railing. It had been stolen three weeks ago, which had made me shriek, thinking I would have to buy a replacement, but two days later it was returned, crusted with mud but otherwise uninjured, as though someone had simply needed a bicycle for a few days and then brought it back. Which was probably exactly what the thinking had been: no guilt, just some pragmatic rationalization about whose need at the time was greater. Kate pointed out it might have been that kind of logic that got me the bike in the first place, but her casualness about it just made me more pissed off.

I suspected someone at the neighbouring house, occupied by a large, noisy family of native Hawaiians, none of whom seemed to work and who greeted me with some version of "hello, crazy *haole*" when they saw me. I was supposed to laugh and pretend that didn't bother me, but of course if I'd countered with some racial insult of my own, well, that wouldn't have been acceptable, would it? The locals, as the native Hawaiians here liked to call themselves, were not exactly the ones you saw pictured in the guidebooks, smiling and handing leis to visitors.

It was raining lightly, as it did most nights, and by the time I pumped up Mohouli Street and Komohana Road and turned into the upper University Park site that housed most of the telescope centres I was dripping wet and cursing myself for forgetting my raincoat.

I left the bicycle at the rack, beside Robert Ito's smashed-up Toyota that the staff had decided to leave there as a reminder to all of us who went up the mountain that we couldn't get complacent about it, that, especially if we spent the night at the observatory and didn't want to sleep at the dormitory at the halfway point, we were in danger of dozing off coming back down. At that altitude fatigue was a major problem. It could hit us so hard that just climbing a flight of stairs was utterly exhausting. Plus the thin air did dangerous things to our perceptions. There had been some close calls, mostly with visiting scientists, who had gotten disoriented and wandered off. Every time I'd gone up the mountain I'd gotten a headache and upset stomach that lasted the whole time I was there. When I described the nausea to Kate she said I was skysick.

Fortunately I didn't have much need or desire to go up. I knew there were astronomers, even the major guys, who still made the trip regularly, maybe just out of respect for the profession and the telescope, but it was the computers now, the whole electronic network, that did all the work. Computers aimed the telescope; computers monitored and adjusted; computers whisked the data off the detectors onto storage tapes. Even when that data came down to me in my office, it was still a computer I was relying on to do all the detailed analysis.

I could barely imagine what it must have been like before that. Astronomers would have had to spend hours on end in a focus cage, a kind of crow's nest high above the primary mirror, sliding photographic plates in and out, fine-tuning the telescope by hand to keep it from blurring as the Earth turned. When the dome was open the cold would become intense. One of my profs talked about how he'd worn an electrically heated suit, designed for fighter pilots, but he said it wasn't much help. Now at least there are nice heated control rooms in every observatory.

But heated control rooms weren't enough incentive for me to put up with the time loss and the nausea, and as long as the telescope kept sending me the data I needed I had no reason to visit it. And if anything went wrong up there it wasn't up to me to fix it, anyway, even if I could. I was one of the few people who understood how Orlovski's instrument worked, but if something went wrong with it — and oh dear God my blood ran cold at the thought — I wouldn't have had much idea how to repair it. Fortunately we had technicians a lot more skilled and experienced than I was.

I was at work even earlier than usual. I liked this time, this feeling that the building was still drowsing. But I could hear some kind of cleaning machine running on the floor above me, and I assumed it was Hale, doing something janitorial. I'm not sure what shifts he worked or what his job really was. The other day I saw him outside, stacking up palm leaves a hard wind had ripped off.

The biggest branch had hit Perry's new Datsun. We all stood around saying the usual "ah, Jeez" and "tough luck, man" at the dent in his hood, and then Hilde said something in German.

"Huh?" said Perry.

"Oh, just something from Goethe, I think. It means, sort of, 'Nobody walks under palm trees unpunished.'"

So everyone but Perry had their immune laugh at that. But it gave me a chill somehow. As though it would be my turn next.

I opened the door to my office. The room smelled of garlic. I wished to hell Bruno wouldn't eat in here. Yesterday I was cursing my computer because it kept freezing, and then I realized I'd been rolling the mouse over something green and gummy. I was damned sure it hadn't come from me. It took me ten minutes to scrape the ball clean.

I logged in. My password, "Planetboy," was sounding too cute and cocky these days. I checked to see that the computer had been grinding away all night, and then I went down to the staff lounge, dumped some coffee into the machine. I sat there watching it burp and drizzle into the pot. For the first time I found myself dreading going back to my desk, going through what the JCMT had sent down that night, even though I knew how important it was to analyze things as they came in, not let them start piling up in disks and tapes. But half of last week the telescope was down because of bad weather (and not even cloud or rain, just extra moistness in the air, which submillimetre telescopes hate), and before that it had been working on some special TAG projects that had dropped my research out of the queue, so I'd had more than enough time to catch up and review my data.

But I had nothing. It was the end of December, the end of 1995, and I had nothing. *Überhaupt nichts*, as Hilde would say. Everything sounds more ominous in German.

I poured myself a coffee. It was too weak and had grounds in it. I'd probably done something sloppy with the filter.

I picked up the copy of the December interview with the US astronomers Marcy and Butler in the *Chicago Tribune* that was sitting on one of the tables. I guess it was paranoid, and probably because of that damned dream, to think someone had left it there on purpose for me, as though I might not have seen it, as though I needed to have my nose rubbed in the fact that Marcy and Butler were strongly hinting they had evidence of a second planet in the 51 Pegasi system. They were working their asses off, determined not to get scooped again.

How could I imagine I could find something before they did? They were the pros. They'd been at it for years. And who knew how close Mayor and Queloz in Switzerland were to something new? For all I knew there was already a discovery, just waiting for verification. Orlovski's work hadn't give me any kind of shortcut.

Maybe the instrument he'd developed and installed for the JCMT simply wasn't up to the job. Maybe the precision it was giving of three metres per second, which was pretty incredible, still wasn't enough. Maybe I needed to reassess all my computer requirements. Maybe I should just go home and shoot myself.

Someone was standing beside me. I jumped.

Louisa.

"Hi," she said. "I don't often see you in here."

"Yeah, well. Today I needed a break before I even got started."

She sat down opposite me. She was wearing an oversized blue cotton blouse, but instead of her usual jeans she had on a long paisley skirt. She pulled her feet up underneath it so that it looked as though she had no legs at all.

"They're getting close, aren't they?" She gestured at the newspaper.

"Yeah. They can probably see the little green men and little green women."

"Oh, I don't think they'll get that far."

I shifted uncomfortably. I could see this getting us into the religion thing again, that anthropic principle.

"Well, I don't really care," I said. "I'd just like to find a planet so that I can get rich and famous and be envied by my peers." I'd meant to sound heavily ironic, but it came out sounding heavily honest.

She laughed. I didn't think she had it in her. She got up, poured herself a coffee, and came back over and stood beside me. She put her hand on my shoulder.

And I suddenly knew that if I wanted to I could pull her down onto the carpet and make love to her. I'm hardly one of those macho types who thinks every woman is after him, but there was something in that hand on my shoulder that might as well have been saying it out loud. But even as I was processing that, I knew I wouldn't act on the invitation. I wouldn't cheat on Kate.

I patted her hand, in what I hoped was an innocent and collegial way, nothing rebuffing, nothing encouraging.

"Well, back to the computer," I said. "Who knows, maybe this will be The Day."

"Good luck," she said. Her voice exhaled its usual whiff of frost. By the time I set my coffee cup on the table and stood up she had gone.

This was not, of course, The Day. In fact it seemed worse than usual. I'd spent half of the last week writing more computer code, plugging it in, and then today I deleted most of it. Shit, shit, shit. I was sick of tweaking the data. Everything just seemed royally buggered. Whenever I thought, hey, is that something, could that be something, could that be sinusoidal, could that be a wobble, it would be gone the next day. I was having a lot more sympathy for poor old Peter van de Kamp who spent his whole life poring over his two thousand photographic plates of Barnard's star, insisting he detected planets there even when critics had proven that if he'd seen anything at all it was probably produced by a flaw in his telescope.

What was I even doing here? I'd have been farther ahead if I'd stayed home and just reviewed archived data at the centre in Victoria. It was collecting all kinds of stuff from the Hubble and the other telescope on Mauna Kea co-owned by Canada, the Canada-France-Hawaii telescope. Maybe that was the one I should have applied to work with. It was the one that had already done some major extrasolar planet research. Going with Orlovski and the JCMT seemed like a huge mistake.

I had asked Bruno a few days ago why his father had chosen to work with a submillimetre telescope in the first place, and he looked embarrassed and said, "You'll laugh when I tell you."

"Laugh, cry, whatever."

"He had a dream."

"A dream?"

"He was lecturing and Einstein walked into the classroom and wrote on the blackboard, '*Such im Untermillimetre.*' Look in the submillimetre."

"You are fucking kidding me."

"My father was a bit, well, superstitious."

"We are here — let me get this straight — because your father dreamt Einstein walked into the room and told him what to do."

"It's not as lunatic as it sounds," Bruno said, getting defensive. "There are lots of cases of scientists struggling with something and then seeing an answer in a dream."

"Well," I said, realizing I had better back off, "I guess geniuses get inspiration from strange places."

"Sure. You know how when Pauli gave his speculative talk on particle physics and then said to Neils Bohr, 'You probably think these ideas are crazy,' and Bohr replied, 'I do, but unfortunately —'"

"'— they are not crazy enough!'" I chimed in. We laughed.

Not crazy enough. Maybe that had been Orlovski's problem. Maybe it was my problem. My dreams weren't quite crazy enough. Only a few hundred years ago people like Giordano Bruno and Kepler and Tycho Brahe had to worry that they'd be killed for what they believed and discovered. Grad school is a more benign oppressor, I suppose; it doesn't usually require murder. But it does punish. The irony is that what's now punished is not originality but the failure to be original enough.

I began writing up some results from last week, plus a summary of my program modifications. I'd told myself I had to keep up with this, to be ready at a moment's notice to just plug in that final brilliant conclusion, or I'd have no hope of getting my findings published in *Nature* or *Science*. Everybody wanted to publish there, the big prestige journals, even though it meant there could be no leaks to the newspapers, not even any prior presentations at academic conferences. And what was expected wasn't just exclusive rights but results that were new, new, new. I'd heard complaints about how the increasing pressure was encouraging some researchers to rush into publication too soon, with so-called "quick and dirty" experiments. I wanted my paper to be quick and clean.

But today working on it seemed particularly pointless, like polishing the glass in an empty frame when I had no idea if I could ever find the picture to go in it. I knew what the picture would look like. I only had to glance at the photo above my desk of the Mayor and Queloz discovery data. But it was seeming less and less likely I would ever find my own. I needed about a dozen more computers and a hundred more hours in each day.

What was it Kate had once said about housework, about how it was an exercise in futility but she supposed that was better than no exercise at all? I rubbed hard at the tight muscles at the back of my neck, did a few shoulder rolls and clicked open another window on the screen.

The lights flickered. I could hear the beeps from the UPSes, the uninterruptible power supply units that all our computers were plugged into. I had one down by my feet, and it was bleating at me now. It wasn't the first time: the island's power system wasn't the most reliable. But the lights stayed on, so I guessed there was no reason to shut my computer down. The UPS, which was really just a big battery that sat between the main power and the computers, could handle a longer power interruption than this.

But it seemed like a good excuse to just shut down, anyway, and go home early. I'd be there for supper for a change.

When I came in the door I saw Kate in the living room with her feet up reading a novel, and it put me in an even fouler mood.

"Why don't you cook us some dinner?" I said. "If you're not too busy."

She put a bookmark in her novel and set it down. Science fiction. Lovely.

"Okay," she said. "I didn't think you'd be here for supper."

Her cheerfulness irritated me even more. "Well, I am. I had a shitty day."

"I'm sorry." She trotted out into the kitchen. "A sandwich all right?"

I dropped myself into a chair, tossed my backpack onto the coffee table. It had more force than I'd intended and it collapsed the taped-up leg of the table.

"Christ!" I yelled. "Is everything in this place broken?"

Kate came back, wiping her hands on the dishtowel.

"Pretty much," she said.

A muddle of papers and other debris Kate left piled on the coffee table had tumbled off onto the floor, and when I bent to look at the coffee table leg I saw among the the papers some photos that had slid out of their folder. They were mostly of an older couple, in tourist poses, and the yellow Post-it note on the folder said, "Just a few shots from our trip to Europe. Love, Jan and Peter."

Jan and Peter. Lovely. David's parents.

I held the photos out to Kate. "When did these come?"

She had the decency to look uncomfortable. "A few days ago. I didn't think you'd want to see them."

"You're right about that." I slapped them down onto the arm of the sofa. "I don't know why you insist on staying in touch with them."

"They're Sandy's grandparents —"

"Sandy. Fine. Let Sandy be the one to keep in touch."

"They're my friends."

"They're your ex-in-laws. Doesn't it seem a tad, oh, let's see, *unfair* to me that you're still hanging on to them? You're supposed to be with me now, with my family."

And I knew I was goading her, daring her to say that my parents weren't good enough, that I didn't even want her to be friends with them, and I suppose this was such a stupendously obvious thing for her to say that she didn't bother, and this pissed me off even more.

"I'm sorry you saw the pictures," she said. "I didn't mean for them to upset you."

"I don't expect you to *hide* them from me. I expect you to be, to be, moving *on*, for God's sake."

"I know."

"You *know*. You *know*. For most people that answer means they're doing something about it. But not you. For you it means you just don't want to argue."

"Well, I don't."

I sighed. Hopeless. Bloody hopeless.

I crouched down and jammed the splintered table leg back together and wrapped the tape around it again. When I stood up, I bumped the top-heavy floor lamp made from a stem of ragged bamboo through which a cracked electrical cord had been threaded. I caught the damn thing just before it fell, though I had to fight the urge then to heave it against the wall. I spotted an abandoned coffee cup on the floor beside the sofa, picked it up, thrust it at Kate.

"Look at this! It's got pieces of mould floating in it!"

Kate took the cup. "So it does. Sorry."

"What did you say we've got to eat? A sandwich? I'm sick of sandwiches. Can't we have a real meal for a change?"

"There's not much in the house, I'm afraid. Not much that you'd like. Maybe we could go out."

"Out. Sure. Your daddy send you more money?"

"No," she said. I had gotten to her. Finally. I recognized that tenseness in her lips. "Actually," she said, "I sent some money home to Sandy today. She needed a new printer."

"Wonderful! Wonderful! We can't bloody afford to eat, and you send Sandy money."

"I *am* earning some of my own, you know."

"Oh, right. And that belongs just to you, whereas mine belongs to both of us. Sweet."

She shrugged. "Well, if we're low I could always ask Daddy to send us more."

Childish, we were both so childish.

KATE

Childish. Oh, we both were. I had to stop myself from laughing. I knew I was pushing Avey's buttons, but only because he would paint them bright red for me.

Of course, he was pushing my buttons, too. Was I colluding with him in that? Am I imagining now that I was more in control of my emotions that day than I really was?

When I made the sandwiches I could have cut up the leftover chicken breast for them, but I suppose I wanted the meal to seem as meagre as possible. Peanut butter and honey, a salad of browning lettuce and flavourless tomato, and a big bowl of poi, which I knew Avey found faintly repellent but which was nutritious and cheap so he couldn't object. I wiped the counter and then balled up the dishcloth and threw it into the corner of the sink, where it would annoy Avey if he found it. Everybody knew dishcloths were supposed to be rinsed and wrung out, folded in half and hung on the faucet.

We ate. The honey dripped off the bread onto the table, onto our fingers. Everything Avey touched on the table seemed to snap and bristle with argument. We didn't look at each other. The old fan in the corner turned its rusty wire face from Avey to me, from me to him, as though curious about our silence. Its breath came and went on my legs. The little green gecko sat motionless on the wall, watching all of us.

I don't know why this day of all days I chose not to say something conciliatory. I wasn't *that* irritated with Avey. It wasn't as though we'd been arguing about anything new, or even that I thought he'd been particularly unjust in his accusations. Maybe it was because talking about David's parents had made this odd but vivid memory trickle into my brain.

I was nineteen, I think. David and I hadn't been married long. We were visiting his parents. David's father, a large, hearty man I liked very much, enjoyed reading biographies, and, as I was coming back down the hall from the bathroom, I heard him guffaw and read to his wife a remark made by the daughter of David Lloyd George, prime minister of England, about her father's mistress: "She was a thick pile of carpet into which one's feet gratefully sank."

"Remind you of anyone we know?" David's father asked.

"Not me," his wife said. They both laughed.

I stood frozen in the hallway. Was it me they were reminded of? Was that the person I had become, had made myself into?

I told David about it that night. He was amazed I could have seen myself in that remark, assured me his parents were probably talking about his aunt and her stoic affair with a married man. David put his cold, bare feet on my thigh and scrunched up his toes and made me shriek.

"See?" he said. "You're not even a carpet. You're a hardwood floor."

I looked at Avey now across from me, and I had the urge to tell him about that incident. I'm not sure why. It would just have made him more angry. Maybe that would have been the point. Maybe I wanted him to tell me I was not just a hardwood floor but one with splinters in it.

I didn't say anything.

It started to rain. Even if I hadn't heard it on the roof I would have heard it dripping into the pail in the bedroom. Slowly, a drip or two a minute. It was happening now almost every time it rained, whether there was wind or not. When I'd pressed the landlord about it, he said he would have to wait until he could find the right kind of patch before he could fix it. I had to hope that wouldn't fall into the same category as replacing the boarded-up front window. He'd said he had to wait until he could buy the glass.

Avey got up, went into the kitchen. I could hear him running water, washing the honey off himself. I hoped he wouldn't open the fridge and see the leftover chicken.

When he came back he said, "I'm going to go up to the office again."

"It's raining," I said. "It's late."

"I can't sit around here doing nothing. I'm not like you. Sometimes I wish I were."

"Oh."

What I'd almost said was, "Well, I never wish I were like *you*." I'd thought better of it, fortunately. Besides, I wasn't sure if he had meant his remark as an insult or just an observation. But I could see my lame little "Oh" made him feel he had hurt me.

But I hadn't felt particularly insulted. Later I tried to convince myself that I had, but it wasn't true.

Avey made some sort of gesture at me that might have been apologetic before he put on his jacket and went out. When I took my plate into the kitchen I saw the dishcloth folded neatly over the faucet.

It was after midnight when he came home. I pretended to be asleep. The next morning I had to check a new couple early into one of the condo units so I actually was up before he was. Although it was sunny at the moment, before I left I made sure, as usual, to empty the bucket in the bedroom in case it started to rain again. The Big Island had more diverse weather than any comparably sized piece of land in the world, with eleven of the planet's thirteen types of climactic zones, right from tropical and monsoonal to desert and glacial, but "monsoonal" seemed like the one that hovered over our house.

It was the abundant rain, of course, that made everything here so lush. And I suppose I had, as the man in the store had advised me the day after I came here, changed my attitude. Except for the rain that leaked into the house, I didn't mind it now as much. It could come up suddenly and leave just as quickly. It was always warm. If I got caught outside in a shower I made myself laugh. You get wet. You dry off. It seemed quite simple. And my skin had never felt better. Usually in winter my hands needed to be laminated with creams or they chapped so mercilessly I could practically have Velcroed them together. My neck, which usually got stiff and sore in winter, felt so flexible I might have grown a few new vertebrae.

I remembered the way Avey in Edmonton had suddenly reached over and pulled the scarf from my neck. It was an odd moment. It wasn't as though I thought he was going to strangle me if I didn't go with him, but I did think he was pretending he would. Instead he'd thrown the scarf across the room and told me I wouldn't need it any more. I'd looked at the scarf on the floor, the way, lying there, it was freed of function, something no longer what it was, something that could pick itself up and become anything. Maybe I came to Hawaii because of a scarf.

As I got onto my bicycle, I waved at Keke next door. She was standing at the side of her house yelling at one of her kids. It was a noisy family (Avey said their voices could pierce a bulletproof vest), but I'd had a few pleasantly laconic chats with Keke, who worked part-time at one of the stores downtown. Her name, she'd told me, would translate into "Kate," and we'd had a laugh about exchanging our lives for a day or two. She might appreciate the break from the kids, she'd said, but my husband looked too serious for her.

She returned my wave. "Go back to bed," she shouted. I wasn't sure if she was talking to me or the child, who was naked and giggling and hiding inadequately in the shrubbery.

Keke went back inside, which was a relief, because I didn't have time to "talk story," as the Hawaiians called it. It was rude to refuse, even if it made you late for an appointment.

I headed down to the beach. The air smelled of plumeria and of something rich, humid and jungly I had grown to like. There was no trace in the air of vog, a nasty mix of water vapour, carbon dioxide, and sulfur dioxide, most of the latter belched out by the Kilauea volcano to the south of Hilo. Close to three thousand tons of it a day, apparently. It reacted with sunlight, oxygen, dust and water to form a variety of alarming sulfur compounds — sulfuric acid was the only one I could remember. Trade winds carried the vog down the coast where onshore and offshore breezes batted it back and forth. Fortunately, Hilo was not badly affected. The other side of the island, the Kona side, where all the tourists went, was much worse.

It was useful information to have for the people at the condo, who sometimes seemed less than charmed with the isolation and the lack of tourist facilities on this side of the island.

A small cloud rolled in from the west, and soon I could feel the sprinkles on my face.

For our honeymoon David and I went to Europe and cycled in the Black Forest where we got lost and it began to rain and we huddled under an overhang of rock and roots and fell asleep and were nosed awake by a heavy-fetlocked horse with a long, kind face.

I was taking a longer route than I needed to, but I preferred cycling along the bay, especially early in the morning. The sun was just coming up. A pair of mynah birds, the yellow skin outlining their eyes giving them a shrewd and clerical look, shrieked at me as I turned down Manono Street.

The horse's owner was a small woman who wore a straw hat with half the brim missing, and David and I would talk about this later, about the missing brim, conjecturing as to whether it had been broken off deliberately or by accident, and she led us out of the forest to a village where she left us with the Burgermeister, who asked if we had been swimming in the rain.

There was little traffic, and I could hear the sea, could see the waves roll in, withdraw, return. It was open ocean as I'd never seen it before coming here. The only time I had ever seen the Pacific was in Vancouver, where the gulf islands gentled the tides and where only during a severe windstorm did they get real whitecaps.

Yes yes, we said, swimming in the rain, and we were cold and shivering and soaked to the skin and I was never happier, and on the plane back David said, The horse must have eaten it, of course, and how I didn't have to ask, Eaten what?

I stopped my bike, stood there at the side of the road leaning on one leg. I closed my eyes, listened to the thud and retreat thud and retreat of the waves.

"You okay?" A truck had slowed almost to a stop beside me.

"Yes, yes," I said. "Sorry."

"No problemo." He accelerated away.

I took a deep breath, held it in my stomach, let it out slowly, completely, until I was empty and ready for the next breath and the next, and then I pressed my foot down hard on the pedal and kept going. The rain cloud had disappeared, leaving only a few feathery wisps in the sky. Far above me three wide-winged frigate birds floated on a thermal.

I crossed the little bridge over the Wailoa River and went past the flat, grassy park where Avey and I had gone for a walk. Since then, every time I'd ridden past the clock at the side of the road on Kamehameha Street, with its hands frozen at 1:04 a.m. from the 1960 tsunami, it had given me a chill, knowing how vulnerable we were, how dangerous it was to live on any Pacific coast.

I sped up the road, crossed the inlet at Mokupane Point, going uphill now, away from any gathering tsunamis. On my left somewhere was Bruno's house, and beyond that rose the huge parabola of Mauna Kea.

If I looked closely I could see three or four small, gleaming white bubbles on top: the telescopes. I wasn't sure if I could see the one Avey worked at; he'd never pointed it out to me or taken me up the mountain to see it. I don't think he himself went up that often. Still, I had pictured him there, staring at the stars, at mirrors. One fanciful time I had imagined him looking for his opposite self in some parallel universe, looking for his reversed twin with whom he had somehow accidentally changed places at birth.

I turned off onto the small road near Lauhue Point Lookout where the condo complex was. It was built into the slope so that every one of the ten units had easy entry at the top level, where the guests could park their rental cars, and also at the bottom level, where they could walk out onto private gardens and go down to the beach. Every window had an ocean view. A huge swimming pool was built on the south side and landscaped so that swimmers looking out from it had the illusion of the pool merging with the ocean on the skyline. It was the most dazzling such complex I had ever seen, designed by a famous Brazilian architect.

I went into Unit Three, in which I had been staying, pulled a branch of orchid blossoms from the vase I kept on the counter, and took the branch into the adjacent suite for the new guests. I kicked off my runners and walked barefoot through the kitchen with its white marble tiles veined with pale grey. I remembered a builder in Edmonton telling me of the first time he installed marble tiles, in a house overlooking the river on Saskatchewan Drive. As usual, he wrote numbers in felt pen on the bottom of each tile so that he would place them in their earmarked positions. Later, to the shock of the owners, numbers slowly began to appear on their kitchen floor. Marble, apparently, is porous, and the ink simply bled through. But nothing was bleeding through this marble except a welcome coolness. I curled my toes on it, feeling the slightly uneven textures that our feet were supposed to prefer.

I left the orchid branch floating in the bathroom sink in the master bedroom. The original aloha tradition was to leave it in the toilet bowl, but after one guest phoned me in a panic about some creature that must have come up from the sewers I began leaving the orchids somewhere less frightening.

I took a glass of ice water from the dispenser on the refrigerator door and went down to the middle floor, which was basically a huge and expensively furnished living room with one bedroom off to the side. The other two bedrooms were on the floor below. I opened the sliding doors and watched, for a while, the waves bulging and smashing on the rocks. A pair of storm-petrels flitted low over the sea, then virtually stopped and hovered, looking for food and pattering their feet on the surface, for which they had been named "petrel," alluding to St. Peter who allegedly walked on water. When they disappeared into the distance I lay down on the chaise longue on the lanai and waited for the tourists to arrive.

When they did, I took a proprietary pride in their delight with the place.

"This is so much nicer than the Kona side of the island," the woman said.

"Oh, I think so, too," I said. I had never actually been to the Kona side.

I went back to Unit Three. It was booked by an Australian family for next week; I would miss it. Unit Ten would be empty by then, but for part of January all the suites were reserved. I would have to go back to spending my days in what I now called the Pupuka, a word I'd acquired from Karen, who was taking a class in Hawaiian at the university. "Pupuka" meant "ugly," and "puka" meant "hole," so the term seemed doubly appropriate.

The condo was a bit of a joke, really: luxury to excess, and it was a relief to know it wasn't a place I would want to live for more than a holiday; but I suppose a more important thing I learned about myself that year was that the Pupuka fell below some lower level of my expectations, too. Maybe, in my rebellions against my parents, I had thought I had no such limits.

Avey had never come out here. He was always too busy, and I was actually glad he showed no interest. It would just have made him envious, angry that there were people who could afford such things, and he might even have wanted us to start staying overnight here, to more or less move in, and I knew that would have been frowned upon by the owners.

I wondered if he thought I was still upset about last night. Even if I had been annoyed with him then, I wasn't any more. I knew how much stress he was under, how I was just an available target. I could let myself be that for him, could turn my irritation into an indulgent sympathy.

When I think back on this day, it's that thought I return to: that I wasn't angry with him. I've kept trying to convince myself that I was, but I wasn't.

It was Karen's fault.

I'd told her to drop by for coffee and a swim in the pool if the guests weren't using it. Of course, what I didn't expect was that when she came she would have Hale with her.

I stood at the door and my first thought was of Joe, Karen's husband: a nice, rather pudgy, shy man, and now Karen was cheating on him.

No, I have to be honest. That was my second thought. My first was oh my God oh my God be careful be careful.

Karen probably read all of this on my face, because she gave me a wink as she brushed past me.

"I hope you don't mind," she said. "I told Hale about this gorgeous place you had."

"I don't really have it," I said. "I'm just the caretaker."

Hale murmured something which I couldn't quite hear and walked past me to look out the dining room window. I hated the way I was watching him, a light to which my mothy eyes were drawn. He was wearing cutoffs and a white T-shirt with "da kine" written across the back. An insect settled on his ankle and he dislodged it by moving his foot slightly, without looking down. His legs were taut and muscular, as mine as had become, and I supposed it was for the same reason, riding a bicycle.

Karen took hold of my arm. The pupils of her eyes were enlarged. Large pupils were apparently once considered a mark of beauty, which is why women sometimes applied an extract from the poisonous herb deadly nightshade to their eyes: it dilated the pupil, hence its other name, "beautiful woman," or belladonna. I doubted that Karen had been using deadly nightshade, but I suspected she had been taking some other drug. Everything about her seemed hyper, excited, her whole body grinning.

"Just a little present for you," she whispered, tipping her head towards Hale, who still stood with his back to us looking out at the ocean, at Hilo to the east cupping the bay.

"Karen. Good grief. What are you doing?"

She giggled. "Nothing. He offered to show me the Botanical Gardens just up the road, that's all. They're gorgeous. You have to go sometime."

"But what are you doing with him in the first place?"

"Oh, don't be priggish, my sweet. I'm not sleeping with him."

"Why did you bring him here?"

She set the champagne bottle she had brought onto the kitchen counter. "I told you. A present. *Mele Kalikimaka.* Merry Christmas. A little belated but oh well."

I had to choose between being insulted or being amused. I can see now it was a mistake, but I chose the latter.

"Well, thank you. We really must get you some gainful employment."

"Yes, yes, devil, work, idle hands." She broke a banana from the bunch I had sitting on the counter and peeled it halfway down, took a big bite. "*Starving*. You know when the real downfall of the old Hawaiian religion came? It was when the wives of Kamehameha struck it a fatal blow by persuading the king to break two of its most sacred rules. He allowed men and women to eat together and allowed women to eat bananas. No lie. Not making that up. God, I'm hungry." She shoved the last of the banana in her mouth, bulging out her cheeks, and said something else I couldn't understand.

"Pardon?"

"I said —" She wiped away some banana leaking from the corner of her mouth. "Must dash. I promised Joe I'd bring him a computer chip he wants to try." She turned to the door.

"You're not leaving him here?" I stared at her.

"I'll be back in a couple of hours. He does have some conversation, if you prod him. Show him the garden. Take him for a swim."

"Karen!"

"I haven't the nerve," she said. "Maybe you do."

She was backing out the door. I grabbed her arm. "No!"

Hale had come up behind us. I had no idea how much he had heard. "It's okay," he said. His voice was barely a murmur. "I don't really want to swim in the pool."

So then I had to turn and say, "Oh, no, really, it's fine, it's just that I wasn't expecting you —"

And when I turned back to Karen she was in her car, flicking her fingers coyly at me through the windshield as she pulled away.

"This is embarrassing," Hale said, in his low voice I had to strain to hear. "I didn't know she was going to ... do this. She just said we'd stop. See the place. Maybe go for a swim."

I made myself smile, not step away from him, not run after Karen's car and grab hold of her bumper and demand she take Hale away with her.

"Karen can be impulsive," I said. "I suppose it's what makes her an interesting friend."

Hale picked up the champagne bottle. "She left us this," he said. "We might as well have some."

I couldn't think of any way to refuse, so I let him open it and pour us two glasses. I tried not to watch his mouth as he drank. His lips, so like David's, all the same small, delicate movements.

I showed him through the suite, and he would murmur something occasionally, though it seemed more out of politeness than admiration. The view, after all, was likely one he had seen every day of his life. I heard myself lapsing into the language of the realtor showing a non-committal client through a property.

On the ground floor I took him out into the private garden, and here, at last, he allowed me his opinion of something.

When I remarked on the brilliant red poinsettia hedge, about how at home we could only see the plants in little pots at Christmas, he said, "You should be glad. It's a weed. It doesn't belong here. It was imported from Mexico." He pointed at a small jacaranda tree with purple blossoms. "That — imported from South America. Even that —" and he pointed at the curving wall of bougainvillea dividing this garden from the adjoining one "— doesn't belong here. It was brought in from Brazil." He gestured at a bush of red, cone-shaped flowers. "Shouldn't be here. Comes from India. And that one. Anthurium. Doesn't belong here. *A'ole pono*. And there — oleander. From Asia. Our vegetation is a hodgepodge now of imported stuff."

His voice had accumulated considerable vehemence. I could only glance at the flowers as he pointed to them before my eyes went back to his face.

He knelt down, pushed aside some pothos vine, and fingered the plump, deep green leaves of a plant with a spike of yellow flowers from which long orange stamens protruded. "And this. Why would they plant this? Kahili ginger. Not only a foreigner but ... a very aggressive one. It will soon crowd out everything else."

"It's pretty. I suppose they didn't think beyond that."

He moved his hand to another plant, nipped off a cluster of white, waxy trumpet-shaped flowers. I had a sudden fear that he might be planning to weed the non-native flora from the garden and was relieved when he stood up, twirling the cluster in his fingers.

"Of course," he said. "They're all pretty. But the point is ... that they don't belong here."

I pointed at the bamboo along the back of the property, its strong brown stems regular as fence railings. "What about that? Or the coconut palm? Or the banana and breadfruit and taro? Weren't they essential to Hawaii's early development, but weren't they imports, too, brought here over a thousand years ago by the Polynesians? Canoe plants, aren't they called? How far back do you go before a plant is really, truly native?"

I'd tried to make my voice sound casual, just mildly curious, but I was holding my breath now. Who was I to ask such questions, I with my tourist brochure knowledge?

He frowned, twirling the cluster of flowers faster in his fingers. "That's true," he said finally. "But the canoe plants made it possible for people to ... live here. These new plants —" he looked around the garden "— they're brought only to ... amuse people. And they kill off the native species. Since your Captain Cook arrived, Hawaii has ... the world record for greatest number of extinctions."

"That's very sad," I said inadequately. I didn't want to say anything about "your" Captain Cook, since I supposed he was more mine than his. I gestured around. "So what *is* truly indigenous, then? What *does* belong?"

He thought for a moment, his eyes flicking around the garden, which I now, too, had to see as a kind of botanical imperialism.

"I belong."

He said it with such seriousness that I wasn't tempted to smile.

"And these." He reached over and slid the cluster of white flowers into my hair.

I suppose it was then. The way his hand stayed in my hair. The faint smell of coconut oil coming from him or maybe from the air or from the flower. The mouth that was so familiar, that was David's mouth, David whom I would love forever for all the denied possibility of our lives, his mouth, this mouth, that I needed to kiss, beyond all reason, my whole body yearning toward him, wanting to belong.

Five

If all astronomical activity in Canada ceased
tomorrow, almost no one would care.

— RICHARD A. JARRELL *(from his 1988*
history of Canadian astronomy)

A V E Y

Of all idiot things, a power failure. Perfect way to start the day. The UPSes were beeping all through the building. A systems administrator finally came down the hallway and told us someone had shot out a bunch of transformers at an electrical substation, and that we'd be out for four or five hours. That was way longer than our UPSes could keep us running. You could hear the moans and screams echoing up and down the corridors. We had no choice but to save whatever we were working on and shut down our computers. The whole building seemed suddenly amazingly quiet.

"Ah, well," said Bruno. "I didn't feel like working today anyway."

"You never feel like working," I said.

At least we hadn't lost any data. I was compulsive about backing up everything, anyway. I didn't think Bruno bothered. If he lost something, well, it was less for him to have to look at. I didn't know how he could be like that, coming in like a clerk paid by the hour and putting in minimal time and energy. I did three times the work that he did.

Hale was at the door, leaning against the jamb.

"Want something?" I said.

I hadn't meant to sound that curt. But it annoyed me, him lounging there, not having to worry about the power being off, in fact probably glad of it. He'd been hanging around my door more often lately, and I'd had a sudden suspicion that he might be gay and sizing me up. It wouldn't have been the first time that happened. Another of the perils of being short, probably. Of course Hale was a gorgeous man, and if I'd been gay I'd probably have been gaga over him, but I wasn't gay, and I wished he wouldn't hang around, with that funny little smile on his face. Even Bruno had noticed and said something insinuating about it yesterday.

"No," Hale said, straightening. "But, well, I have the Jeep today. I wondered ... if you might want me to run you home. Until the power comes back."

Out of the corner of my eye I could see Bruno grinning.

"No, that's fine. I've got my bike."

"Okay." He shrugged, strolled away down the hall.

"Shut up," I said to Bruno.

He laughed. "I'd be thrilled to have him look at me with such interest."

"I'll bet."

"Well, maybe he's using you to get to me. Don't I wish."

And suddenly I realized that Bruno wasn't really joking. "Jesus, man," I said. "Are you gay?" Subtlety and I are not exactly close friends.

"Apparently."

"Oh."

"Is that a problem for you? Sharing an office with someone gay? I mean, tell me if it is."

"No, no, hell, no. Is it a problem for you, sharing an office with a rude, short, straight neurotic from Edmonton?"

Bruno laughed. "Not usually."

"Well, that puts you in another minority."

Still, gay: funny how that made me look at him differently all of a sudden, imagining him with another man. But it didn't bother me in any kind of homophobic way, and maybe I have dear old Dad, ironically, to thank for that. When the parents of one of his students told him the boy was gay, he came home and fisted his hand into my shirt and said, "If I find out you're one of those perverts I'll cut the thing off. You hear me?" So deep down, somewhere underneath the fear, I'd thought, I hope I am gay, maybe not yet, while he can still hurt me, but later, when I can hurt him. In any case, it gave me more sensitivity about the issue than I might otherwise have had.

I got up, clapped Bruno on the shoulder and said, "Well, they're saying now the Y chromosome is shrinking so eventually we'll all be women, anyway."

"Gay women, I hope," Bruno said.

I turned back to work, got a little shock at seeing the computer's blank grey face. "Shit. Right. I'm one of those guys who keeps flicking the light switch on twenty times even though he knows the power's off."

"Actually," Bruno said, "I suppose Hale was right. There's no point sitting around here with the computers down. I think I'll go home. I could drop you off, too, pick you up when the power's back."

"Okay. All right. Kate might scream when she sees me. She's probably forgotten someone else even lives there. Or maybe she's at the condo today, I forget."

We went out into the hallway, past a few people still wandering around with bewildered looks on their faces, and out the front door. In the parking lot we stood blinking like nocturnal creatures forced into relocation during the daytime. What a job this was. And we weren't even astronomers the way the public thought of them, night owls, peering up through huge lenses into the sky until dawn. Radio telescopes could work both day and night, but of course even optical astronomers could now let the telescopes and computers work the night shift while they worked in the daytime. But squinting into computer screens all day was not the big liberation I'd first thought it was.

I followed Bruno to where he'd parked his Tracker. "Hey, man," I said, "you've got grey hair." I was amazed. I hadn't noticed it in the office, those wiry white threads around his ears. He was my age, for heaven's sake.

"Yeah, well." He scratched at his head above his right ear. "Maybe it's just dandruff."

"Scurf."

"Huh?"

"It means dandruff. My mother called it scurf. She had a kind of eccentric vocabulary." *Had.* As though she were dead. Or as though once I moved out she stopped talking. Maybe she did. It would have been safer that way.

Bruno unlocked the doors. "Want to take the scenic route? Along Banyan Drive?"

"Where's that?"

"Oh, my boy — haven't you been down to the peninsula with the hotels and banyan trees?"

"I guess not."

Bruno shook his head. "You have to get out more."

We drove down Kanoelehua Avenue, which I thought I had been on before, but to my surprise when we crossed the Bayfront Highway it turned into Banyan Drive, a winding street with huge banyan trees leaning over it on either side.

"Each tree was named after the person who planted it," Bruno said. "There's one by Amelia Earhart, and one by Babe Ruth. And Richard Nixon. Though the first one Nixon planted was washed away on election day when he became V.P."

"Weird trees," I said. "All those rooty things hanging down."

"The trees grow to be giants. I think the Hindus consider them sacred."

"Should we park, get out and walk?"

"It's called Banyan *Drive*," Bruno said, "not Banyan *Walk*."

I realized it wasn't just the omnipresent chip bags on Bruno's desk that were responsible for his bulk, which seemed to be increasing every day. I had finally persuaded him to throw away his favourite brown shorts whose zipper had stopped gritting its teeth at what was expected of it and pulled so loose of the fabric that you could see his underwear.

At least the bicycle was forcing me to get some exercise, though I probably wouldn't have bulked up like Bruno: I'd have turned into some shrivelled husk, some brain on a stalk.

The drive curved past three or four hotels, the first ones I had actually seen here. Hilo wasn't exactly a tourist destination. The hotels didn't seem particularly luxurious, but since they were on the water they were probably expensive. Country Club, said one. In front of another a vanful of tourists as fat as Bruno and draped with cameras was disembarking. I didn't envy them. Kate would say that was because I didn't know how to enjoy myself. I would say it was because we weren't made to waste our time and money waddling around overpriced resorts letting our minds turn to slop.

A delivery truck had spilled several cases of Coke on the road in front of us. We could have gone around, but Bruno pulled over and parked under one of the big banyans, Nixon's, I think, and we sat watching the driver clean up the mess.

"So this being-gay thing," I said. "Does it come with any perks? Is there a network of gay astronomers who are going to recommend you for jobs?"

"I wish. I'll wind up teaching junior high school Science, if I'm lucky."

My father had taught junior high Science. Thinking of it brought a sourness to my mouth. Of course, people who didn't have to go home with him at night thought my father was a great teacher. Maybe he was.

"Oh, come on," I said. "With your father's magic name to open doors you should be able to get a research position, a cushy postdoc fellowship, somewhere."

"In astronomy? You know how few working astronomers Canada has."

I sighed. Yeah, I knew. Maybe things would have looked more promising if the great Canadian planet hunt had been successful. In the early 1980s a Canadian team from UBC, working out of the Canada-France-Hawaii telescope here, undertook a major, painstaking twelve-year-long search for the first extrasolar planets. They found nothing that could be verified. Looking back on it now, it's more than a little ironic, because a few years ago some celestial powers re-evaluated the Canadian study and conceded that, yeah, well, maybe they *did* find a planet orbiting Gamma Cephei. But back in 1995, all we had was the footnote, the rung-in-the-ladder credit, the special disappointment of "almost."

"Teaching Science to Grade 9 wouldn't be all that bad," Bruno said. "Grade 9 is where you can get them hooked. That and elementary school. I'd like to teach elementary school, actually. Except that when you say 'gay' and 'elementary school' to anybody it's like, oh, you must be a pedophile."

I was going to say that if I wound up teaching either elementary school or Grade 9 I would cut my throat, but I had the sense to swallow the remark. I wanted a job in astronomy. Everything else sounded like failure.

"Well, who knows what will become of us," I said. "Who knows what options we'll have, what choices we'll make, what we'll discover or not discover."

Bruno nodded, watched a fat seagull hop onto the hood of the car and cock its head optimistically at us. Then he said, "Once when my father was head of his astronomy department and doing his annual budget applications he thought he'd plump them up with a list of some of the department's greatest achievements over the years, so he sent off a questionnaire to all the alums he could find, asking them, 'What's the most important discovery you ever made?' Some of the answers were pretty funny. One man said his most important discovery was learning his wife was having an affair with one of his grad students. There was another one I remember. It said, 'My most important discovery was my self.'"

"His self, huh. Was it out there orbiting Jupiter or something?"

Bruno laughed. "Of course, my father was asking people at the end of their careers. They weren't our age, living on grants and peering hopefully through other people's windshields." The seagull seemed to know it was being spoken of and hopped closer. Bruno turned on the wipers and startled a squawk and flap of wings from the bird, but it didn't fly away.

"So," I said, "send me a questionnaire when I'm eighty. I might say, 'Hey, I discovered my glasses were on top of my head the whole time.'"

"That's happened to me already."

"Well, there you go."

The driver of the truck had the road cleared by now, and he gave us an elaborate sweeping bow to usher us back onto the road. If that had been me I would have been pissed right off at two jerks just sitting there watching me work.

When Bruno dropped me off at the house, or, as Kate called it now, the Pupuka, I found her in the kitchen, washing dishes in the shoebox-sized sink.

She had obviously been crying.

Oh, hell. What had I done now? I was pretty sure she wasn't still upset over what I'd said a few days ago about her being a Daddy's girl and all that: she'd seemed back to her usual self the the next day. Brooding about things was not a skill she had ever mastered.

The TV was on in the living room, some variety show, the singing blurring into static every few minutes because the aerial on the roof had more or less rusted through and finally keeled right over. Bruno said it looked as though a bicycle rack had fallen from the skies and embedded itself in the roof. I turned the volume down, went back into the kitchen, remembering to avoid the soft spot, a sag in the floor that had developed a few weeks ago and that had made us think the linoleum was the only thing keeping us from sinking through the rotting floorboards.

Kate was grinding the dishcloth around and around a plate as though she wanted to wear a hole in it. She was trying not to look at me. But it was pretty hard not to notice her puffy red eyes, her whole untidy look that she got when she was upset.

Shit, shit, shit. I didn't want to deal with this.

"What's the matter? What happened?"

"Nothing," she said, keeping her eyes on the dishcloth. Scrub, scrub. She was wearing her old oversized blue striped shirt she was so unaccountably fond of, and the sleeves she'd rolled up over her elbows kept drooping into the dishwater.

I picked up the dishtowel and began drying the plates and cups she'd piled on the counter. Kate said once that drying dishes with a dishtowel was one of the stupider wastes of time when the air would dry them just as well, but I hoped the gesture might lessen the importance of whatever my transgression had been.

"You're upset," I said. "Don't pretend. Tell me. Is it something I did? I'm sorry."

"How can you be sorry when you don't even know if it's something you did?"

"Well, I'm ... preemptively sorry. I mean, I'm sorry that you're upset. Whether it's my fault or not."

She handed me the plate. She hadn't rinsed it, and I didn't want to seem to be correcting her so I dried it anyway, blotting off the suds.

She turned to me then. "Oh, Avey," she said.

I got scared then. "What? What?"

Tears were running down her cheeks. She shook her head.

"*What?*"

At last she said, "I was thinking about David."

KATE

"I was thinking about David."

I was ashamed as soon as the words left my mouth, because although it was the truth it was also a lie. Remembering David was what I was doing to stop myself from remembering Hale, to give myself some excuse.

"Oh," Avey said. I could hear the relief in his voice, could almost hear him thinking: well, at least it's not something that's my fault. I must have really alarmed him; usually he hated it when I mentioned David.

For one mad moment I wanted to tell him what I'd done. But I knew such confession would be only for myself. The last thing Avey needed to deal with now was knowing his wife had slept with someone he worked with.

So I gave him a sturdy smile and said, "It's okay. Sorry." I turned back to the dishes. "What are you doing home so early?" I forced my voice to sound normal.

"Power failure. Bruno gave me a ride. Maybe it's even fixed by now. I hate these interruptions. At least my data —"

The phone rang and he went to answer. I heard him say, "Okay, thanks," and then hang up. I could never believe men were able to keep calls that brief.

When he came back he said, "That was Hale. Power's back on."

Hale. That he would phone here at all, even just to give Avey a message, made my stomach jump with panic. I shoved both hands deep into the dishwater, pressed them on the bottom of the sink. I might have been trying to drown something.

"I'll call Bruno to come pick me up." Avey patted my shoulder. "You going to be okay?

"Yes, yes, of course. Call Bruno."

After Avey left, I sat down in the living room, staring at the TV set. The figures on it seemed to stretch and distort off to the left, then suddenly break apart entirely into horizontal lines, then just as abruptly snap back into recognizable shapes. It was not unlike the way I was feeling.

Three days ago I had fallen into bed with a man I had just met and let him make love to me. No, that sounded too passive. We had made love to each other. I had been in a kind of delirium, needing, wanting, clinging. I had apparently been too deranged even to care about using a condom, though Hale had provided one, thank God. After, it was all I could do to look him in the face. He was very gentle with me then, laying his hand lightly on my forehead like someone bestowing a benediction or checking for a fever and then sort of just disappearing from the room. I heard the front door close. And suddenly it did feel as though my head was being flooded with fever, the blood panicking through every brain cell.

I leapt out of the bed and stared down at it, my hand pressed over my mouth. How *could* I have? Every appetite passes in twenty minutes, I'd read. What was wrong with me? Couldn't I just have waited twenty minutes? Sex with Avey was less than I might have wished for, but it wasn't non-existent. I wasn't starved of it.

I stripped off the sheets and stuffed them into the washer. I sat on the floor, my head leaning against the machine, listening to the muted cycles, the rustling forgiveness of water. Forgiveness: how could I possibly be forgiven? When the last spin cycle started I began to cry, huddled there inside the enormity of what I'd done. I remembered a teacher saying people thought "enormity" just meant "largeness," but primarily it meant great wickedness, an offense against what was right and decent. When the laundry was finished and I put away the detergent I noticed the cupboard door had a loosening hinge, and I kept opening and closing it, looking at the hinge, thinking, that's me, I'm becoming unhinged, I'm a door just waiting to drop from its frame.

Karen called me that night. Her words were ones of apology for the way she had dropped Hale on my doorstep like some unwanted pet and driven off, but her tone was unashamedly inflected with curiosity. Badly as I might have wanted to talk to someone about what I had done I had the sense not to confide in her.

"I was a tad stoned," she said. "I hope Hale didn't behave as badly as I did?"

"No, he was good." I nearly began laughing hysterically. "A good sport," I added.

I might not have gone to the condo the following day if I hadn't had to check some people out and wait for the new couple coming that afternoon. But of course there was no point in staying at the Pupuka, pacing about and berating myself. I had to continue my life as I was expected to. I remembered to bring along a screwdriver and tighten the hinge on the cupboard door in the laundry room. The washing machine beside me was just a metal box, I told myself: it wasn't a witness, it had no memory unless I allowed it some. I didn't trust myself to feel that objective about the bedroom, and I avoided even walking past its closed door.

When the doorbell went and I could see from the side window who it was, I knew I could just not answer, but I had promised myself I wouldn't hide from what had to be done.

I couldn't help smiling when I saw him. He was wearing shorts and a green T-shirt but also a hibiscus blossom in his hair, and around his neck he had a lei made entirely of the trumpet-shaped waxy flowers he had picked for me the day before.

"May I come in?"

I could have said what I intended to right there, but that seemed too rude. He'd done nothing wrong. We could be civilized.

I stood aside, and he came in. He pulled one of the flowers from the lei and reached over to slip it into my hair, but I leaned back, avoiding his hand.

"What I did yesterday," I said, talking too fast, my words sounding distressingly brisk, "was a mistake. I'm married. I don't want to cheat on my husband. He'd be terribly upset. It's flattering that you wanted me, because I know you could have any woman you choose, but I feel bad about what happened. So we can't, you know, do it again."

Hale stood there looking at me, twirling the flower in his fingers. I noticed how perfect his hands were, the nails cut square across, the knuckles both delicate and strong.

"Wasn't it ... something you liked?"

"Yes, of course it was. It was quite ... lovely. But I'm not someone who can have an affair and think it's just fun. I couldn't hurt Avey like that. He deserves better from me." My hand went to my forehead, brushing away a strand of hair that didn't actually seem to be there.

He set the flower on the kitchen counter, took a moment before replying. I could barely breathe.

"I'm sorry," he said. "I had hoped."

I thought he would say more, that this was just one of his strange speech hiatuses, but he didn't.

"I like you," I said. "You're an interesting person. Perhaps we can be friends."

"It's hard to be ... friends with a woman."

I laughed. The petulance in his remark made me realize how young he was, such a boy. And if I had feared his mere presence would disarm my rational brain I suppose I was reassured. He had been here five whole minutes and I was not swooning; my body was not rabid with desire.

"You're wrong," I said. "Women make very good friends."

"I had hoped," he said again. He took the lei from around his neck. I took a step back, and if he had been intending to put it around my neck he changed his mind and set it in the sink. The smell of the flowers was very strong, like a bucket full of hyacinths, perfuming the whole apartment.

"We call them *pua male*," Hale said. "Wedding flowers."

"Ah."

He put the stopper in the sink, turned on the tap. We watched the lei tremble, lift, float. He turned the tap off. We didn't take our eyes from the flowers. The water had released an even stronger scent.

"All right, then," he said. "Since you want me to go I'll go." He turned, went out the front door without closing it.

I stared after him. It had all happened so fast. He picked up his bicycle from the driveway, got on, pedalled away without looking back.

Was there some disappointment in me? Had some dark, primitive place in me wanted him to refuse to leave, wanted him to kiss me, to press me down onto the bed, to say he desired me beyond all denials? I shuddered. No, surely not. Surely as I closed the door I felt nothing but relief, relief that it could end so easily, that my terrible lapse of judgement the day before had simply been some hormonal error, and that Hale seemed willing to see it as I did and had left without more obvious resentment. Back in Edmonton my boss at the realty company had a code he would use if an offer was about to be accepted. "IWW," he would scrawl on Post-it notes or on file covers. It meant: "It Went Well." I was hoping that was what I could say about this negotiation with Hale.

When the new couple checked into Unit Four I gave them the lei. They were delighted.

None of which explained why several days later, cleaning up the breakfast dishes, I had found myself crying, ashamed and angry with myself and full of fresh recriminations. I had begun thinking of David, and then I would tell myself he was just an excuse I was giving myself, pretending I had seen Hale as some reincarnation of the love I had lost. I'd put on David's old blue striped shirt, one of three of his I'd saved, but it didn't give me the comfort I'd sometimes find there. Avey didn't know the shirts were David's, of course, though if he'd looked closely he would have been able to see the buttons were on the wrong side for a woman's shirt.

It was barely half an hour since Bruno had picked Avey up when the phone rang.

It was Hale.

He'd known Avey would have left for the JAC. He'd known I would be here alone. My breathing felt stiff, as though I were forcing my lungs against a heavy weight.

"I was thinking," he said, "that if we are friends, if as you say we are friends, and since I have the Jeep for the day ... and it's still early ... I could take you to see the lava flows. You shouldn't leave the island without seeing them."

I twisted the phone cord around my fingers. *If as you say we are friends.* Yes, I had said that. And if I meant it his reasoning wasn't wrong, was it? And perhaps if we did something as friends it would confirm for both of us that there was nothing deeper between us. It might even make me feel less ashamed about what I'd done; it wouldn't really have just been about sex, then. And I could tell Avey where I was going and with whom — I could be honest about it. Avey wouldn't care; he'd be glad someone was showing me places he had no time or desire to see.

"Kate?"

"Yes, sorry. I was just thinking about it. And, all right. Why not? Yes, we're friends. Yes, I'd like to see the lava flows."

Of course I can see now how foolish I was. I had talked myself into it, the way a child might, making cheap ethical bargains with herself, telling herself not only that her intent is innocent but that if it is innocent all will be well.

I left a note for Avey saying, "Hale called again and offered to show me the volcanoes today, so I've driven up there with him. See you later — I'll probably be home before you are." Maybe I was leaving the note for myself as much as for Avey.

I sat outside on the front steps waiting. On the step below me a large blue fly sat waiting for something, too, wringing its tiny black hands.

Hale picked me up in a white Jeep that I assumed belonged to the JAC. I wondered if he had permission to take it for an excursion such as this. As I got in he gestured at the boarded-up window on the house.

"When did that happen?" he asked.

"Who knows? It was there when we moved in. The landlord said he'd replace it, but we're still waiting."

"He's a local." It didn't seem to be a question.

"I assume so."

"There is some ... resentment of *haoles*."

"That's hardly fair," I said. "He makes a living off us."

"Maybe he resents having to make a living."

Like me, Hale was wearing a long-sleeved shirt and jeans and runners, and his eyes were hidden behind large sunglasses. I usually disliked talking to people wearing sunglasses, but it was probably a good thing that I could see as little of him as I did. We sat primly beside each other, careful not to touch. Every time his hand went down to the stick shift, my eyes would flick to it, as though I needed to make sure it was not transgressing towards my knee.

He nodded at a thermos on the floor. His hair was starting to blow free from the rubber band with which he'd fastened it, and tendrils were whipping at his face. "Why don't you pour us some *awa?*" he said. "There are two cups."

"*Awa?*" I unscrewed the top of the thermos.

"Kava. I grow it myself. I make it from the root. I don't contaminate it the way some people do, with soda and stuff."

I poured us each some. It had a muddy, slightly green look, like watered-down pea soup, and it smelled a bit like pea soup, too. I took a sip. It was foul, the taste cooked grass might have, with a slight bitterness. Almost instantly my tongue and palate went numb.

"Is it like a narcotic? Could it impair your ability to drive?"

He took such a deep and deliberate drink it made me wince. "I'm used to it. It's just to relax. It's not illegal."

I looked nervously at the thermos, estimating how many cups it still held. Two, maybe.

We were heading southwest of Hilo to Kilauea, the most active volcano in the world. It was, Hale said, the home of Pele, the Hawaiian goddess of fire, who was chased from island to island by the goddess of the sea until she found a home in the Kilauea caldera.

"Pele is the last of the old gods to survive," Hale said. "When the lava flows come towards their homes there are still people who ... make prayers and offerings to her. Sometimes she listens. Sometimes she doesn't."

"She's like most of our gods, then."

It was a short drive, perhaps only thirty miles, up the lava dome on the southwest flank of Mauna Loa to the road that circled the caldera. The slope was surprisingly smooth and gentle. This was a shield volcano, so called because it had the curve of a Roman shield lying on its side. I could feel the sun getting hotter as we climbed, and Hale insisted I replace my own sunglasses with the pair of heavier, thicker ones in the glove compartment. There were several there. I knew astronomers could suffer vision damage from exposure to the intense and unfiltered sunlight at observatories. Kilauea wasn't as high as Mauna Kea, or even as Mauna Loa, the other active volcano on the Big Island whose peak we could see to the west, but it was high enough for a drop in atmosphere.

Far below I could see the ocean. The whitecaps were tiny scallops on the shore. I looked for the different colours of beaches — black, green, white, golden — that the island, because it was still so young, was supposed to have, but I was too far away to see such detail. At the island's southern tip was Green Sand Beach, named for its deposits of olivine, a green volcanic rock, but the island seemed simply to dissolve there into a white haze.

As we drove around the crater rim, Hale pointed things out to me: the thick cracks in the land surface from which lava had issued; the spouts of steam and smoke coming up from the vents, from fumaroles, along the rift zones where the magma was near the surface; the yellow sulphur deposits left by the gases that seeped out with the groundwater; the flows themselves, black and brittle where we looked but still new enough that it was easy to imagine them red and molten, rolling slowly down to the ocean. We were driving on a flow that was only twenty years old, and to the east we could see the most recent flow, which had begun in the early eighties and was, according to Hale, the largest and longest eruption in history, and which showed no sign of ending.

I came from a part of the world where the volcanoes were much more explosive, where Mt. St. Helens in the Cascades had shaken homes hundreds of miles away like a huge bomb going off. These were much gentler eruptions, the lava crawling so languidly and at such a small degree of incline down to the sea that people could have picnics beside them, watching the lava turn from red to black, watching it cool and harden into basaltic rock or ooze at last, sizzling and steaming, into the sea. I tried not to think of "the great crack" on Kilauea's southern flank, the eight-mile-long fissure up to seventy feet deep that acted rather like a huge hinge. Most scientists believed it would someday break off this part of the island and slide it into the sea, creating a tidal wave a thousand feet high.

I asked Hale if he ever thought about that.

He shrugged. "It won't happen in my lifetime. Are you afraid it'll happen in yours?"

I laughed. "No. But it's, well, *there*. This massive lurking. When it happens it will be devastating."

"It wouldn't affect you Canadians, anyway."

"On the west coast it would. Though Avey and I live far inland beyond the mountains, so I guess the problem isn't on our doorstep or under our feet as it is here."

"Then I suppose you're lucky. Here no matter what we do or think Pele has her own plans."

"That's rather fatalistic."

"Maybe being around the astronomers has influenced me."

"Are astronomers fatalistic? Maybe they're really building themselves safe, high places on Mauna Kea to escape from the flood. Maybe their work has nothing to do with the stars."

He turned his head to me, his eyes invisible behind his sunglasses. I gave him a toothy smile, to show I was joking.

We got out of the car and walked for a while, following a rough path across the lava. Grey lichens and the occasional spike of fountain grass had found purchase in some of the rock, but mostly it was black and bare. In one spot a pile of strange, thready rock looked more like filaments of spun glass than lava. We continued down the trail to the edge of what Hale called a *kipuka*, a small island of vegetation untouched by the lava.

"I like these places," he said, squatting down, fingering a low-growing shrub with thick, reddish leaves. "The untouched parts. The original parts. The parts the lava hasn't killed."

"But the lava is making new land, giving something else a chance, maybe."

He frowned.

I knelt down beside him, pointed at a piece of rough, chunky lava whose texture reminded me of an aerated chocolate bar. "This is *aʻa*, isn't it? Someone said that if you fall on it you'll know why it's called *aʻa*. And that over there —" I picked up a smoother, shinier oval of black lava "— is *pahoehoe*." I was surprised that I had remembered. Even my pronunciation had been credible. "I learned the words at school. They're the ones geology books use."

If I had expected him to be pleased that Hawaii had given a name to something in a Canadian textbook I was wrong. His frown only deepened.

"Let them find their own names. Why do they want to steal ours?"

He straightened, started walking back to the Jeep. I trotted along behind him. I was still carrying the piece of *pahoehoe*.

When we got to the vehicle, he turned to me and said, "For the tourists and geologists, the lava is fascinating. For us ... it comes and can destroy our homes. The insurance companies might pay us something for lost houses, but not for loss of access to property. My uncle in Puna —" he gestured to the east "— his house was in a *kipuka*, and the insurance company said, oh, you were lucky, no damage, so even though his house is now worthless because he can't get to it he got no compensation."

"I can see that's not fair."

"My brother in Puna had a house on the ocean. The lava took it, but it made his property bigger, right? Accreted land, they call it. But the new lava land ... belongs to the state. My brother loses in every way."

"How ... unfortunate," I said. I couldn't seem to find a better word.

"Yes, unfortunate." He got into the Jeep, slammed shut the door.

I sighed. Fatalism was obviously not Hale's consistent philosophy.

I should have said I wanted to go back then, but I felt responsible for his bad mood, so I suggested we have a coffee at the restaurant that overlooked the caldera. Maybe the coffee would work better than the kava had. He shrugged.

"If you want," he said.

A part of me was glad he was in a bad mood. Probably there are men who wear such an attitude attractively, who glower sexily, but Hale wasn't one of them.

The restaurant was in the complex called Volcano House, which had existed there in some form for two centuries and was carved right into the rim of the crater. It offered a panoramic view of the caldera, which was really just the top of the giant lava dome that had collapsed in on itself, making subsequent eruptions less intense. It reminded me of icing on a huge cake. Sometimes flames shot up from the caldera in fountains of molten rock. Most of them fell back into the cauldron, but some of them exploded into fiery embers that drifted on the wind. It was an altogether amazing sight.

The restaurant was busy servicing the two tour buses parked outside, and there seemed to be many families with overactive children. When Hale took off his sunglasses people stared at him, as people always did. He only glared back.

"You know what someone told me once?" he said after we ordered. "She said, 'Oh, you look just like a postcard.' I said, 'No, the postcard looks just like me.'"

I laughed. "Good answer."

"She said I was rude and should learn how to take a compliment." He picked up his coffee spoon and ran the edge of it, hard, around and around on his placemat. "You know the United States stole Hawaii. None of the *haoles* belong here. None of the Japanese. They all come here and steal what's ours."

How did he expect me to respond? Even if I didn't object in principle, I was personally implicated as a *haole*. He put his sunglasses back on, looked out the window. I could see reflections in them of fiery embers.

I knew I was inviting trouble, but I said, "Well, the lava was here before anybody. I suppose the islands really belong to it."

I could have said something even more querulous, about how the current Hawaiians were probably originally from Tahiti and how they had aggressively taken over the islands from earlier settlers from the Marquesas Islands. But who was I to make such judgements? I was a privileged descendant of Europeans who stole Canada from its aborigines. I was already regretting what I'd said about the lava. It was as insensitive as what I'd said about the canoe plants. I don't know why I felt this urge to say things to him that I knew would surely be annoying. I wasn't being, well, *nice*. Maybe I wanted to prove to both of us that I was immune to him. Of course, what I had said to him so far did not compare with what I would say to him before I left the island.

Hale didn't answer, sat staring out the window at the steam rising from the huge, round caldera. There was a smell of sulphur in the air.

"I suppose we should head back," I said after a while.

He nodded, finished his coffee. When the waitress brought the bill I picked it up. Hale offered no objection.

"Let me pay you for the gas, too," I said.

"The tank was full."

I didn't pursue it. I hoped that somewhere back in Canada this wasn't my tax money at play.

We got in the Jeep. My foot knocked over the thermos, and Hale frowned at me. "Oh, don't give me your stink-eye," I said.

I expected a surly reply about how I shouldn't try to talk like a local. But to my surprise Hale smiled.

"You been makin' house too much with that Keke," he said. "She too *uji* for you."

"Nobody is too *uji* for me." I had no idea what *uji* was.

"Except me, maybe," he muttered. But he couldn't pretend he hadn't smiled. He'd smiled. Even his posture had eased its scowl.

He put the key in the ignition, then pointed at the piece of *pahoehoe* I had set on the floor.

"You don't want to take that with you," he said.

"Why not?"

"It's bad luck. Pele would be angry."

"She knows how to make more."

He shrugged. "Every year the park wardens at the Volcano House get hundreds of pieces of lava mailed back to them. Some of them are addressed to Mrs. Pele. People include terrible stories ... of the bad luck it brought them."

I picked up the *pahoehoe*, ran my thumb over its ropey striations. It felt like a piece of smooth driftwood. "Well, then. It's a challenge, isn't it? I'll have to keep it now."

He didn't answer. I had no idea what he was thinking, if he was annoyed or amused or indifferent. I dropped the lava into my jacket pocket, where it eventually worked its way into the lining and stayed there until, years later, in Canada, it fell out as I was bundling the jacket up with a package of clothes for Goodwill. I remembered then everything about this day, and I wondered, briefly, if I should send the lava back to Pele.

We pulled out of the parking lot. The sun had heated up the Jeep, and I rolled down the window, then rolled it up again as the cold air pulsed inside. I rubbed at the goosebumps on my arms.

"So," Hale said, tilting his head to the north at the snowy head of Mauna Kea, "has your husband found his planet yet?"

"Not that I'm aware of."

"What does he look for, anyway, when he's sitting there ... staring at his computer all day? I look at their screens and nothing makes any sense to me."

I thought about it for a minute. "I suppose it's a language they have to translate. Avey said once that what he looks for is an anomaly."

"An anomaly? That's something that doesn't belong."

I smiled. Hale was the expert on what belonged. "I guess that's not from the point of view of the planet."

"So maybe if he does find one it would be ... like Captain Cook discovering us. What would the planet have to say about it? I wasn't lost, it would say. I didn't need to to be found. Maybe you're the ones who are lost." He turned back onto Crater Rim Drive. "One more thing you have to see. Nahuku."

"What's that?"

"You'll see."

He drove south a few miles, then pulled into a lot at the side of the road. The sign said "Thurston Lava Tube." I'd heard of it. I assumed this was Nahuku. I didn't ask him about the discrepancy, though I remembered what he had said about *a'a* and *pahoehoe*, and I wondered if he preferred that we *haoles* did bring along our own names. It was quite confusing, trying to please Hale and Pele.

"The place is usually full of tour buses," Hale said. "We're lucky."

We headed down the trail, which was steep and slippery, into the pit crater and into an unexpected forest of ferns, brilliantly green, haloed with a variety of birds flickering and calling overhead. The air was delicious, moist and full of oxygen and subtle perfumes, making me a little heady after the sulphurous smells above us along the crater rim.

Hale reached over, brushed a bug with long pincers on its tail from my sleeve.

"What was that?" I watched it scuttle under a vine. "It looks like what at home we call an earwig."

"It *is* an earwig. Another nasty import. It likes it up here where it's cooler."

"I used to think they'd crawl into my ears at night."

"They don't. But cockroaches so. My cousin works at the hospital, and he says it's one of the most common causes of visits to the emergency room."

I shuddered. "I still don't think I've gotten rid of all those in our house."

"We have a saying: 'There's always another cockroach.'"

"I'll embroider that on a pillowcase."

The entrance to the lava tube, Hale explained, was actually a collapsed part of its roof. It was hung with mosses and ferns, but the tube itself seemed almost man-made, like a tunnel perfectly formed and leading into a mine. It was hard to imagine lava flowing like this, underground, creating a kind of plumbing system for itself, but it probably would have been very efficient, an outer crust that hardened and provided an insulation for the molten lava inside.

We entered the tunnel, Hale behind me. The sudden blackness made me stumble, pull my sunglasses off, and reach for the wall for support. Some lights had been installed in the walls, but they were very dim, and I stood blinking at the strange darkness, at the sudden cool air.

"It's so dark," I said.

"They shouldn't have put lights in at all. It spoils the effect."

"It's spooky enough even with the lights."

"There were lava stalactites here once, too," Hale said, "but people broke them off and took them. For souvenirs."

He was so close behind me that I instinctively began moving forward. The floor was fairly smooth, and perhaps had even been paved, but my feet found it hard to walk, my steps wanting to be too high, not trusting a surface my eyes could not see. Overhead I could detect roots of trees and other plants dangling down from the thick rainforest above.

"How far does the tunnel go?" I asked.

He was right behind me again. "Not far. Some lava tubes go for ten miles. This one goes for less than half a mile. We can climb out through another crack in the roof."

"I don't think I want to go all the way."

"We can go a little farther."

I took a few more steps, then stopped, turned. The entrance to the tunnel seemed a long way back, just a pinprick of green light, and not where I had expected to see it. The tunnel had been curving. My eyes had adjusted a little to the dark, and I could see sections of the walls, but then I realized that was mostly because they were covered, eerily, with white ashes.

Hale was just a few inches from me. His shirt brushed my arm.

"We should go back," I said. "I'm getting a little claustrophobic."

He put his hands on my arms, and then he was kissing me. I turned my face to the side, my whole body stiffening.

"No," I said. "Hale. For Pete's sake."

"Kate. *He wahine u'i.* You're so beautiful."

And I started to laugh. "How do you know? It's almost pitch black! You can't see me!" And that sounded so absurd that I began laughing even harder. The echoes bounced wildly off the walls.

"I do see you. I want to make love to you again."

"Oh, Hale. We agreed. We're friends, that's all." I pushed myself away from him, out of his arms.

"I want there to be more."

"I'm married. I'm not free to be with you. I thought you understood that."

"Why did you come with me today, then?"

"To see the volcanoes! Oh, I'm sorry, I'm sorry. I shouldn't have come. I've completely given you the wrong idea."

He was a dark shape between me and the small, distant spot of light. I kept my eyes on it, as though it would blink out if I didn't. I started to stumble back toward it.

Hale put his hand on my shoulder, not quite stopping me, not quite letting me walk away.

Was I afraid then? Of him? I was afraid of the darkness, I know. But I don't think I was afraid of Hale. And it was over so quickly, really. I pulled free of his hand and walked back toward the entrance, to the growing circle of light, which was suddenly blocked by a busload of Australian tourists being urged so relentlessly and recklessly into the tunnel by their tour guide shouting about being behind schedule that it was like a lava river bearing me backwards, and it was only when Hale took my arm and we both strained determinedly forward that we were able to flail our way out.

Six

*If you do not expect the unexpected,
you will not find it.*

— Heraclitus

Avey

Sandy came to visit. It was just after New Year's.

She had almost come for Christmas, but she hadn't wanted her grandparents to spend it by themselves. I guess she thought they would miss her more than we would. I'd told Kate to go back to Edmonton for Christmas if she wanted, but she said no, it wasn't fair to leave me here alone. I'd have been just as happy to spend Christmas Day at the office, but even I knew that if anyone saw me there it would have been too embarrassing. So we'd had a little potluck thing at Bruno's, eight of us with nowhere else to go, and it was okay. Joe and Karen were from somewhere in northern England with a foul climate, and Dieter and Hilde were from somewhere wintry in Bavaria, and with Bruno and Kate and me from Canada we could sit on the lanai in our shorts and T-shirts, drinking our mai-tais, and make fun of Ravi, who came from India and complained how he was cold here all the time.

"I can't believe we're on the same latitude as Calcutta," he moaned.

"Yeah, those darn trade winds," Bruno said, "keeping us in this deep freeze."

"They are blizzards, really," Hilde said. "Let's call a card a card." Her mastery of English slang was proximal at best.

"You bet," I said. "And when that Pineapple Express blows its way up to Canada the temperature drops fifty degrees in ten minutes."

"Just imagine how nice the islands would be if they weren't buried under all this snow," Bruno said.

"And under that is the permafrost," Karen said. "I don't know how the volcanoes can break through it."

"A *furchtbar* climate," Dieter agreed. "*Schrecklich.*"

Ravi sat with his jacket on and shivered obligingly for us through dinner.

And now here was Sandy. She was as close to a daughter as I would have, I guess, thanks to a vasectomy eight years ago that I suppose I had done partly because I knew it would upset my father, who had assumed he would inflict his genes on endless generations. Partly I had it done because my girlfriend at the time had announced she was pregnant. It scared me to death, seeing my academic dreams vanish just like that. She took one look at my horrified face and made an appointment for herself at the clinic.

Sandy was twenty now, taller than both me and her mother, pretty enough with her curly dark hair that she streaked with blond, her deep-set blue eyes and her full lips with the little brown mole at one corner. But she had a harder look to her face than Kate did, as though she always carried some irritation at the edges of her mouth and around her eyes. Her face was the same oval shape as Kate's, but unless you looked closely you would say it was square. She had none of Kate's laid-back, shrugging nature. Her voice was unexpectedly deep, too, and I imagined men must have found it a disconcerting blend of sexy and mannish. When one of my profs met her he told me she was gorgeous but that he had to keep looking at her Adam's apple to make sure. Jerk.

Sandy and I were a lot alike, actually. It didn't mean we had become great friends or anything, but we got along okay, none of those aggrieved stepdaughter tricks. What we shared was ambition, a need to accomplish something. With Sandy it had the added component of what she called feminism but what I called self-interest with a built-in excuse. She was at university now, going into pre-law, and I could imagine she'd make a good lawyer. I wouldn't want to be facing those interrogative eyes in the witness stand.

The house, of course, made Sandy shriek. "It's dreadful! It's a slum."

"We've gotten used to it," Kate said.

"There's a smell." She wrinkled her nose, looked around suspiciously. "Have you shampooed the rug, if that's what that is?" She gestured at the brown carpet in the living room. It was worn through to the underlay in spots.

"Well, no," Kate said.

"And the walls? Have you at least washed the walls?"

"Mostly," Kate said.

"You could have told me it was this bad. I could have stayed at a hotel."

I could see Kate pursing her lips, but she didn't say anything. She was used to Sandy saying exactly what she thought without passing the remark through the usual diplomatic censors. Sandy called it "being straightforward."

I gave an exaggerated sigh. "Must be nice to be a student and afford hotels."

That, at least, made her hesitate. We all knew she was living shamelessly off her grandparents.

"Sorry. But you must admit this is a bit, well, rustic." She scratched at a mosquito bite on her upper arm where I could see she'd had removed, not quite successfully, the tattoo of the scorpion she'd gotten during her Goth period, which had lasted about three days. I guess law school frowned on such overt symbols of the predatory.

"At least the window is fixed," I said, gesturing at it. Someone had come, hallelujah, two days ago and had even left some curtains for it.

"And we'll only be here another month or so," Kate added.

Another month or so. I stumbled against Sandy's suitcase as my feet moved, involuntarily, it seemed, toward the door. It was January, 1996. 1995 was over and I had nothing to show for it, nothing.

I said, "I've got to go to work."

"It's almost five o'clock," Sandy said. "I thought you didn't work nights."

"I've got stuff to review. It's not a nine-to-five job."

"We'll talk about you when you're gone," Sandy said.

"Ha ha. Unfortunately I'm more worried about my work than about you and your mother."

Sandy laughed. "I like a man with his paranoias prioritized. So — shall I give you a lift?" She had rented a car, paid for of course by the grandparents.

"It's just as easy to bike," I said. My hand was on the doorknob.

Only another month or so, only another month or so.

But at the office I couldn't seem to concentrate, my eyes drifting repeatedly away from the computer. I should have stayed and had a meal with them, at least, driven around with them a bit. Sandy was only going to be here for two days. Plus they were going to talk about me if I wasn't there, ha ha.

I checked my email, found a new message from Rob Charchuck, my old office mate at U of A. We'd shared the office with an exchange student from China, one of those brilliant guys I couldn't bring myself to resent because he had the best giggly laugh I'd ever heard and because he was even shorter than I was, a little shrimp of a guy. He liked astronomy, he told us, because it made everyone else feel small, too. Once he showed Rob and me the Chinese ideogram for *opportunity*. The first part, he said, drawing it, was the symbol for *dwarf*, the second for *giant*.

"See?" he said. "Dwarf turns into giant. Opportunity."

"No shit." Rob gave me a shove. "You live in the wrong country, Fleming."

"You live on the wrong planet, Charchuck." I gave him a punch.

The exchange student giggled. He liked it when we did that insulting and physical stuff. He was never sure if we meant it. I wasn't always sure, either. We had the maturity of twelve-year-olds.

Rob's email today was continuing another reciprocally insulting argument we'd been having since he'd told me he didn't think we needed to reconcile Einstein's theory of general relativity with the discoveries of quantum mechanics. I couldn't believe he was serious: how could we accept the division of physics into two separate theories, one with rules for stars and planets and another for the world of atoms and electrons? He'd said he could live with two separate theories because the gravitational effects on atoms or particles are so unobservably tiny. I'd said tiny didn't mean non-existent, and how the hell could he want to stop looking for one unified theory? He said having the two theories had been working all right for the last seventy years. I told him that was the biggest copout I'd ever heard.

His message today said, "Ah, Fleming. The trouble with you is that you have no negative capability."

Negative capability. He probably thought I wouldn't know what that meant. He forgot we'd taken first-year English from the same Keats fanatic.

"Charchuck," I typed. "Ooooh. No negative capability. You've like so hurt my feelings. You must be majoring in English now. I can see how you'd be more comfortable in a field where poets say we shouldn't be fretting over those darned annoyances of fact and reason."

I pushed *Send.*

Okay. Play time was over. I had to get back to work. *Abeunt studia in mores.* I hated still remembering that. It was what my father used to say. It means something like: Diligent labour will become a habit.

As I waited for my computer to reset I picked up the new issue of *Icarus* on Bruno's desk and skimmed the article by George Wetherill. He was talking again about how 51 Pegasi B orbited so bizarrely close to its sun, considering its mass and the fact it was a gas giant. It was a hard thing for astronomers to get their heads around. I suppose I wasn't the only one hoping there'd be an explanation other than that this was some freak. Of course there were still a few scientists who didn't believe there was a planet at all, just a pulsating star.

Wetherill went on about how the planet was also way too close to its sun to be some super-Earth and that the chances of an extrasolar Earth located at just the right distance to evolve life were not great in any case. Well, I didn't care about that. I wasn't planning to move there.

But the rest of the world did care. For them it was all about finding Earth-like planets. That was going to be the whole new next thing. That was where the funding would go. Maybe even if I could find another gas giant all the hype would be about who could find the first Earth-like planet. The current Doppler method couldn't find one. Those of us using it would be obsolete, we'd be dinosaurs, Mayor and Queloz would be old news, and the guy who discovered the second gas planet, well, who would care, nobody would even remember his name. So what if I was the first North American, so what if I scooped Marcy and Butler in the US? I was just deluding myself that finding a second planet would matter. It wasn't the *first,* was it, it wouldn't matter unless it was the *first* —

Ah, Jeez. I was making myself nuts.

I tossed the periodical back onto Bruno's desk. And I saw Hale standing at the door, leaning on a push-broom, looking at me.

"Christ, man," I said. "You gave me a scare."

"Sorry. Just wondering if there was anything you wanted before I went home."

Why would he think there was anything I wanted from him? "No, no," I said. "I might pack it in early tonight."

"For you, early means before midnight."

I had to concede him a laugh for that. "Thanks for taking Kate out to see the volcanoes, by the way. She said she enjoyed it."

He raised one shoulder slightly, let it drop. "My pleasure. She is ... easy company."

Was there something just slightly insinuative in his voice? I squinted up at him. No, of course not. What was I thinking? Kate was cute, but she had more than ten years on Hale. Of course she had almost that many on me, too. But surely Hale would have had enough girlfriends his own age he'd have to beat off with a stick. And he was just a janitor here, for God's sake. He'd know enough not to try something with the wives of the academics.

"Yeah, I guess she is," I said. "Her daughter's visiting now. She's a university student." Just in case he had misjudged Kate's age.

"Well, I'd be glad ... to show them both around. If they'd like."

He had this irritating way of pausing in the middle of a sentence, as though his words sidled up to his teeth and then didn't know how to step over them. It might have been some sort of speech impediment, or something he'd learned to cure one, but more likely it was a deliberate mannerism, an actor's trick, to force your attention.

"The daughter's got her own car, thanks."

I turned rather pointedly back to the computer. It took longer than it should have before I heard Hale walking away down the corridor.

I clicked open the file I'd been working on. Okay. Maybe this would be the night the dwarf turned into the giant.

It wasn't, of course. In fact, by the time I left the office I think gravity had sucked more spinal fluid than usual out of me.

The next morning I made myself stay and have breakfast with Kate and Sandy. I could tell they were both surprised. We had toast and cereal, though Sandy could have made not quite so big a deal out of the fact that we didn't have soy milk. We made her jump a foot when we both yelled at her as she was about to step on the soft spot on the kitchen linoleum.

"Sorry," Kate said. "It's the floor's fontanelle. Though I don't think it will ever knit itself together."

Sandy eyed the floor as she sat down. "I think I saw a movie about this house. *The Hilo Horror*."

I stayed for a second cup of coffee, which surprised Kate even more, and I even unearthed an entertaining anecdote: Bruno had come home last week to find a mongoose had gotten into his house. It had taken him two days to finally get it out. Well, it was a funny story, though not for Bruno.

"Mongooses are vicious," Sandy said. "I wouldn't want to find one in my house."

"They were imported to control the rat population," Kate said, "but nobody considered that rats are nocturnal and mongooses are diurnal."

"Like astronomers compared to the rest of the population," Sandy said.

"Since you must be talking only about optical astronomers, I won't take umbrage," I said.

"I wonder what predator they can import to keep astronomers under control," Sandy said.

"Anyway," Kate continued, "the imported mongooses became almost as big a problem as the rats. They've helped to decimate the nene, for instance, by eating its eggs."

"The nene is the state bird. It's a relative of the Canada goose." I'd picked that up somewhere.

"It mustn't be the same kind of survivor," Sandy said, taking the last piece of toast. "When I was in London as soon as anyone heard I was from Canada they yelled at me to take those geese home. Guess they were brought in to some of the ponds and parks and were so aggressive that they completely took over."

I laughed. "Good for them."

"They shouldn't have brought them in in the first place," Kate said. "Hawaii is a good example of how imported species destroy the local plants and animals. There's very little left that's indigenous. Hale — he works with Avey — told me over a third of the plants and almost all of the birds that were here when Captain Cook arrived are gone."

"Hale took your mom up to see the volcanoes. Now I think he's got a crush on her."

Ah, shit. I had sort of been enjoying this just sitting here, this joking around, and now I'd spoiled it. Kate was looking embarrassed and upset.

"A crush," Sandy said. "Sounds interesting."

But neither Kate nor I seemed able to find anything to say to that, and the silence lasted long enough for Sandy to raise an eyebrow. Shit, shit, shit.

"Well, your mom should be flattered. Hale's a hunk," I said. But my words had only a crudeness, a false comedy, to them. Damn it. This was why I didn't do chit-chat.

I set down my coffee cup. "Well, gotta go."

Sandy didn't offer to drive me, even though it was raining. I suppose I shouldn't have thought there was any kind of rebuff in that, since I'd refused her offer before, but I did.

The morning was half gone. I'd never been this late before. The rain had stopped by the time I finally turned onto Nowelo, and there was a rainbow arching over the university campus below me, but my eyes weren't on the rainbow as I cut the corner left onto A'ohoku. They were on the JAC at the end of the street.

And I realized too late a car was turning right from A'ohoku. I avoided hitting it only by slewing the bike onto the shoulder at the last minute.

I went down, the bike on top of me, both of us skidding into a bush.

"Jesus, man!" shouted the driver of the car as it swerved past me. I could see his wide-open eyes, his wide-open mouth. Then he just drove off.

Bastard, bastard. Okay, the accident was mostly my fault, I'd been slicing too casual a curve around that corner, but the guy should have stopped. I got up, cursing, inspected first the bike and then myself for damage. The bike had landed on me and didn't have a scratch, but the side of my knee was starting to throb, and I could see gravel ground into it. I picked out some of the bigger pieces, hobbled down to the JAC, washed out the rest in the bathroom, then went back to the front desk and asked Kani for some bandaids. She'd done something strange to her hair. It was cut shorter on one side than the other and had dark purple streaks.

"Ouch," she said at the sight of my knee.

"Some asshole trying to run me off the road," I said.

"Lucky it's not worse, then." She opened her bottom desk drawer and handed me a roll of gauze, some surgical tape, and a tube of antiseptic cream.

"Whoa. You're well-stocked."

"You'd be surprised what you boys do to yourselves," she said.

I sat down by the front door, smeared on some antiseptic, then slapped a big clumsy bandage over the whole mess and limped off to my office. Kani was right, I suppose — I was lucky this wasn't worse. But I wasn't feeling lucky as I hobbled down to my office. I was in a royally foul mood.

But maybe if I hadn't had the accident that day I wouldn't have seen what I did when I opened my office door and stepped inside. Maybe I wouldn't have bent down and prodded at the bandage and then looked up at just the right time, just the right angle. Maybe I wouldn't have seen what I did.

The curve.

The new planet.

K A T E

"The new planet? You *found* it?"

I had never seen Avey this excited. His face was flushed, his eyes so intense they looked unnatural, and he was shifting so quickly from one foot to the other that lava might have been boiling up under the linoleum. A little blood was seeping from his knee where he said he'd scraped it falling from his bicycle, but he waved away my sympathetic murmurs.

"It was perfect, *perfect!* A forty-sigma detection. Most major detections in science are lucky to be three-sigma, meaning they're only three times the size of their errors, but this was a forty, damn it, a *forty!*"

He dashed to the kitchen sink, ran himself a glass of water and gulped it down, so fast half of it ran down his chin, dripped onto his T-shirt. He didn't seem to notice.

"So there couldn't be a mistake —"

"I can't see how. But look, you can't tell anybody. I mean *any*body. This is really serious. *Anybody*. Not Sandy, not anybody. I have to verify it first. I have to be completely, absolutely one hundred per cent, sure. Double- and triple-check everything. It'll take a few days."

"Oh, Avey. This is wonderful." I gave him a hug, and he actually danced me across the living room floor, then let himself drop breathlessly onto the sofa. The front of my shirt was damp with his perspiration and the spilled water.

I suppose I was only now starting to really understand. Avey had discovered the second extrasolar planet. This was what a lot of astronomers had been dreaming of, and Avey had done it. I hadn't actually thought about what would happen if he found it. The odds had been so much against him.

"It has to get peer review and all that, of course," Avey was saying, "but they'll fast-track it. And it's going to be a whirlwind. A fucking whirlwind. The phone won't stop ringing, trust me. And I'll have to travel. There are a dozen conferences that'll want me. Ah, God. And jobs —" He gave a wild laugh. "The offers will be coming from everywhere. Where do you want to live? Pick where you want to live."

I laughed. "Slow down, slow down."

"You're right, you're right. I have to be calm. I have to be careful. One wrong move and I could screw this up. But I'm just so sure, there's just no doubt, it was the same damned curve Mayor and Queloz had, almost exactly the same. It's a planet. I know it is."

He got up, ran his hand through his hair, which stood up in little spikes, as though it, too, had had a thrilling experience. I noticed he had an erection. I considered commenting on it, saying something funny about how we shouldn't let it go to waste, but of course he had other things on his mind, and I didn't want to have him think that I believed, as I suppose I did, that it was his work more than his wife that had aroused him.

"Did you tell Bruno yet?"

"God, no. Bruno's the competition."

"It's a shame you couldn't both win."

Avey winced, shrugged. "Yeah, well. It's his bad luck, that's all. Someone's bad luck is always someone else's good luck. It's the Exclusion Principle. Only one of us gets the seat on the bus."

"Well, in that case I'm glad it's you."

"So am I. I want it more than Bruno does." He snapped a look at his watch. "Gotta go back now. Don't even know why I came home. Just had to get out of there. I was afraid I'd go yahooing down the halls or something. I'll be up there until God knows when. You and Sandy can manage without me."

"Of course, of course. Go."

"By the way ..." He paused. "About this morning. What I said about Hale. Sorry. I sounded stupid. I didn't mean to embarrass you."

I was astonished. In the midst of the most exciting day of his life he was apologizing to me for something he'd had every right to say. "Oh, Avey. It's all right. You were just making a joke. And I shouldn't have gone up to Kilauea in the first place with him."

"Why not? I'm glad you got to go, with a local who knows the place. And Hale's okay. He's a nice guy, really. And, look, I'm going to be so hugely busy now, there's no way I can take you up the mountain to see the observatory. I know you wanted to see it before we leave. So Hale can take you. He has to go up there a lot, you can go along sometime."

"Oh, that's not necessary —"

"No, really. I insist."

What could I say? If I resolutely refused he would wonder why. He was already at the door, talking more to himself than to me about what he needed to do.

I poured myself a coffee and stood looking out through our new window at the bougainvillea spilling so far into the driveway that Sandy, coming back now from her trip to the store, had to park in the street again. When she got out of the car, for a few seconds I actually didn't recognize her, this grown-up and confident and rather intimidating woman who looked about the same age as I still felt myself to be. I waved at her through the window. I was going to take her to the condo, which I knew would impress her, and we could have lunch on the lanai. I would have to try not to think about being there with Hale. And I would have to be careful not to say anything about Avey's discovery.

Avey had found his planet.

If he was right, everything about our lives would change. He would become the celebrity he wanted so desperately to be.

And I would have been so happy for him, so unqualifiedly happy, if only he hadn't insisted I go up to the observatory now with Hale. It was as though he had found just the right punishment for me.

*

He must have said something to Hale, because the day after Sandy left Hale called and said he had to go up the mountain. One of the technicians had been, of all things, tightening the lens of his eyeglasses and had dropped the small screwdriver somewhere down into the telescope mechanism, and Hale had to go up to try to retrieve it.

I twisted the phone cord around and around my fingers. I would have to go with him sometime. It would probably be better to do it now, before Avey broke the news of his discovery.

"All right," I said.

I tried not to think of our trip to Kilauea, the way he had behaved in the lava tube. We had barely spoken during our ride home, although when we parted he said he had enjoyed my company. I looked at his face, his eyes invisible behind his dark glasses, and had no idea if he was being ironic.

He picked me up in a four-wheel-drive Ford Explorer. I knew a rugged vehicle was necessary. As Sandy had discovered, the rental car companies would not allow their cars to be driven on the Saddle Road, which linked the Hilo and Kona sides of the island through a saddle-shaped pass between Mauna Kea and Mauna Loa and which connected with the even rougher road up to the observatory.

I felt a bit foolish, wearing my pyjamas under my clothes and carrying an extra shirt and sweater, but I knew I would be needing them. It might have been a little chilly atop Kilauea, but it would be freezing on Mauna Kea. Hale gave me an appraising look and nodded before he opened the car door. He was dressed in jeans and a T-shirt but I could see a parka in the back seat.

"The window," he said. "It's fixed."

It took me a moment to understand he was talking about the house. "Yes. What a relief. The landlord even brought curtains."

Something in Hale's expression: and I knew with a sudden certainty that he had been responsible. I waited for him to explain, but he didn't. Perhaps he expected me to make the connection and say something. But the whole idea was unsettling: I didn't want him to do me favours. Taking me up to the observatory was bad enough.

"All right, then," he said. "Let's go. *Mauka*. Toward the mountain."

"I really don't have to go, you know. You don't have to take me."

He shrugged. "Your husband asked me to."

"But that's not enough reason."

"He's been ... generous to me. I ... broke something at work, and my supervisor ... wasn't pleased. I would probably have been suspended except that your husband asked I not be."

I tried to hide my surprise, and my unease. What was Avey doing? Had he interceded for Hale for my sake? Was taking me up to the observatory the price Hale had to pay for Avey's help? I had the urge to jump out of the vehicle, run away from all of it. But I only nodded as though I knew what had happened between them. The proverbial tangled web was settling on me, so thick I would soon need wirecutters to free myself.

We started off. At the end of the street I could see the pair of battered, red carpet slippers still sitting by the sidewalk, and I stared at them with an émigré's hunger, as though they were a last, comforting memory to take with me to a dangerous new land.

Hale headed west out of town, down Kaumana Drive. The floor on my side of the vehicle was littered with empty Coke cans, and I kept shoving them out of the way. No matter where I tried to wedge them they came muddling back. Then the road began to climb, and they rolled and settled somewhere under my seat. Kaumana Drive turned into Route 200, the Saddle Road. When I looked behind me, through the trees I could get glimpses of Hilo, receding, a small speckled patch on the edge of the huge ocean pulled like a sheet of glistening cellophane around the rim of the planet. The beaches seemed to be melting with light.

"You shouldn't look back," Hale said. "Isn't that one of your Christian ideas? You'll turn into a pillar of salt."

I laughed. "Pillar of lava here, more likely," I said. "Aren't we driving on one of the flows that almost wiped out Hilo?"

He nodded. "People watched it come for seven months. When it was half a mile from the town ... they begged Princess Ruth to ask Pele to stop. Princess Ruth was a huge woman. When she came from Honolulu on a steamship she had to be hoisted out in a cattle sling. But she managed to get to the edge of the flow. She threw a bottle of brandy onto the lava ... and prayed to Pele to stop, then slept there through the night. In the morning the lava had stopped."

"What a nice story."

"It's not a story. It's true."

"Oh. Well, hurrah for Princess Ruth. Your history has some powerful women in it. And Pele is female, too. No-one turns her into a pillar of salt for looking in the wrong direction."

"Pele is the turn-er, not the turn-ee," Hale said.

I smiled. Maybe, I thought, the trip would be okay.

"Of course," Hale went on, "the US army takes credit for stopping some of flows heading into Hilo, too. They dropped bombs on them."

"How did Pele like that?"

"She got her revenge. There was a big eruption just after the attack on Pearl Harbour ... when the islands were under a strict blackout. Her fires ... were like a big beacon for the Japanese planes."

We continued to climb. Lava flows flanked the road, the vegetation becoming more and more sparse and stunted, with dead-looking trees apparently unable to survive on the limited nutrients in the lava. Other stretches had no vegetation at all or just simple pale lichens. We hit patches of cloud and mist. Hale drove faster than I would have liked, considering the road. It had been built in a hurry for military vehicles during wartime, and it was narrow and hilly, with unbanked and blind turns. Still, it was paved and in better condition than I had thought it would be. Perhaps the stories of its poor condition were invented by both the astronomers and Hilo locals who didn't want the tourists from Kona coming over on it.

We reached the crest of the Saddle Road in less than an hour, and then we turned right off the main road and headed up towards the summit. Above us and to our left a lenticular cloud floated over Mauna Loa. The wind conditions here could be just right to sculpt them, their strange, round, layered shapes that were surely often mistaken for flying saucers.

I could feel the air getting thinner, and we needed the heat on in the vehicle now. We passed a kind of pastureland and a forest, mostly of scraggly kiawe trees, that seemed to have survived the lava. I glimpsed something moving among the trees: perhaps it was one of the feral sheep or goats that had been brought in for hunters. I tried not to think of men with guns, camouflaged as chunks of lava, waiting to kill the life that could endure here.

At last we pulled into the lot of the Onizuka Visitors' Center, where we were supposed to wait for half an hour before continuing on, to get used to the altitude. We were at 9,000 feet above sea level now.

Inside the building, which seemed brand new, I looked at the displays, the pictures of the telescopes, the diagrams explaining the electromagnetic spectrum. Although there were over half a dozen cars in the lot, we and the clerk were the only people in the place. I bought a T-shirt with a picture of the observatory on the back, and on the front it said, "Mauna Kea: Clearly The Best." The young woman working there couldn't take her eyes off Hale. I wondered what it must be like to be the girlfriend or wife of someone who looked like him.

"I'm going outside," he said. I could tell the woman's gaze was annoying him. "You can come look at some of the plants here if you want."

I followed him around to an enclosure at the end of the parking lot. The fence, Hale said, was there to protect a remnant of subalpine forest that had once covered the slopes of the mountain. I recognized a plant called silversword, which looked like a soft cactus. After twenty years it would flower once and then die.

Hale gestured at several large trees he called the *mamane* and then to smaller plants at their base. He gave me the long Hawaiian names, then said, "I can't tell you the English names. They don't have any. Though that one is a relative of the geranium." He pointed to a shrub that had silver leaves, which probably helped it to reflect the severe solar radiation at this altitude.

"Geranium. At home they're our most common houseplants."

"Houseplants. Another name for plants that shouldn't be there in the first place."

I sighed.

We walked around for a while, not speaking, waiting for our bodies to be ready for the final ascent to the observatory. Large, greyish birds flew around the *mamane* trees, and lower down smaller green birds were probing flowers for nectar. Their calls sounded like zippers being pulled up.

I could see, not far up the hill and blending brownly into the landscape, the dormitories, called Hale Pohaku, in which the astronomers could sleep after spending a night on the mountain. The place had housed a lot of scientists over the years, and now was more like a private, non-profit hotel. Avey told me that once a homeless man had even found his way up here, and when someone over supper asked him at which observatory he worked he said it was the Canada-France-Hawaii one. When asked his name, he said, "Chateaubriand." The Canada-France-Hawaii Telescope people had of course never heard of an astronomer by that name.

Avey had stopped at Hale Pohaku a few times, though not to stay overnight, just to get something to eat and allow his metabolism to return to normal. No one spent twenty-four hours at the summit — the fatigue and impaired judgement and other health problems made it an unacceptable risk. I had to be grateful for the computers that now made it possible for Avey to work in Hilo; obsessed as he could get, I could well imagine him spending more than twenty-four hours at the telescope, and that was with his judgement operating as usual.

It must have rained here heavily recently, because when we got back to the parking lot we noticed several large pools of clear water. Hale stopped by one of them, looked down into it. I came and stood beside him, gazed down at our two reflections in the water.

"This reminds me," I said, "of a science fiction story I read. It's set on Mars, which humans have colonized and settled for some time. There are only rumours of original inhabitants, original Martians. The children in this family keep begging their father to show them a real Martian, and one day the father says, okay, he'll show them a real Martian, and he takes them out to a lake and he tells them to look down. They see their own reflections, of course. And the father says, there, those are the real Martians."

Hale didn't respond for a while, and then he said abruptly, "Why did you tell me that story? Did you want it to be some sort of lesson for me about how invaders eventually become the natives?"

"Well, not exactly, but —"

"The real lesson is that the original inhabitants have all been destroyed, haven't they?"

"It's —"

He pushed his foot into the water, dissolving our faces into fragments. "This is what we all become. Pieces. Broken things."

I thought: how little I know this man. Does he think of himself as a broken thing?

I put a hand on his arm, and said — what *did* I say? I can't remember. Some murmur of comfort, a gesture and words he took for something else, because he turned and put his arms, hard, around me.

"I want us to be together, Kate."

"Oh, Hale. For heaven's sake." I tried to push myself away, glancing at the Visitors' Center, where the clerk might be watching us. Hale's arms were so tight around me that it was easier to just lower myself until I could slither clumsily out from beneath them. "How many times do I have to tell you? It's impossible. Absolutely impossible. I mean — even by your own arguments, I don't belong here. Avey and I will be leaving soon."

He pushed his foot again into the pond. I could imagine water seeping into the frayed stitching of his runner, and in my urge to tell him to stop I recognized something absurdly maternal.

"You don't have to go with him."

"Of course I do. Look, you say Avey did you a favour, and now you want to make love to his wife." Perhaps an appeal to whatever manly agreement they had made might carry more weight than my own protestations.

"I know you're refusing me because you think this would hurt Avey. But would he have told me to ... take you up the mountain if it wasn't okay for him?"

"That's not the same as our sleeping together!" I waved my hand in the air, as though it were full of corroborative evidence. "Oh, I'm sorry I came, Hale. I shouldn't have. I'm a — what's your word? A *hupo*. I'm a *hupo*. An idiot. Let's just go back to Hilo. Let's pretend this didn't happen."

Hale didn't look at me, kept nudging his foot into the water. A dark-skinned man wearing a flannel shirt and huge hiking boots drove up, nodded at us, went into the Onizuka Center.

"I told your husband I'd take you to see his telescope. He'll be ... angry with me if I don't. And I have my job to do there."

I looked yearningly down the hill. I wondered if I could simply fake a visit to the telescope for Avey, wondered if I could pay the man in the hiking boots to drive me back to Hilo.

"I promise," Hale said, looking up at me at last, "I won't touch you again."

"You promised that before."

"Even *I* know ... when there's no more point."

I had to laugh. Everything about this was absurd. We were both *hupos*. The man in the hiking boots came out of the building carrying a package. He nodded at us again, got into his van. I didn't seem to be running over to him, entreating rescue.

"All right," I said. "Let's go see the telescope."

"We won't have to stay long," Hale said. "Just until I find the lost screwdriver."

I headed for the Explorer, but Hale said, "No, we have to change vehicles here. We need one better tuned for the altitude." He opened the door to a Jeep with thick, wide tires. I had no choice but to get in.

We drove on. The pavement ended abruptly and the road turned to cinder, rutted and very steep, with many curves and switchbacks and potholes. I could see why on my map it looked like a seismograph printout after a quake. There were no guardrails despite some steep drop-offs. I didn't dare to look down.

Around us the landscape had become completely barren, just rough chunks of lava everywhere. The only colours now were the blacks and greys of volcanic ash, rocks and mud. Cinder cones dotted the landscape like huge mole hills. A moonscape: the Apollo astronauts had done much of their training here.

We passed a spot where the repeated frost heaves had created a surface sorting of sand and pebbles. It looked like a field with carefully tilled and even rows, a crop of rocks.

I could feel the wind buffeting the Jeep, and Hale turned the heat up as high as it would go.

He pulled a bottle of water out of a side compartment in the door, flipped up the lid, drank, handed it to me. When I was slow in taking it, he said impatiently, "You have to keep hydrated. It helps with the altitude sickness. We have to climb about four thousand feet in just nine miles."

I drank. I was beginning to feel dizzy, nauseous, perhaps from the altitude, perhaps from the jolting ride and many turns. It seemed to me Hale was driving much faster than was safe. When the James Clerk Maxwell Telescope was opened, Prince Philip came to dedicate it and rode to the top in a Rolls-Royce. I wondered how he had liked the trip. He would, at least, have had more confidence in his driver than I did in mine. I was feeling queasy enough without having to worry about Hale. I remembered his arms around me, so hard, a sudden rope, a tightening lasso, and I made myself take deep breaths, sucking what oxygen I could from the thin air.

I was just going to ask him to drive more slowly when the road suddenly became asphalt again. It would be paved now, I could see on the map, for the last four miles. When it was icy, though, it would actually be safer to drive on the cinders. We passed through a wispy layer of cloud, and I assumed that now we were above the tropical inversion layer which separated the peak from the lower moist air and gave the summit its exceptionally dry and clear atmosphere.

Hale shifted into a higher gear. "You look nervous," he said. "Are you afraid I'm going to deliberately drive us over the cliff?"

"Not deliberately."

"It's going down that's more dangerous. Especially after you've been up on the mountain long enough to get altitude sickness. The downhill speed limit ... is twenty-five miles an hour, but some Frenchmen decided to set a record ... and took it at sixty."

I shuddered, looking down at a sheering drop-off. At least there were guardrails here. Sheets of icicles were draped from them like washing on a clothesline, some of them blown and frozen sideways from the wind.

"Did they set a record?"

"Oh, yes. They did the drive in nine minutes. If you like we can try to match it when we go back."

"No thanks."

"We're almost there," Hale said. He shifted, abruptly enough to make the vehicle lurch, into a lower gear. A gust of wind slapped at us, hard, pushing the Jeep into the centre of the road.

We rounded a curve, and then, suddenly, there they were: the observatory domes like fat, white bubbles glittering in the hard sun. The lava mounds around them had a slightly reddish, ferrous colour. Straight ahead I recognized the Keck, or "mighty Keck," as I had been told we must call it. The second Keck dome was there, too, but wasn't yet open. There were eight telescopes here now, phenomenal creatures that held almost every record in the world for one dimension or another. And there were more to come, including a giant observatory funded by Mitsubishi. The University of Hawaii, which controlled the summit, had already leased eleven separate sites.

Hale pointed to two domes on a ridge to the right. "Those were the first, from the late nineteen sixties. They were built by the University of Hawaii. The others —" he gestured ahead, at the Kecks, and then to the left, where we were turning "— came later. When other countries realized what we had."

We were veering to the west, down what I had heard Avey call Submillimetre Valley because of the electromagnetic wavelengths used by both the telescopes here, plus a projected one they were all excited about called the Submillimetre Array. In the distance I could see the massive Mauna Loa, and, in the glittering ocean, other islands: Maui, Moloka'i, another one whose name I didn't remember.

We passed the Caltech Observatory, and then there it was, at the end of the road: the James Clerk Maxwell Telescope. Avey's telescope. It was a cylinder more than a dome like the others. The large sliding panel at the top wasn't projecting backward, as I'd seen in photographs, so that meant the roof was closed and the telescope wasn't observing, which it could do in the daytime, unlike its optical cousins.

I was surprised to see no other vehicles in the parking lot. I hadn't seen any in the lots of the other sites I had glimpsed, either. Of course, it was Sunday, but still I had expected more activity. It was a different kind of astronomy, I thought, all these amazing machines working here without noticeable human supervision.

We got out of the Jeep. The wind hit us so hard I stumbled from its force. I'd heard it could get up to 200 miles an hour. I snatched my hat before it could spin away and felt my hair pulling straight out behind me. My heartbeat had accelerated to what seemed like twice normal.

The cold was intense. I shoved my hands into my jacket pockets but the warmth there seemed already to have been sucked away. When I exhaled, the moisture in my breath disappeared almost instantly in the dry air and the wind.

Hale lifted a tool kit out of the back seat, and I followed him to the small door at the bottom of the building. He unlocked it, and I stumbled gratefully inside, into a small entrance hall, but if I expected the sudden reassurance of warmth I was disappointed, because although we were out of the wind the temperature was still freezing.

"It's not heated," Hale said, seeing my expression. "What did you expect?"

"Heat, I guess."

He nodded upwards. "There's a small control room up there, and that's heated. But the big chamber, no."

We took a few steps up to a circular corridor with some small rooms along it on the outer edges.

"We're on the ground floor now," Hale said. "But everything above us rotates 360 degrees. We have to find where the steps are to go up."

It seemed odd to me that he wouldn't know where the steps were, but then I realized that since the stairs were attached to the rotating level of course they would move around.

We found them only a few yards from where we stood. They were metal, raised several inches from the floor we stood on. I stepped onto them warily, as I might onto a merry-go-round that had only temporarily slowed to let me board.

"The next level is the carousel level," Hale said behind me.

"Carousel! So it *is* just a big merry-go-round." I laughed. The effort left me breathless. "It's not going to move while we're here, is it?"

"Probably not."

We emerged in a cavernous room. I could see the telescope here properly for the first time. It was amazing, a huge, delicately balanced reflecting dish made up of hundreds of aluminum plates whose undersides I must be looking at. The dish was about fifteen metres in diameter and crisscrossed and filigreed with support rods, giving it a meshed, honeycombed look. It seemed to sit in an enormous egg-cup-like metal holder, with a network of scaffolding and thick tubes that were probably adjustable pistons. The bottom of the cup, I assumed, was a pivot that could move the dish up and down. Catwalks clung to the walls at several levels, connected by metal stairs. To my right I could see the small control room Hale had referred to.

"Wow," I said.

The whole telescope structure sat on a round base, a paler colour than the platform on which we were standing. It was level with ours, but Hale pointed to a circular gap, less than an inch, between the two floors.

"The telescope can rotate separately from the floor we're standing on," he said. "But our floor rotates, too, to line the telescope up with the doors it needs to look through."

"Circles within circles. No wonder my head is spinning."

"Astronomers like circles."

"Well, there aren't a lot of square stars and planets." I pointed to a metal box, narrowing at the base, that seemed to be attached near the bottom of the telescope. It was large enough for someone to stand upright inside it. "What's that?"

"The receiver cabin."

"Is that the instrument Dr. Orlovski had installed? The one Avey uses? That gives him the more precise readings?"

"How would I know?" Hale said irritably. "I'm just the janitor."

He began screwing together parts of a tool. I saw it was essentially a long rod with both a mirror and a magnet at the end.

"Do you know where the screwdriver fell?"

"He told me, more or less. Wait here."

I would rather have gone with him, but I stayed obediently where I was and watched him climb to the first catwalk, then to the second. Clang, clang, clang: his steps echoed in the huge vaulted room. He disappeared around the side of the telescope.

I waited, taking deep breaths to make up for the depleted oxygen. It was apparently less than forty per cent of its value at sea level. Did that mean I should be trying to breathe in over twice as much as usual? Was my body already making more red blood cells, making what doctors called "thick blood," to compensate?

The dome creaked and moaned from the wind. I squinted up at the roof, at the huge, white Gore-Tex wind-and-dust screen covering the viewing slit. It stayed there even when the roof was open and the telescope was observing, an arrangement that was easier to understand when I reminded myself the screen was transparent to radiation at submillimetre wavelengths. I kept forgetting this wasn't the usual kind of telescope that looked up at the sky with more or less the same kind of eyes I had.

I began jogging in place to keep warm. I wondered if, when the roof was closed, as it was now, the building could be heated. Probably when the roof was open it had to be kept cold inside to equalize with the outside, or the temperature differences between the metal and air could cause a turbulence and blur the reception. But maybe even with the roof closed it wasn't a good idea to expose the dish to temperature fluctuations. The plates were so delicately balanced that I imagined even the slightest expansions and contractions would be problematic.

I blew into my hands. My ears were getting icy, and I rubbed them, pulled my hair over them, wishing I had brought something that could improvise as earmuffs or scarf.

"Hale?" I called.

No answer. There was no sound in the room. The clanging of his footsteps had stopped. How long had it been? Fifteen minutes? Twenty? Half an hour? I felt the first pricklings of anxiety.

Carefully I approached the huge cutout circle on which the telescope stood and started up the metal stairs to the narrow catwalk level. I pulled down my sleeve to cover my fingers before I took hold of the railing. I didn't know if my bare hand would have frozen to it or not, but I relied on my Alberta instincts. I walked all the way around.

"Hale? Hale?" My voice echoed in the cavelike room. Hale, Hale. His name in Hawaiian meant "house," I thought irrelevantly. I had the urge to laugh wildly. Impaired judgement, I reminded myself: be careful. I held more tightly to the railings, thankful for the places where a meshed screen under them added to the level of safety.

I went up to the next level. My anxiety had turned to something deeper now. I kept swallowing, trying to gulp down the nut of fear in my throat.

There was no sign of Hale. I was starting to feel dizzy, and I stopped, closed my eyes, counted out ten deep breaths. My heartbeat felt dangerously fast, and I wondered if this was normal for the altitude or if I could just possibly be on the edge of a heart attack. I leaned over, propped my hands on my knees, the posture of runners after a long race. It felt so good I had to force myself to straighten up.

I turned back down the catwalk, stumbling, almost falling, then clattered down the stairs to the carousel level. My legs were weak, threatening to collapse under me.

I found the small control room Hale had mentioned, but the door was locked. The walls were mostly of glass, and I peered in at the tightly packed, cramped space, at the jumble of computers and racks of electronics and wires, at the chair in front of one of the computers that suggested a human being sitting there. The space was heated, Hale had said. I began banging on the door, rattling the knob, knowing it was pointless but unable to stop.

"Hale!" I was screaming now.

He wasn't here.

He was hiding.

He had fallen.

He had gone outside.

He was leaving without me.

I could feel the hysteria in me, hear the small moaning sobs of panic in my throat.

I had to find him. I had to stop him before he left, before he left me behind.

The stairs to the ground floor: where were the stairs? Hale said sometimes they moved. Or was that only from the level below? Had this level been moving? It could have been. Would I have noticed?

I made the circuit twice before I found the stairs. My breathing was so laboured, the inhalations crowded together into a thick wheezing, that I had to stop, clutching the railing, before I could start down. I let myself sink onto the bottom step to rest, massaging a cramp starting to knot itself into my calf. But now I was back to the circular corridor: I remembered it — it felt like a victory, a triumph of memory over disorientation.

And there was the door where we'd come in. Nothing had moved. But I had to hurry, hurry: was that hum the sound of the Jeep motor?

I staggered down the last steps to the door, flung it open, gasped with relief. The Jeep was still there. Hale hadn't left yet — if I ran to the vehicle right now I could still catch him.

Perhaps there was a logical part of my brain that said, stop, think, what if the door locks behind you, at least prop it open, but the terrified part thought only of getting to the Jeep. I could almost see it moving, pulling away.

I ran to it, frantically, screaming, "Wait! Wait!"

When I reached it, Hale, of course, was not inside. And the doors were locked. I walked around and around the vehicle, peering in, as I had done at the control room, seeing the extra sweater and shirt and pair of gloves in the back seat, trying all the doors, over and over.

I don't know how long I did this. It was only fatigue that made me stop, made me stumble back to the entrance to the building. The wind was vicious, not gusting but steady and shrill, bringing the temperature, I knew, with the wind chill factor, far below zero. I had to keep swallowing to stop from throwing up: there was a raw, sour taste in my throat.

The door to the building wouldn't open.

I jerked frantically at the handle, screaming. I pounded on the door, so hard I knew I was bruising my hand.

"Hale! Hale!"

Had the door locked automatically behind me? Or had Hale done it?

I sank down, whimpering. Somewhere my sunglasses had fallen off, and the intense light seemed to be burning right through my head. I looked around at the other telescopes visible from here. But their parking lots had been empty. Going there would be pointless. I was alone here, on this frigid moonscape.

The Keck. Someone would be there, surely, surely. The mighty Keck. Would they leave it completely unattended?

But it wasn't close; it must be over a mile away — down, then up, a switchback road. Still, now that my mind had grasped the possibility of rescue, it seemed my only chance. I began walking down the slope, following the road. But I was actually walking away from the Keck. If I cut across to it at an angle I would get there more quickly. It was uphill, but it seemed a better choice. I left the road and stepped onto the rough lava.

It wasn't the smooth, ropey *pahoehoe* one could easily walk on. It was all hard chunks and cinders, sharp enough to cut. My runners twisted and slewed, and I knew it wouldn't be long before I fell, and then it would be like hitting broken glass. *If you fall you'll know why it's called a'a:* I whimpered, remembering saying that to Hale, a joke. There were patches of snow, too, hiding the surface. It was hard enough to keep my footing here, but to reach the Keck I had a steep climb, steeper than it had first appeared. The wind seemed to be trying to rip away the whole mountaintop from under my feet, the telescopes the only things nailing it down in the far corners. I squinted at the Keck domes above me, castles on a hill, so close, so impossibly far.

"Help!" I shouted up at them, the wind disintegrating the words so quickly even my own ears didn't hear them. My breath was sticking in my throat, cold metal on warm flesh.

I would have to go back to the road.

But the road wasn't where I thought it was. I turned and turned, looking. Nothing was familiar. Everything was so brilliantly white I thought I must be going blind, but, no, blindness was darkness, wasn't it? I began to laugh, spittle flying from my mouth. I was going blind, and it was white: like death, not the blackness at the end after all but the white light at the end of the tunnel, the white, safe light at the entrance to the lava tube.

My fingers had gone numb. I breathed on them, held them over my mouth. I had to make myself move, try to find the road. My foot skidded off a rock, and I went down on one knee, a twisting jolt of pain. The hand I had instinctively flung out to stop myself from falling landed on a piece of cinder; the grit bit into my palm. When I looked at it I could see the grains embedded in the flesh, tiny specks of blood forming around some of them. I picked up one of the larger grains, examined it, as though I had found something amazing. My whole palm seemed to look amazing, speckled with dirt and blood.

I must have stood there for several minutes, immobile, my brain slowing down the way the rest of my body was slowing down. My heart didn't seem to be racing any more. Perhaps I was in one of the stages of freezing to death, I thought. It didn't seem terrifying, just rather sad.

And suddenly someone had hold of my arm, was pulling at me, shouting.

"What's the matter with you? What are you doing? Come away from here!"

I stared at him. He was huge, blocking the sun. My feet braced themselves, resisted his tugging. He was dangerous, my mind was saying, he was not to be trusted, he would hurt me, I couldn't remember how or why but it seemed important I resist him.

"Kate!" He began to shake me. "Try to concentrate! We have to get back to the Jeep!"

The Jeep. Yes, I had wanted to get into the Jeep. It would be warm. And I could see it now, behind this man, not too far, the motor running, a thin tail of exhaust being whipped by the wind.

I let the man drag me toward it, both of us stumbling over the lava, until, at last, my feet felt the smooth reassurance of asphalt under them. The man opened the passenger door, pushed me inside.

The heat overwhelmed me. It seemed to come from every part of the vehicle, flooding over me, painful almost. I closed my eyes, turned my face toward the front vents with the heaviest flow, held my trembling hands toward them.

The man behind the steering wheel kept saying my name. "Kate. Kate. Are you all right?"

I looked at him. It was Hale. My mind snapped to clarity. I remembered exactly what had happened.

"Yes," I said. "I'm all right." My lips felt numb, the words coming out slurred.

"What made you do that? Leave the building like that?"

"I waited for you. You disappeared. I went searching for you."

"I was looking for the screwdriver. When I found it I came back and you were gone."

"I waited and waited. Over half an hour. I called your name. You didn't answer. I searched the building for you. I thought you'd gone out to the car."

"It wasn't half an hour. And I never left the building. You have altitude sickness. It distorts things."

The warmth was slowly penetrating, my body everywhere tingling. My knee was throbbing from the fall, my palm prickling as though it had been poked with pins. I made a gentle fist around the pain, held it in.

Could he be right? Could everything have had an innocent explanation? Could I have been disoriented right from the beginning?

All I knew was that I needed to get away from here. I would say whatever I needed to. It was only six or seven miles down to the dormitories, the Onizuka Center, other people. It could be dangerous for me to argue with Hale here. Whether that reasoning came from paranoia and altitude sickness or not, it was also survival reasoning.

"Let's just go," I said, trying to make my voice neutral. "I think I've had enough of Mauna Kea for one day."

Hale put the car in gear, and we headed off. I caught a last glimpse of the Keck domes to my left, and then we were leaving the summit. The Coke cans that had rolled under my seat on the way up came tumbling back around my feet. I was glad to see them. It meant we were going down, down. Hale drove slowly, carefully, perhaps unnecessarily so. I could sense him glancing over at me, but I didn't return his gaze.

"I'm sorry," he said. "This hasn't been a very good experience for you."

"No," I said, "not exactly."

I had never felt so relieved in my life as I did when we rounded the last curve and saw the Visitors' Center below us.

When Hale parked the car in the lot and we got out, I turned to him and said, "I'm going to stay here, Hale. I'll call Karen to come and pick me up. I don't want to go the rest of the way with you."

I could see the alarm on his face. I didn't care what he felt, what he thought I might tell Karen or Avey or the woman in the Visitors' Center.

"What do you mean? You have to come back with me."

"I don't."

"You have to. Please, Kate."

"No, I don't!" My voice was loud. "I just — I just don't want to go any further with you. I won't say anything to Avey, if that's what you're worried about. It's just — all this — the mountain. I almost froze to death!"

Somehow I was able to stop myself from accusing him; somehow I was able to tell myself it mightn't be his fault. But my confused anger at him was still there, and it pounced clumsily on the next closest reason: "This belonging and not belonging. You use that as an excuse. To feel superior. To be selfish and disagreeable. Anything you don't like about your life you blame on that. Your ancestors drove off the people who came before. So, so, it's all ridiculous. Everything comes from somewhere else. You came from somewhere else, too — like the canoe plants. Maybe you're the bamboo, you've squeezed out what came earlier. I'm tired of hearing about being first, about being special because you're first, first, first!"

"Kate."

I was crying by then. I started to walk to the Visitors' Center. I thought Hale would follow me, but he didn't. And I didn't turn around. I remember thinking I should, that I had been ranting and cruel and unfair, but I was afraid to, afraid of what could happen when you turn around and look back, afraid of being paralyzed by apology and regret.

PART II

Vancouver

Seven

*Give me matter
and I will construct a world out of it.*

— IMMANUEL KANT

A V E Y

When I come back from the Faculty Club I see Joan is out and has not just left the door to the outer office unlocked, she's left it wide open. I've told her a thousand times not to do that even if she's only going across the hall. Just last week one of the Fine Arts offices had computers snatched while the secretary was fixing a paper jam in the copy room.

I slam the door shut behind me and lock it. If she doesn't have her key with her she can hunt down a janitor.

I see my mail is still in my pigeonhole by the door so I pick it up and head for my own office which adjoins the main one. At least Joan hasn't left that unlocked. She values her life too much. I sit down behind my desk, a nice one, oak, with rounded corners and capacious drawers, and I glance, as I always do, out the window at the view of the North Shore mountains which I know is the envy of the faculty on the south side of the building. More pleasing to me, it's the envy of the Physics Department, which predicted darkly I would regret getting Astronomy hived off into a separate department and separate building.

I drop most of the papers — a faculty newsletter, a notice of a lecture in Geology, some advertising — more or less directly into the recycling bin, but the last few items are student assignments. I write "LATE" across them in red felt pen before sliding them into my class file.

The last piece of paper is a poem, photocopied from a book. It's by Walt Whitman. I've read it before. It's the one about astronomers.

When I heard the learn'd astronomer,
When the proofs, the figures, were ranged in columns
     before me,
When I was shown the charts and diagrams, to add, divide,
     and measure them,
When I was sitting heard the astronomer where he lectured
     with much applause in the lecture-room,
How soon unaccountable I became tired and sick,
Till rising and gliding out I wander'd off by myself,
In the mystical moist night-air, and from time to time,
Look'd up in perfect silence at the stars.

Shit. Who left this? One of the students with the late assignments? Surely nobody would have been so obvious.

Maybe it was one of my colleagues. I wouldn't put it past any of them. I'm aware I'm not popular, that as chair I am considered too rigorous ("despotic" was apparently the word one of the sessionals used).

So this might be just another prank like what they did after the verification committee concluded, finally, that my planet wasn't a planet after all. It was a brown dwarf. I found a ceramic leprechaun, painted brown, on my desk. Ha, ha. I knew I should have chuckled and been a good sport about it, that there were even people who might have taken it as some sort of affectionate kidding, but all I could see was that it was people laughing at me. I was even too pissed off at Rob to answer his email from that lame college in Manitoba: "Hey! You didn't change into a giant after all! You just got brown." If it had all happened ten years later I'm sure I would have had to suffer through all the demotion jokes about being plutoed.

I shouldn't have cared — hell, I'd taken my pick of tenure-track job offers by then, and I'd played the whole thing right all along, no extravagant claims, just submitting my data and waiting. But of course I was disappointed at the final verdict. A brown dwarf, well, sure, it was a significant discovery, and mine was only the second ever definitively identified, but it wasn't the first, was it? Finding the second planet would almost have been as good as finding the first, but who cared about another brown dwarf? Even their name has made astronomers grimace. Shiv Kumar, who published the first papers on them in the 1960s, called them "black dwarfs," but because that term was already used to describe white dwarfs (don't ask), it got changed to "brown dwarfs." That name was "stupid," Kumar said, and other astronomers agreed, calling it "lousy," "idiotic," "ridiculous," saying "crimson dwarfs" or "infrared dwarfs" would be more accurate. They blame a grad student for choosing the name. When in doubt, always blame a grad student.

Well, I didn't care what they called them. All that mattered to me was that what I'd found wasn't a planet.

At least that's the verdict I had to accept.

But could they be considered planets? Yes, no, maybe. Essentially they're failed stars without enough mass to ignite nuclear reactions, but ever since the 1960s the argument about whether they could be considered planets has been about as vicious as the one about their name. At first, mass was used to make the distinction: if the object was comparable in mass to Jupiter it was a planet; if it was ten or more Jupiters it was a brown dwarf. But between one and ten Jupiters was a grey area. Looking at composition could be another way of making the distinction, since a planet has more heavy elements than a sun, but this test was almost impossible to apply. Formation theories at the time made the distinction based on the likelihood that brown dwarfs, even those that orbit stars, form the way stars do. Oh, the arguments, like the dwarfs themselves, were hot and heavy.

Ironically, when I was hunting frantically for that second planet twelve years ago I would have argued against the inclusion of brown dwarfs, but that was before my own discovery was downgraded to one. People probably expected me to weigh in then on the debate, but I was smart enough to feign neutrality. "I don't have an opinion," I would lie demurely. "I have a vested interest."

Noble of me, people thought, classy. They didn't know that I'd have argued to have a lump of shit called a planet if I'd thought it would make any difference.

"If our own solar system had a brown dwarf, we would've been calling it a planet now for centuries," I fumed at Kate. "We were quite ecumenical, after all, in welcoming the gas giants into the family, and they were completely unlike our solid Earth and the other inner planets. But a brown dwarf — ooooh, it's weird, it's scary, it's just too different from us."

"We don't like to change our definitions of things," Kate said. "Can a slave be a person? Can a woman be a person? Can an ape be a person?"

"Can a brown dwarf be a planet? Apparently not."

"Or not yet."

"Well, that's where I'm living. In the not yet."

So now my name will always have that asterisk beside it in the history books, that faint stigma of having almost found another planet, of having just missed. Just missed: and that's about the literal size of it, too. It turns out I'd found a T6.5 dwarf, still one of the coolest and smallest ever identified: as close to being a real planet as it could get. Close but no Nobel. Kate reminded me that sometimes the most important discoveries come from finding something other than what you've been looking for, that even Columbus was a failure at finding India, but somehow I didn't think brown dwarfs were ever going to be as popular as North America.

Last year one of the undergrads showed me a picture from the local paper of what purported to be a photographic image of an exoplanet, and I snorted and said, "Practically every day somebody's claiming to have taken a picture of one and then, oops, it turns out to be a mistake." I tapped the page. "I'll bet this is, if anything, only a brown dwarf."

Only. I winced to hear myself use the word.

Actually, brown dwarfs have become sexier lately. The latest research shows that there's likely an unbroken continuum between heavyweight planets and lightweight brown dwarfs and that they can form inside circumstellar disks the way planets do, not from collapsing clouds the way stars do. Plus they have all these meteorological effects: clouds, dust, magnetism, temperature ranges. Nobody's calling them *planets*, of course. Maybe what's exciting most astronomers about them, though, is their damned profusion: there might be a tenth as many as stars. That's thirty million in our galaxy alone. They probably make up most of the dark matter in the universe.

If I hadn't been so disappointed not to have found a planet, I could have made myself a brown dwarf specialist. I could have been one of the experts the papers call now when there's some new discovery about them. But I let it go. The average graduate student in my department probably knows more about them than I do. Another lost opportunity. Another miscalculation.

And so who did get the credit then for the second exoplanet? Not the little pissant from Edmonton, obviously. It was the planet-hunting darlings from California, the ones everyone had expected would find the first one: Marcy and Butler. A few weeks after my own discovery they announced not just one but two new planets, around 70 Virginis and Ursae Majoris. By the time the year was out they'd identified six new planets. I've lost track of how many they're credited with now. Over a hundred, I expect. They're the undisputed masters in the field. Still, they weren't the first, were they? It must have been especially galling because if they'd only analysed earlier their data sitting for years on their computer tapes their discovery *would* have been credited as the first. At least until the recent re-evaluation of the Canadian study made the question of who was really first even more murky.

Ah, the first, the first: that unfortunate legacy of primogeniture. There's one winner and there's the runner-up. There's a T-shirt saying, "Coming second means you're the first loser." There's the race-car driver's remark about how the only ones who remember you if you come second are your wife and your dog. There's the joke about how nobody cares what Buzz Aldrin said when he stepped onto the moon.

Joan's come back into the outer office. It took her long enough. Of course she might have had to hunt down someone with a key.

When I go out to her desk she gives me her "measured look," apportioning just the right amount of grievance, but she doesn't say anything about the locked door. She generally has the dourest look of any woman I've ever known. The two lines that deeply bracket her mouth must have been achieved when her last smile so shocked her face it left permanent scars.

I find it hard to make eye contact with her now that she's had the laser surgery, a ridiculous vanity at her age, which is somewhere in the fifties. I miss her glasses with the red frames. They put her at a more comfortable distance. Now when she looks at me her eyes seem bigger, and she seems always to be staring, reminding me of a cat we had who went blind and antagonized other cats by seeming to stare at them. Apparently the laser procedure for people her age fixes one eye permanently to be long-sighted and the other to be short-sighted. I keep thinking I should find out which is which so I can approach her at the proper angle, as you would a walleyed horse.

I hold up the piece of paper with the Whitman poem on it and ask, trying to sound casual, "Did you see who left this?"

"What is it?"

"A poem."

The stare she's giving me now is insultingly incredulous. "Someone wrote you a poem?"

"Sort of. It was at the bottom of my pile of mail."

"There were a couple of students leaving assignments, and then the regular inter-campus mail, but I didn't see anything else." I can see her trying to read the poem, but I fold the page in half and run my fingers across the crease.

"I expect it was a student," I say, trying to sound dismissive, as though students gave me poems every day. I turn back to my office.

And I suppose that's as close as I'll come to finding out who it was. Shit. It *must* have been a student. I'll be looking at them all tomorrow, all those closed-up faces, wondering throughout the whole lecture which one did this.

But what if it wasn't a student? Or a colleague?

What if it was Hale?

I sink down onto my chair, my legs suddenly so weak they can't hold me. The paper is burning my fingers. I throw it across the desk, where it begins to creep open at the crease, large white eyelids with their iris of words watching me.

The inter-campus mail had come in a lump and was at the top; then there were the three student assignments; then the poem at the bottom. It wasn't in an envelope, so that meant it had been hand-delivered.

Could Hale actually have been here, in person?

My hands are shaking. I clench them into each other. The thought of Hale coming back into my life fills me with a dread that has pure blackness at its core. We were done with each other when I left Hilo. What right does he have to come back now?

I open my top drawer and look again at the postcard I'm sure is from him. The observatories on top of Mauna Kea, the one-word message: "Remember." It's been a week since it came. I was a fool to think, to hope, that was the end of it.

But is Hale bright enough to even understand a poem? If he wanted to send me something else to upset me, would he choose a poem? Maybe it *is* just from a student.

I snatch up the page, slide it into my pocket, tell Joan I'll be out for half an hour, and, as though I have to be furtive, I avoid the elevator and bolt down the side stairs.

It's colder than it should be for March and blustery and drizzling, the kind of weather my mother had an old English word for: "cluttery." For that moment when the sun might suddenly break through in a power of heat, she had another old phrase I seem doomed to remember: "hot spong." I used that one only once in my life, on a school playground, and I'll never forget the derisive whoops. How was I to know it was an archaism?

I've stupidly forgotten my jacket so I wrench my shirt collar up and make a hunched dash down University Boulevard. The wind slaps my tie across my face. I pass the Biological Sciences Building, glancing as I always do down Main Mall to the old Geophysics and Astronomy Building with the two observatories on the roof. My first office was right under one of them, and every time a big truck would go by and rattle the windows I'd look up and think, oh hell, is this the earthquake that's going to bring it down onto my head? I am damned glad to be out of there. Earth and Ocean Sciences has the building now, and they're welcome to it.

Half a block more and I'm on East Mall, brushing the rain off me under the big overhang of the UBC Bookstore. Inside, the place is virtually empty except for what looks like a Japanese tour group being shown up and down the aisles of sweatshirts.

I find the sections for English, feeling my old annoyance at how many there are, when it should be the Sciences that get the lion's share. It's not that I'm opposed to English courses; it's the way they've managed to become compulsory for every bloody program. I'd like to be able to make every first year student take Astronomy. In the long run they'd be better off understanding how the sun works than how a sonnet works. Some of my colleagues reserve their sneers for the Social Sciences, mostly because they dare to use the word "science" (and, face it, it's ludicrous that a sociology course can have the same number of credits as an astronomy course), but it's English that pisses me off the most, the way it force-feeds its courses down all our curricular throats, a kind of gavage that fattens students up without giving them real nutrition. But any criticism of Literature and, hey, you're a redneck, you're a reactionary, you have no soul.

The bookstore shelves are pretty empty this time of year, but I find a scattering of first-year English texts, most of them used. I leaf through the index of a couple, and then there it is, in *Approaches to Literature*: Whitman's "When I Heard the Learn'd Astronomer." I unfold the page I've brought and compare the two.

The one I have is definitely a photocopy of this text. Even the page number is the same. I hear myself giving a snort of relief. So it *was* a student. It would be too much of a coincidence for Hale to have found this particular anthology. I'm grinning so much when I leave the store that the clerk takes it personally and smiles back.

It takes the rain to dampen my sense of deliverance and remind me that now I still have to deal with the fact one of my students was obviously trying to insult me. Of course, the textbook made it easy. I'll bet that if I had something in one of my texts that ridiculed English instructors there'd be such howls from Liberal Arts I'd be fighting a formal grievance.

At the door to my building Louisa is shaking off her umbrella and collapsing it awkwardly with one hand, and I catch the door for her so that she doesn't have to set down her briefcase. The umbrella is small and pink with some kind of girly fringe, and the briefcase is big and black and mannish. I suppose those two accoutrements could tell people something about the contradictions in her nature. She's wearing her ridiculously Arctic coat whose collar puts a furry frill around her neck and makes her head look as though she were serving it up on a platter.

"Thanks," she says, giving her hair a little doggy shake as if it might have filled up with water, too.

Of all the people I met in Hilo the last one I would have expected to see again, let alone wind up working with, was Louisa. But here we are, in the same department. I was already chair when she applied for a position, and she thought I was responsible for her getting hired, a misconception I admit I have done nothing to correct. The truth is that of the selection committee members I was by far the least supportive of her, remembering her religious proclivities and also that embarrassing fumble we had in the staff lounge at the JAC. But we couldn't ignore her credentials, which placed her far ahead of the other new PhDs on the short list. Plus the dean was giving us pressure to hire a woman.

My misgivings about Louisa were quickly allayed, however, when I discovered that my two causes for unease about her seemed to have been more or less eliminated. She'd had a crisis of faith, it seemed, when her sister was killed in a car accident, and if she still believed in her Great Designer it was at least without missionary enthusiasm: he was not someone she was recommending to everyone. In fact, whenever "God" was mentioned in any cosmological way she would flush and look away, as though an old boyfriend had been spoken of. Well, maybe he had. In any case, there was (and herein the allaying of my other anxiety) another boyfriend in the picture now. She had shown up at several faculty functions with a stubby middle-aged man from the private sector whom she introduced as "her partner." I was very pleased to meet him.

So I get along rather well with Louisa, which is more than I can say of the other department faculty, who seem constantly to be wanting to exchange their teaching responsibilities for research projects or whining about how they need more TA support or running off to unauthorized conferences. Nobody here is lazy, but maybe it's harder to keep a bunch of workaholics in line than a bunch of layabouts. Yesterday one of the postdocs asked me if I could find an extra five thousand in the budget for computer software he needed by tomorrow. Tomorrow!

"How's the 303 turned out this term?" I ask. Louisa is particularly grateful to me this year because I let her teach the 303 when it was really my turn. I didn't tell her that I actually preferred the 102.

"Great." Louisa pushes the elevator button. I notice the grey in her dark hair, like hundreds of little cracks. "Only a dozen students. Every one of them got all the galaxy classifications in the last assignment, and one brilliant fellow did the arm and luminosity classing, too. His explanations were so good I'm tempted to steal them."

I smile. "Yeah, we aren't doing enough to discourage these geniuses. Who needs the competition?" I was joking, of course, but maybe in some way that I didn't want to overanalyze I was also talking about why I preferred to teach the first-years.

"How's your 102 been?"

We get into the elevator. "Okay," I say. "Not stellar."

We laugh. For a moment I consider showing her the poem, but then the elevator stops at the third floor where some gabbling and overperfumed secretaries get on, and the impulse passes. By the time we reach our floor I'm shuddering at the very idea. If I've learned anything, it's to hold my failures and vulnerabilities very close to my chest.

Joan's at her desk clicking away so fast on her mouse that I'm half expecting to see a computer game at the end of it, but by the time I reach her the screen shows some word processing document, maybe the curriculum revisions I've been nagging her for weeks to finish. She always has some excuse, something she doesn't understand. I swear the woman would need to read the manual fifty times just to learn how to fart, and then she'd probably do it backwards. She reminds me of Mrs. Hu-Wiggins, from those Carol Burnett skits I saw as a kid. Though I doubt if Mrs. Hu-Wiggins ever prepared a contract and under the witness signature line typed "witless." That was just last week. Thank God I caught it. It did give me some jokes about having a secretary in the Witless Protection Program. If ever there was an argument against union seniority clauses it's sitting right in front of me.

I read a novel once where an acerbic character calls old people "the results." An apt corollary for seniority clauses, I'd thought. Of course you'd have to say that about tenure, then, too. The results. Aren't we just.

"Get me a list of any English courses my 102s are taking this term," I tell her.

She stares up at me with her larger-than-life eyes. "What for?"

"Just get them, please."

In my office I dig out the late assignments that were in this morning's mail. David Velikovsky. Chrystal Sherk. Gregory Patch. Quite the names. I try to remember the faces behind them, imagine each of them smirking, sliding the poem into my mailbox. Damn it. This is going to gnaw at me. Thank goodness the term is almost over.

The assignment is one of my favourites, having the students imagine finding an Earth-like planet and doing spectral analyses and then seeing if they can tell whether the system is made of matter or anti-matter. But only the improbably named Chrystal Sherk gets it all right. Velikovsky and Patch make the same initial stupid calculation error for the stellar spectrum, and there's no reason for them both to have done that unless one copied from the other, so I give them both an F, though I know they're going to bitch at me about it because I could have given them part marks for having the process right.

It's about time for Peterson's class to end, and I know if he comes back and finds me here he'll want to come in and chat. He's a nice enough kid and the only PhD student I've got this year, but once I made the mistake of telling him he reminded me of myself at that age, and good lord he took that as a compliment. So he likes to come by and waste my time. Once he just wanted to show me all the mnemonic phrases he'd come up with for the spectral classification sequence. Lately he's been hinting that he'd like an extension for submitting the second draft of his thesis, but I'm not about to give up part of my summer so I can work through his exasperating dissertation. My mother would call it "longsome."

I am grateful to Peterson for one thing, though, and that is for alerting me to the fact that what I had considered a perfected look of disguised seething impatience was not perfected after all. "Are you feeling all right?" he'd asked, solicitously, interrupting himself in the middle of an explanation in sub-atomic detail of something he'd found on the NASA website. What was giving me away? If I'd Botoxed them I couldn't have been more certain there were no betraying twitches or tics; my intermittent eye contact was simulating interest and attention; I'd programmed my random interjections of mmms and uh-huhs to cut out when I detected the rising inflections of a question. My smile: that had to be it. When I checked it in the mirror I confirmed that it looked not only phoney but downright distempered. I knew that what betrayed an insincere smile was not the mouth but the eyes, that those little muscles around them needed to be engaged, so I practised the smile for another week before I brought it out to any faculty meetings, where it armored me nicely against the lethal monologues of the bores in Liberal Arts.

I pack up my briefcase and tell Joan I am done for the day. I want to ask her if she's found the class lists, but I don't want to sound impatient. Well, maybe it's better if I don't know. What I really wanted to find out I did, and that is that it wasn't Hale who left me the poem.

As I leave the building I think I see the oversize black coat housing Peterson come flapping around the corner, the belt as usual dragging behind him like the leash from an escaped idea, but I pretend I don't and stride away.

By the time I get home, an easy ten-minute drive through the Endowment Lands to our house in Point Grey, the rain has stopped, and when I get out of the car I notice the new things in the garden: the snowdrops under the cherry tree, the first miniature daffodils along the side of the house in their nests of ivy, the yellow spears of forsythia. Kate does the gardening and seems to enjoy it, thank God, because for me all of it would be drudgery.

I wish she'd take as much interest in the house, or at least make more of an effort to hold up her end financially. We still owe her parents for their help with the down payment on the mortgage. All she would need to do is sell another house or two each year and we'd be okay, but it's as though she deliberately slows herself down at the point at which she could make real money. I've actually heard her decline listings, telling clients she had enough at the moment and passing them on to someone else in the office. She thinks it's funny, doing things like that. The more she does it the more popular it makes her. I'd like to try that at my job.

Her car is out front so I know she's home. "Hello?"

K A T E

"Hello?"

Avey's home. He's not usually this early. I didn't hear his car, the new Lexus so quiet it could sneak up on the cat.

I don't know why I don't respond to his shout, why I don't call back, "I'm in the garden." I simply freeze here, hunched in the periwinkle, holding up the trowel with its small cargo of soil. I must have the look of someone burying a dead body instead of hyacinth bulbs.

It's not exactly that I don't want Avey to be home. We see so little of each other. He comes home only to grab a change of clothes, a quick sandwich; there is always a committee meeting, a lecture, a conference somewhere. It's just that now the house will be filled with his noise and impatience, the air agitated and stirred into restless eddies, and for the moment I am reluctant to surrender the peacefulness of this earthy garden. Sometimes I think creation should have stopped at the plant kingdom. To pay for ambulation animals have become such a noisier lot. Surely photosynthesis is better than all that shouting.

Finally I brush the dirt from my hands and head to the back door, pausing to glance at the section of the garden I have weeded and edged, where the narcissus and daffodils will come up. Already the ground is unbuttoning snowdrops, crocuses, tiny violets.

When the job offers came in for Avey, I begged him to take the one at the University of Alberta, but he said I must be crazy not to want to move somewhere with a better climate. I suspect it was the proximity to his parents as much as the harshness of the winters that made him so eager to leave.

I missed Edmonton terribly the first few years. I still miss it, miss my history there, miss the way I regularly would run into people who'd known me all my life. I miss Sandy, my parents, David's parents, my co-workers at the agency who were more casual and less competitive than the ones here. I miss my friends: Laura, whom I've known since Grade 2 when we cut each other's hair with pinking shears; Melanie, who always made me laugh with her droll stories of incrementally awful boyfriends; and Ingrid, my best friend — I still think of her that way, my best friend, though how long can I keep doing that when we are separated by hundreds of miles, when we see each other only a few times a year?

I even still miss the Edmonton winters, those clear, crisp, white days. Here it will drizzle on for weeks at a time, the clouds so dense and low and scowly it's hard to remember there must still be a sun behind them making its daily rounds. Snow is infrequent and rarely beautiful. It stays only long enough to make people whine about it.

It has puzzled me, too, how people can live here knowing the fault lines under our feet will, eventually and inevitably, bring everything to ruins. When I ask people about it, they always say the same thing: "I don't think about it." When once I raised the subject at work my boss came over and told me in a low and unpleased voice that he didn't want to hear "the e-word" used when clients were in the office. If they specifically asked about earthquake dangers I was not to lie, exactly, but to give dismissive answers such as, "Doesn't seem to worry anybody else here," or, "Hasn't been a problem lately."

If Avey were to tell me he had a job offer from U of A and did I want to move back there, I would say yes. This is still not home. In some odd way I feel as though this is the planet Avey found, and it is newer and rawer and less stable than the one I came from. Here the crust is still thin and too ready to tear, and there is a molecular uncertainty to things that makes me feel I should tiptoe around.

Still, I have tried to fit in, to be a loyal parishioner at the west coast altar, respecting the local scriptures and silencing my disbelief: I keep an earthquake kit in the garden shed; I have designated a table in each room as the one I will crouch under; I have bolted the bigger bookcases to the wall; I keep thick-soled shoes under the bed; and I tell my parents when they fret about the dangers, "I don't think about it." Much of the time now that is true. Much of the time now I look at the thick greens in my garden in winter and think, well, all right, this is better than blizzards.

When I reach the back door, I see that soon I will have to cut back again the bamboo at the east side of the patio paving stones. After years of dormancy, it has decided to grow alarmingly quickly. I wish someone had told me that bamboo is something you must be prepared to have in your garden forever. I wonder if I will live to see it flower. It does so only once every 60 to 120 years, and it happens simultaneously worldwide for the entire species. Did I read that somewhere, or is it something Hale told me?

Hale. The postcard was surely from him. *Remember.* What does it mean? I've tried not to think about it.

But ever since the card arrived a week ago I haven't been able to stop looking at the garden with his eye, thinking of what is native flora and what isn't. The pretty evergreen dwarf salal by the hedge: that is native, I know. What else? Perhaps those sword ferns under the dogwood tree? There isn't much that hasn't been imported. We seem not to care about that here, seem in fact to value plants in direct proportion to how alien they find our soils and climate. In Vancouver they also seem to be valued more if they cannot also grow in Alberta or Toronto: some sort of botanical braggadocio.

The saddest foreigner in the garden must be the espaliered apple tree planted along the south wall by the previous owner. It reminded me too much of something crucified, so I removed the restraining wires and posts, but the tree has only managed to lean out from the wall, not grow straight, no matter how much I urged its twisted arms upwards.

When I remarked on this to Avey, he said, "So, if you want an apple tree we'll cut this down and plant a normal one."

"I just want this one to be healthy. To, well, become what it was meant to be."

"'What it was meant to be.' Please. It's not a teenager. It's a bush." So the tree stays as it is, incompletely free.

I come in through the back door into the kitchen. It smells of lemons. We have recently had the kitchen remodelled, adding, among other things, a skylight and new windows, each with nine panes of glass separated by muntin bars, the narrow strips that hold the panes. They are vinyl but made to look like wood. The window over the sink has a curved top and three extra muntins radiating out from the top horizontal strip. I suppose this is all stylish, some neo-colonial look.

The stainless steel appliances and new granite countertops are glittering from the ministrations of the maid this morning. My parents had a maid, and I promised myself I would never have a house large enough to need one, but apparently I do and I do. After she leaves, the house has a frightening perfection, the glasses spaced in the cupboards in order of size, the spice rack re-alphabetized in case I'd put the cumin before the cinnamon again, the newspaper sections reassembled meticulously on the coffee table, the ends of the toilet paper folded into origami. The woman's name is Phyllida and Avey adores her. I can't blame him for finding my own housekeeping too lax. I know that as Department Head he must have a home in which he can entertain and impress, often at short notice.

For me, though, the house, old but completely remodelled, is much larger and grander than I wanted, with five bedrooms, four bathrooms, and a huge sunken living room. It reminds me in uncomfortable ways of the condo in Hilo, its embarrassing excesses. Surely, I told Avey, there's some compromise between this and the Pupuka. But he insisted that this was the kind of home we were now expected to own. He was delighted when someone told him all we needed was fountains in the front yard and we could call ourselves Bellagio North.

Avey has, as usual the moment he enters the house, put on a CD, Diana Krall, I think, and is pouring himself a glass of red wine, something that is *not* usual.

I wash my hands at the sink. "Celebrating something?"

He gives a snort, swirls the wine in the glass forcefully enough to make it lick the rim of the glass.

"I wish."

"Something happen?" I ask.

I can see him thinking it over, wondering if he should tell me, and then he reaches into his pants pocket and pulls out a piece of paper folded into quarters and hands it to me. "This was in my mailbox. A student, I assume. It's damned annoying."

I read the poem. "It's rather complimentary, isn't it? The astronomer is learn'd. There is much applause. The speaker is moved to think about the vastness of the universe."

Avey raises his eyebrows a bit, pushes up his lower lip. "You think?" He takes a gulp of wine. "It seemed like an insult to me. And the anonymity of it."

"Well, if you were a student and wanted to tell your instructor that he had made you think profound things about the stars maybe you'd be too shy, too, to put your name to a note."

"Maybe."

"You should read it out to your class tomorrow. Make a joke of it."

"Joviality is hardly my style. Besides, I've been giving them all such low grades this year they'd think I was trying to trick them somehow." He pulls loose his tie, opens the top button of his shirt, runs a finger around the inside of the collar. "Well, how was your day? Sell any houses I should know about?"

I pick up the bottle of wine on the counter, pour myself a glass.

Avey gives me a look. "Are *you* celebrating something?"

"No more than you, I'm afraid. There's just something, well, perplexing, something sad, at work that I don't know how to deal with."

I can see more than hear the sigh as Avey's lips part slightly. I know he doesn't like hearing about my problems at work, probably because they seem trivial compared to his or because he knows his advice is always harsher than what I could implement.

But perhaps now he feels he owes me because he asks, "What happened?"

I follow him into the den adjoining the kitchen. The room is several steps down from the kitchen level, giving it almost complete privacy from the street, which is well blocked by the bamboo, the laurel, and the huge rhododendron bushes that keep their plump leaves all year, making the room visible from the outside to only the most trespassing eyes. It's my favourite place in the house, perhaps because it's allowed to become less tidy than the larger, high-ceilinged room on my left we call the living room, though we do little real living there: it's for company, for guests. Avey liked its original ornateness — the chandeliers, the thick carpets, the dark-blue heavy curtains — and has argued to keep it that way. There's a kind of innocence in his home decorating tastes. We replaced most of the furniture there last year, and now it seems as though both the room and the furniture in it are too big. Avey doesn't exactly disagree. He said maybe it was furniture that was ambitious, was moving up. When I said something about how less is more, he snorted, said, "That's just sophistry. Less is less."

We take seats opposite each other in the den, Avey in his leather recliner and I on the love seat, where I have the bad habit of piling up books and magazines on the cushion beside me. On the wall behind Avey is the framed photograph, made up of several segments adjoining each other, the tops and bottoms artfully uneven, of the sectors of space that include the star system where Avey found his planet. The photographs were taken by the Hubble, and in the bottom right hand corner is the inscription from the president of the Canada Astronomical Society that says, "With Recognition and Congratulations to Xavier Fleming." It is probably Avey's most valued possession, especially since the society gave it to him even after the status of his planet was downgraded.

We sip at our wine. I can already feel it, can imagine it turning my whole body slightly pink, perhaps the colour of the walls we had repainted last year. The entryway is one shade darker rose, the stairwell one shade lighter. People have told us it's nice.

At least I resisted the designer's urgings to hire a feng shui expert to assess the house. Just hearing the term made me think of how Karen and I laughed at a feng shui book we had found in the condo in Hilo. All I remember of the book now is that it described how bad luck could enter through a badly placed front door. We spilled rum on one of the pages and it seemed hilarious. "Bad luck! Bad luck!" Karen shrieked. The next time she came to the condo's front door she brought Hale. More bad luck, I think now, with a little shudder.

"So what happened at work?" Avey asks, impatiently.

He shoots the footrest out of his recliner so abruptly his legs almost bounce. Our white Persian cat jumps up on his lap, begins his delicate maneuverings that seem necessary before he can lie down. Avey puts his hand on the cat's back and squashes him down. He stays there. If I tried that I would get bitten. The cat, I think jealously, because he so clearly prefers Avey to me, is some kind of a masochist.

"Well," I say, "it's a listing I have, and I shouldn't care about this problem, I know, but I can't get it out of my mind. It's a house in Kitsilano, with a room in the basement that's been rented out to a Bosnian couple. They were brought here by a church group under some humanitarian program when there was all the ethnic cleansing and horror going on. Well, the vendor, who lives out of town, has given them notice, they're supposed to be out of there already, the completion date is in two weeks, but they just ... well, they just seem bewildered and frightened by it all. We paid for an interpreter and went there one day, but all we could learn was that they had nowhere to go and no money."

What I can't bring myself to tell Avey, for some reason, is what I remember most about that visit. It's the way the couple clung to each other. When we all came into the room, they put their arms so tightly around each other that they had to turn their heads to see us. It reminded me of frightened children, of caged animals cringing at the approach of the experimenter.

"Well, what are they living on?" Avey asks. "They must have some sort of income."

"The church group lost interest in them after their official sponsorship expired. I phoned the church and they said it wasn't their concern any more."

"Can't they work? Can't they earn their own living?"

"I don't see how. They haven't a word of English, and they've no idea how anything operates here. Back home they were farmers, I think. And they're not young. They look sixty. Plus the man is disabled, really. He's missing fingers on each hand. Right now all the couple has to eat is what a restaurant down the street lets them have from what they're throwing out at the end of the day."

"Why don't they go to a food bank?"

"Maybe they do. Food isn't their immediate problem. Apparently the church group registered the couple for welfare, but there's a son in the picture who's turned into some kind of thug, some gang member, and he comes by and intimidates them and takes whatever money they have. I think maybe he threatened the church people, too, and that's part of the reason they don't want to be involved any more."

"Lovely."

"I tried to talk the new owners into letting them stay, but it's impossible. They want the renters out and that's it."

"Well, they're not moving in with us. In case that's what you're going to suggest." He gives a little laugh, to show he knows I wouldn't be seriously entertaining the notion.

"We have the room," I say, not because I had actually thought of this as a solution but to see the doubt flicker across his face.

"Look. Just call immigration, call a homeless shelter, call Social Services, call the police. You're a real estate agent, not a social worker."

"I did talk to a social worker. She said there'd be no room for them in any long-term way, or maybe even a short-term way, at a homeless shelter. And she said it's impossible to live on what welfare pays, and if the couple actually is on it now they'd soon be cut off because there's a two-year limit. The few rentals around are horribly expensive. I had no idea things had become so draconian."

Avey drums his fingers on the armrest. "Okay, abusing the poor isn't civilization at its best. But what has this really got to do with you personally?"

"Well, I feel like I'm throwing them into the street. I was the one who sold their home out from under them."

"Jeez, Kate." Avey snaps the footrest down, jostling the cat, who gives me, not Avey, a reproachful look and jumps down. "If you hadn't sold the house someone else would have."

"I know."

I want to tell Avey about the way the couple clung to each other, but I don't. It's not a detail that would change anything.

He gets up, drains his wine glass. "Sorry if I sound insensitive. Obviously this must be hard for you. Just … let it go, okay? This is not your problem." He glances at his watch, then redoes the top button on his shirt and adjusts the knot in his tie over it. "Anyway, gotta go. The airport. Picking up a visiting lecturer from Boston. Another learn'd astronomer."

Eight

In a field of observation, chance only fosters those
minds which have been prepared."

— Louis Pasteur

A V E Y

Peterson's at the door, poking his long, thin face in at me, saying, "Hi, got a sec?"

"Yeah, okay." I've just sat down, gathered up the things Joan left on my desk. The word "strewn" came to mind.

Peterson's so tall, way over six feet, that he barely clears the door-frame. His arms are about twice the length of mine, and if he ever gets his thesis done the present I'm going to give him is a visit to a tailor's so he doesn't always have half a foot of bony wrist and ankle sticking out of his clothes.

He's tapping a pencil on his clipboard. "Just a silly question. Can you think of any telescopes that have adverbs as well as adjectives in their names?"

I roll my eyes, don't bother to ask the point because there never is one worth knowing.

"CELT," I say, "the California Extremely Large Telescope. And the VLT, the Very Large Telescope."

"Got those," he says, ticking them off on his clipboard. "And the VLA, the Very Large Array, and the VLBA, the Very Long Baseline Array. Any others?"

"Have you got OWL?"

"OWL!" he chortles. "I forgot about OWL!"

OWL stands for the Overwhelmingly Large Telescope, which would have ten times the combined light-collecting area of every optical telescope ever built. Whether the Europeans will actually assemble the billions of Euros needed to finish it is debatable.

I have to ask. "And you're collecting these because?"

"Just something for Diane." Diane is his girlfriend, an English major. "She's doing some paper about adverbs."

I grunt. I can just imagine how astronomy will fare. She won't concede the whimsy in some of those names. Maybe I don't, either. I wish they'd found names that didn't make telescopes sound like big toys.

"Have you rechecked those differential equations for the point mass yet?" I ask. Peterson's never-ending thesis is on gravitational clustering and thermodynamics. If he ever finishes it, it will be brilliant.

He actually flushes, looks down at his feet. Sometimes I think he's emotionally about ten years old. "Not yet." But it takes him a moment before he adds, "I guess I should get to it."

"I guess so," I say. I've never known such a procrastinator.

When he's gone I get back to the papers Joan left for me. First there's the list of English courses I asked for several days ago. Apparently six of my students are in English 110. That hardly narrows it down. Plus for all I know the rest might have taken it last year. Maybe the whole gaggle of them gave me the Whitman poem. A group project. It's not helping the sour feeling I've had all year about this class, mental anorexics the lot of them.

I'm not pleased to see, then, the phone memo from Kilbride saying he has to cancel our lunch. I had been counting on him to give me the lay of the land about Schneider's retirement and whether I had a shot at the deanship. There's nothing in the message about rescheduling. Of course Joan would have been too feeble-witted to ask.

I've been thinking a lot about the deanship. But I'm not about to throw my hat into the ring if it's going to get trampled by some flashy external candidate whose balls I'll have to kiss when he's my boss. My term as department Chair comes up next year, and I have to decide what to do then. I don't know if I can stand to go back to full-time teaching, and as for the research I've about had it with the publish-or-perish miseries. One of my oft-published but underemployed TAs told me once it's really publish-*and*-perish, the way the popularly misquoted phrase is really "do *and* die." Well, if he's right I'm lucky: my last research paper was rejected by two journal peer review boards. And I'm not talking *Science* and *Nature*. Their editorial boards wouldn't even consider my stuff now. My name isn't exactly being mentioned any more with the likes of Marcy and Butler. For a heady little while it was. I try not to think about it. The projects I'm doing seem only to have archival interest at best.

As I suspected would happen, all the buzz now is about finding Earth-like planets. That's where the research money goes, that's where the adverbs go, to say nothing of the adjectives. Geoffrey Marcy estimates that about ten billion stars in our galaxy alone have rocky planets that could support life. Both the SIM PlanetQuest program and the TPF, the Terrestrial Planet Finder, with its interferometers in orbit doing nothing but sniffing for planets, have had huge cutbacks, but for every delay and cancellation there's some new project. The Allen Telescope Array in California is a whole army of telescopes, over 300 of them when it's finished, built specifically to look for extraterrestrial intelligence. That's what my Microsoft dollars are funding: Paul Allen, Microsoft's co-founder, is paying half the shot. SETI must be pissing itself with glee. And Europe, Japan: who knows what they're planning? NASA isn't the only game in town, and everyone wants to find Earth-like planets. We've found the big Jupiters out in orbits where they should be; we've found whole solar systems of gas giants; we've found planets with magnetic fields and atmospheres; we've found rocky planets the size of Neptune. But none, yet, are quite the right size, the right composition, in the right place, to be called Earth-like.

Planets like Earth, planets like Earth. I'm tired of that unrelenting emphasis, frankly. The universe is full of unimagined wonders and all we want is the familiar, to look into space and find a mirror. There's something more than a little desperate about that. Societies nearing collapse because they've outgrown their resources speed up, not slow down. That's us. The closer we get to winking ourselves out, the more frantic we seem to be to find other Earths out there, evolving into the same miserable future we are. Is that supposed to make us feel better?

Well, as I told Kate, I'm a scientist, not a philosopher. And I have the luxury of not having to care about any of it in the same eager way I used to. Especially if I can land the deanship. And for now I'm comfortable enough, I guess. My colleagues still respect me. My credentials are still pretty solid. I'm glad to be stepping back from that competitive research frenzy. Well, a little glad, that kind of conflicted glad people feel as they grow more and more jealous of the young.

The next thing on the pile of papers is a request for PD funds from Louisa to go to a conference in Toronto. I scribble my signature on the form and toss it in the out basket.

Then there's a notice for a lecture series in History, then something about Faculty Club fee changes, then a long report in an annoying font about the repairs to the observatory on the roof of the old Geophysics building. I toss it onto another pile of reports I keep meaning to get to.

There's one more thing: a pink note in Joan's big back-slanted hand-writing, a phone message. "9:10. Hayley called. Wants you to call back." Hayley. Who the hell is that? Why didn't the stupid woman get a last name?

Hayley. Hale.

Oh, shit. Surely it isn't.

The phone number on the bottom is a 604-224 number. If it *is* Hale he was calling from Vancouver.

There doesn't seem to be enough oxygen in the room. I'm taking deep breaths but I'm still feeling faint, my vision getting dark and grainy around the edges. I crumple up the note and shove it into my pocket, and then I take it out again and smooth it flat on the desk.

Finally I get up and blunder my way out of the office, mutter something to Joan about how I'll be out for a while, and head down the stairs. I have to keep my hand clenched on the railing to keep myself from sinking down onto one of the steps. My knees feel painful, each step a jolt, as though I'm on a planet with twice this gravity. When I get outside I turn around, apparently looking for something but not knowing what, and then because I know I have to look purposeful I start walking, and it seems to be toward the lot where I left the car. I'm parked on the second level, off on the east end.

I get into the car, slam shut the door, lock it. I feel instant relief, as though I've outrun something deadly. If it finds me here I can drive away.

I must be cold. I must be freezing. The shaking comes in waves, starting in my shoulders and rippling down to my feet and then starting again. Horripilation. My mother gave me that word. I start the car, turn the heater up. It won't come on until the engine is warm enough, so I sit here waiting it out, letting the shudders run through and through me.

Finally there's warm air.

I put my head down on the wheel, make myself take long, calming breaths.

Hale.

It all comes back then, that day in Hilo twelve years ago.

*

I had just hobbled down to my office.

If the antiseptic I'd put on my scraped knee hadn't made it sting, hadn't made me prop a hand on Bruno's desk while I bent down to poke at the bandage, maybe I wouldn't have seen what I did as I straightened up.

Bruno ran this stupid screensaver that did some kind of Dali-esque warping of his desktop display, making it look as though the windows were melting. I wasn't even really seeing it, wasn't thinking of anything but my knee, and then suddenly I found myself looking more closely at the distortion. There was something about it, something that made me reach over and jiggle the mouse.

Bruno never bothered to log out properly or to lock his computer when he quit working, so the real display promptly flashed back onto the screen. I could see his programs still running in windows scattered over the desktop.

And one of them had just finished calculating and displaying the curve of the planet detection.

I stood there staring at it. It was the curve, the goddamned perfect curve, passing through every dot on the screen, no stragglers. It meant the star was moving both toward and away from Earth, first the former, then the latter, a regular sinuous motion that meant a planet was tugging at it.

It was what I'd spent every minute in this office looking for. And here it was.

On Bruno's computer.

I couldn't believe it. Bruno had done a fraction of the work I had. I'd modified my program so that I knew it was better than his. How could he have found it when I hadn't?

My legs felt so weak I more or less fell into his chair. Carefully, I tapped at his keyboard, ran the program again. No mistake. There it was.

I checked the exact time on his display. This had come in days ago. I'd gone through that data. My program had missed it. It was sitting there on my disks, and my program modifications must have screwed it up.

God *damn* it. Bruno was going to get the credit, Bruno who didn't deserve it, Bruno who didn't even really care about it.

Had he seen this? I closed my eyes, tried to remember what he'd been like when he left yesterday. It was about four in the afternoon. He'd yawned, stretched his arms over his head, said it was time to call it a day. If he'd just had his eureka moment he did a great job of disguising it.

I knew he kept some haphazard notes, a log of sorts, on a yellow steno pad and that he checked it to see where he'd left off the day before. I found the pad without even looking, at the side of his desk. The last thing he'd scribbled down said, "TAV? out, 06:14:20." I didn't know what "TAV" meant, but if the time referred to the place on his data where he'd left off, and if he was working chronologically, then he'd obviously stopped before the curve scrolled up. But I also knew that once he came in it wouldn't take him long, a matter of hours at best, to make the discovery that would change his life. That would change my life. He could walk in right that minute and see, with one glance at the screen, what he had. A cold sweat started running down my chest, my thighs.

Of course I can see now how nuts I was to do what I did next. All I could think was that there wasn't enough time for me to find the data in my own files and to fix whatever glitch there was. I needed time. I needed to buy myself time.

And so I began erasing his files. I knew he never backed anything up. He could recover the original archived data sent down on fibre optic cable from the telescope, but the working files on his own disk where he'd done his teasing and tweaking would be full of holes.

By the time I thought, *what are you doing, this is crazy, stop, he'll know what you've done,* most of the files were toast. So then another level of panic set in. What explanation could there be for most of his disk to just suddenly be wiped?

Some kind of hardware problem. A mechanical problem.

A power failure.

I was down on my hands and knees, crawling under his desk, pawing at the tangle of cords, looking for where his lead plugged into the UPS. I found it. I unplugged his computer.

The machine hum above me ceased abruptly. I stared at the plug in my hands, let it drop to the floor. My mind was bouncing around madly, trying to figure out what to do now. My heart, my traitor's heart, my backwards heart, seemed to be trying to gallop its way to the other side of my chest.

Finally I picked up the plug and nudged it lightly back into the socket, just so it would stick there but not be connected, as though it might have been jostled loose by accident.

Okay. Bruno knew practically nothing about how computers really worked. I'd have to trust that he'd believe a power interruption had screwed up his disk while it was running. It could have, couldn't it? It was theoretically possible. And by the time he retrieved and reconstructed his data I'd have had a chance to go back and fix my own program. Even if there were subtle traces that could distinguish between files corrupted by power loss and those deliberately erased, Bruno would have had to get some forensic experts onto it, and why would he? If I waited a day or two before telling anyone of the discovery, he wouldn't suspect anything.

There were a hundred tripwires in this reasoning, I can see that now, but I could never have anticipated the one I stumbled over when I crawled out from under the desk.

Hale was standing in the doorway looking at me.

I lurched to my feet, bumping my sore knee on the leg of Bruno's desk. I made some little snuffle of sound, some grunt, and then, maybe to distract us both, began to brush at my arms, as though I'd picked up dust from the floor. Maybe it was Hale's gaze I was trying to wipe from myself. He just stood there, leaning against the jamb, watching me. What should I do, what should I say? My mind was empty, empty.

Maybe if I'd said nothing at all I'd have been okay. But though my brain felt as unplugged as Bruno's computer my mouth must have been on battery backup because it began flapping and babbling about how I'd wondered why Bruno's computer wasn't on. And I could see right away — that slight smile, one eyebrow raising just a little — that Hale knew exactly what I'd done. For all I knew, he could have been standing in the doorway watching me ever since I crawled under the desk.

"I was just cleaning in here," he said softly. "The computer was on then. It was ... sleeping, but I bumped the keyboard and the screen lit up."

Everything I thought to offer as an explanation took about two steps and fell into a black puddle.

I was trapped. I couldn't undo what I'd done. Hale might not have known exactly why I'd unplugged the computer, but he wasn't a fool. He'd figure it out when the whole JAC got buzzing about Avey Fleming's new planet.

For one horrible moment I thought, if I knew I could get away with killing him, I might do it.

"Look," I said finally. "I made a mistake. Bruno will be pissed off at me. What would it take for you to tell him that when you were vacuuming you used this socket and accidentally knocked his cord out?"

I held my breath. I had no idea, none at all, how he might respond. I was putting my career, my life, into the hands of a janitor.

It took him forever to answer. He looked for a while at Bruno's blank monitor, then picked at a fingernail, then propped his elbow on the doorframe and ran his other hand slowly through his long hair.

"I could do that," he said.

I swallowed. I could hardly believe what I'd heard. "Well, I'd really appreciate it. That would be so great."

"What I'll ask in exchange ..."

Oh, of course. Had I really thought he was offering to do this as a favour? "What?" I prompted, as he lapsed into another of those irritating hiatuses.

"I would like Kate."

"Kate? What do you mean, you'd like Kate?"

"I mean that I'm very ... fond of her. If she weren't married to you I think she'd like me, too."

I couldn't stop a bray of incredulous laughter. "So you, what, you want me to divorce my *wife?*"

He shrugged. "I would just like for you to ... encourage her. That it's okay with you that we ... see each other."

"What are you saying? That you want me to make Kate have an *affair* with you? Is that it? She's not my property, I can't get her to do that even if I wanted her to."

"I know that. I'm not asking for anything that ... crass. All I would like is to spend some time with her. She feels guilty if she does because she thinks you wouldn't like it."

"Let me be sure I understand. You want me to tell Kate it's okay with me if she ... spends time with you."

He looked into the air for a while, thinking it over. "Yes. I'd like to take her up to the observatory tomorrow, for instance."

"So — you'll keep quiet about what you saw here if I tell Kate it's okay that she ... see you. That it's okay for her to go up Mauna Kea with you."

"I suppose so. Yes."

I'd like to think that I at least had misgivings, that a part of me was shouting, hang on, pal, are we playing with euphemisms when we say "seeing" and "spend time with"? But I'm ashamed to admit that all I was thinking was, shit, could it be that easy, is that all he wants? I wonder what I would have answered if he'd said, yes, he wanted me to divorce Kate. In the state I was in I might even have considered it. I was scared witless, cornered, everything I'd worked my ass off for all my life about to be lost. If that happened, Kate might have left me, anyway. All I'd ever had to offer her was my ambition and the promise of a prestigious career.

"All right," I said. I tried to make my voice sound more reluctant than I felt. Hale had to feel he was getting the better part of the deal.

He smiled. "Good."

"So when Bruno comes in you'll tell him you knocked the cord out by mistake, you'll apologize, right? And for that I'll tell Kate it's okay to ... to see you."

He thought about it for a moment. I could almost see his brain checking back through the steps of our negotiation, a boy checking his arithmetic.

"Yes." He held out his hand.

I shook it. "Okay, then," I said. "We've got a deal."

When he headed back down the hall behind his push-broom he was whistling.

I sank down onto Bruno's chair. A crazy, gobbling laughter was contracting up in my throat. Was it relief? Or just a different category of terror? I pressed my hand hard over my mouth. In the last half hour I had done both the stupidest and the gutsiest things of my life. It was too late to wish I had just stayed in bed all day and let Bruno come in and make his discovery. I had waded in deep, and I had better know how to swim.

I dived over to my computer, skimmed back through my files, found the one I wanted, called it up, and scrolled to the time I'd noted on Bruno's screen.

And there it was.

Jesus, how could I not have seen it? There was nothing wrong with my program. I must have been blind, I must have been asleep. I hadn't needed to erase Bruno's disk. Why hadn't I had the sense to check here first?

I leaned back in my chair, staring at it. The curve. It looked amazing, beautiful, perfect. And now it was where I had dreamed of seeing it, where it belonged, where it would be mine.

I knew I couldn't run around shouting about it right away. Bruno would make the connection between my discovery and his computer going down. I had to wait, act normal. Well, it would give me time to get ready, to plan my big announcement with the right mix of excitement and humility.

Just to be on the safe side, though, I typed up an email to my supervisor in Edmonton, saying I thought I had something but wanted to do more checking. I made some reference to this being Tuesday, even though it was really Wednesday, so it might look as though the message had been languishing in cyberspace somewhere for a day. Edmonton was three hours ahead of us: he'd get it when he checked his morning mail.

And, oh, I'd be his golden boy when my results were confirmed. He wouldn't misspell my name on his reference letters again. He'd be riding my coattails to a full professorship.

I thought of the Leo Szilard quotation he'd given me just before I came here. *You don't have to be much cleverer than other people, you just have to be one day earlier.* I opened my desk drawer, found the page with the quotation, crunched it up, and threw it in my wastebasket. Even there it looked too incriminating. I picked it out of the can, tore it into tiny pieces, tossed some into my wastebasket and leaned over and threw the rest into Bruno's.

As I straightened up I couldn't avoid seeing Bruno's blank computer screen. And I guess it was only then that the real wave of guilt and shame and self-loathing hit me. I was a thief. And God knows what I had signed poor Kate up for.

But it was a wave. It passed. Before another one could hit I gave myself a little existentialist lecture about how there was no damn point to the damage I'd done if I couldn't make myself appreciate what it had gotten me.

*

Over the years that wave has washed over me often enough. Sometimes it would wake me in the night and I'd lie there sleepless and slightly nauseated. Sometimes it would hit me in the middle of a department meeting and I'd have to swallow back some hysterical confession. Sometimes it was a slow and sluggish wave, welling up in the afternoon during the class I'd be teaching, and I would let it push me to a rancid little pub on Granville where I would get drunk and snarl at other drunks.

Still, I always thought that, despite all the ways in which things could have gone wrong, in which I could have been exposed, I'd gotten away with it.

Bruno, poor bastard, didn't suspect a thing. I'm sure of it. It almost killed me, having to keep sharing the office with him, knowing how I'd cheated him.

"Well done, man," he'd said, when I showed him the curve.

I listened for suspicion, anger, irony, in his voice, but I didn't hear any. I didn't even hear any envy. I told myself maybe he was even glad because now he wouldn't have to slog through his own files any more. And he's happy enough where he is now, teaching at some tweedy university in England. He sends me Christmas cards. The last one included a picture of his new partner, a dentist.

What happened between Kate and Hale I don't know. She came back from Mauna Kea upset, so I know they must have gotten into some sort of unpleasantness there, but Kate didn't want to tell me and I didn't press. I suppose I didn't want to know. I was just hoping that whatever had happened it wouldn't make Hale rethink our bargain. Bruno had been more angry with him about his disconnected computer than I had thought he would be, and there was actually talk of firing Hale. So I'd gone to bat for him, told Bruno not to be so hard on him, and it all blew over. Thank God. I shudder to think what would have happened if he'd been fired over the incident. I don't think he'd have seen a trip up to Mauna Kea with Kate, no matter what happened there, worth losing his job for.

But it all worked out. He didn't complain. We had a deal and we both honoured it.

But now he's back. After all these years. It's my worst nightmare.

What could he want? Some kind of blackmail? Kate again? Money? Maybe he's seen the way I'm living and he thinks, hey, I can get some of that, the guy is loaded. He doesn't know that every paycheque is spent before I get it.

Someone taps at my window, making me jump. It's Peterson.

"Hey," he yells, "coming to the staff meeting?"

Staff meeting. Shit. How long have I been sitting here? I glance at my watch. I can't believe it. It's almost four o'clock.

K A T E

It's almost four o'clock. I've just come back from my walk with my neighbour Jenny when the phone rings. I'm expecting a call from a notary, but it's Avey's father.

"Kate! How's my favourite daughter-in-law?"

"Fine," I say carefully. "How are you, Mr. Fleming?" He asked me once to call him "Dad," or at least "Gordon," but I couldn't do it. It had taken Avey about a year after we were married before he told me what kind of a father the man had been, and ever since I've felt only revulsion towards him. What I still feel guilty about is how much I had liked him before that. I knew him before I knew Avey, when he had been Sandy's teacher, and I can even remember thinking that it was too bad Avey hadn't inherited his father's easy charm. "Charming?" my father had said, making a face. "You think he's charming?" Of course he had met Avey's mother and also knew a bit more about the etiology of charm than I did.

"I'm good, I'm good. I sent Avey an email, and he hasn't answered. I'm flying out to a teacher's convention in Burnaby next weekend, and I thought I'd rent a car and drop by."

"Next weekend," I say, stalling. "I think Avey has some out-of-town commitments himself."

"That right? Nothing he can't cancel?"

"I don't think so."

"What about you? You got some time? To have lunch with a poor old man?"

Poor old man: it was what he'd called himself last year when Avey's mother had the heart attack, which fortunately turned out not to be as bad as they first thought, and we'd flown to Edmonton to be with her. When Avey's father saw us in the hospital lobby he collapsed in tears into my arms and said, "Ah, Kate, Kate. Maybe you're the only woman I've got now." I looked at him in horror.

Avey had gotten drunk on the plane. "Stay away from her," he said, too loudly. Everyone stared.

"I'm sorry," I say now. "I'm just too busy." I squeeze my eyes shut, willing him to go away go away go away.

He doesn't answer for a minute, and then he says, "Well, tell Avey to answer his damned email, will you?"

"All right."

I've just hung up when the phone rings again, the notary I was expecting, saying she has my contracts ready for pickup.

I take a quick drive down to her office and get them. On the way back I find myself going past the big white house on Third Avenue with the Bosnian tenants, and I slow down, then turn into the back lane and peer at the basement window. The curtains are drawn but there's a light on behind them. They must still be there, and the new owners will be moving in in less than two weeks.

I pull as close as I can to the overgrown hedge bullying its way into the alley, get out and walk to the back door, their entrance. I don't really expect them to answer my knock; the other times we came we had to enter, without their permission, through the main house.

So I'm startled when the door jerks open and a short but thickly muscled young man in a brown leather jacket and tight jeans stands there scowling at me.

"Oh," I say. "Sorry to bother you. I was wondering if the Karolyis were still here."

"Yeah. So what?"

I realize who he must be. "You're their son?"

"So what?" His voice is accented, but not as heavily as I might have expected.

"Well, I'm glad you're here. I'm the real estate agent, you see, and the house has sold and your parents need to move out, right away, and I'm just not sure if they really understand this."

He lifts his arm and anchors his hand so firmly to the doorframe it's as though he's lowered a guardrail across the entrance. Behind him, at the foot of the stairs, dimly, I can see the Karolyis, can hear them whispering and shushing each other.

"Yeah, well, not my problem."

"You don't understand. They've simply got to leave. You've got to help them. If you don't they'll be thrown into the street."

He shrugs. "There will be someplace for them. Some shelter. Something."

"It's not that easy. Finding new housing is very difficult now. Couldn't they come live with you?"

He snorts. "Are you joking? I live with three other guys in somebody's basement."

"Well, could you leave them enough money to rent someplace else?"

When I say "money" I can see his hand on the doorframe clench into a fist, and I remember how dangerous he might be. He is in a gang, the interpreter discovered; he was involved with drugs; he was arrested; his parents are terrified of him.

But what he does is laugh, a hard thrust of sound. "Money. I got none to spare, lady."

Behind him I can see his mother inching up the stairs. She makes me think of an animal penned up all day in the house, creeping now toward a door left carelessly open. I expect her at any moment to make a dash for freedom, but she stops halfway up and says something to the son in a pleading voice. He gives her a harsh and terse answer, and she says something again, a long explanation or entreaty which he interrupts by saying, this time in English and in that sort of soft voice that can be more threatening than a shouting one, "Shut up."

She does. Our eyes meet, and I smile at her, reassuringly, I would like to think, but of course what am I but an even crueller enemy, here to take away her home. She lets herself be pulled back down the stairs by her husband.

"Won't you do anything to help them?" My voice sounds like the mother's, pleading, female, pitiful. "They really will be evicted. Their belongings will be thrown into the street."

He glances down the stairs, purses his mouth a little, makes me notice the thin white scar that seems to be inserted into his upper lip like a sliver or a piece of jewellery.

"I could take some of the furniture," he says.

"It's a furnished suite," I say, realizing suddenly how I might have made things worse. "The furniture stays. I meant only their personal belongings."

"Yeah, well. Too bad. I didn't ask to come to this fucking stupid country. They were the ones wanted to come, so they can make the best of it. Me, I look after my own self now."

I can only look at him helplessly. He is part of the problem, not the solution. He takes his arm down from across the door, but it is not, of course, an invitation to enter. He steps a little to the right, blocking the entrance now with his whole body, as though I, like his mother, might be attempting to scuttle through.

"They're your parents," I say. "Can't you love them at least a little?"

He doesn't answer, his eyes simply fixed on me, so steadily that I know he must have practised it, this stare that doesn't waver. Then, still staring at me, he steps back and slams shut the door.

I trudge away to the car. I know if I looked back at the house I might see Mrs. Karolyi's face at the basement window, and I couldn't bear it. I think about calling Social Services again when I get home, but they have already told me there is nothing more they can do. If I tell them about the son it just might make things worse for the parents.

When I get home I email Sandy in Edmonton, ask her if she might have any lawyerly advice. She is ferociously busy at her new practice, and I know she won't appreciate yet another demand on her time. "I can pay you your going rate," I type, trying for levity, but then I delete the comment, though I'm not sure if it's because I think she wouldn't find it funny or because she might expect me to pay.

I've just closed the email program and turned away when suddenly I think: you should have asked her about the pictures of David.

A few weeks ago Sandy asked me to send her about two dozen from my album so that she could make copies. I know she got them, but why hasn't she sent the originals back? What if she's lost them? They flash vividly, one after the other, into my mind now, as though I must remember every small detail, in case they are lost. What if they are? Lost, lost. I have to take hold of the seat of the computer chair to steady myself.

I'll send her another email now asking about them. No, email is too slow. I'll phone —

And then, abruptly, the spell of anxiety passes. Why would I think Sandy would have lost the pictures? She's less careless than I am. I didn't tell her I wanted them back immediately. I unclasp my hand from the chair and look at it, puzzled, as though it had been only my hand that had had the panic.

I am used to having painful memories of David ambush me, but this was a new variation. Perhaps it had something to do with the Karolyis. Ambush, bushwhack, bushed: all these words we have about our fear of forest, though now it's more often the forests of our minds we have to fear. I shake my head, make myself utter a rueful laugh. The cat looks up and gives me an interrogative little meow.

"Nothing," I tell him. "Thanks for asking."

The phone rings. When I answer there is only silence on the other end.

"Hello?" I say again, thinking it is probably telemarketers who, as they do these days, compound their irksomeness by making you wait before they get to you.

"Hello. Is this ... Kate?"

That slight pause before he says my name.

Nine

We're now at the stage where we are finding
planets faster than we can investigate them.
— GEOFFREY MARCY, 2000

AVEY

He's late.

The restaurant on Broadway where I told him to meet me is so crowded that I had to put my name on the list and hang around the door for fifteen minutes, but even by the time I got a table he hadn't shown up. So now I'm wondering if I should just have continued to wait in the lobby. It's possible he came, glanced around, didn't see me, and left.

Shit, shit, shit. I'm at a disadvantage now, no matter what I do. I order another glass of wine, a mistake, but I do it anyway. I'm not the kind of brutal drunk my father was, but I don't have a salutary relationship with alcohol.

I keep glancing back and forth between the entryway and the copy of *Nature* I thought to take along. The jazz they're playing is particularly irritating, too loud and nothing but shrill saxophones. It reminds me of my sister blowing at a blade of grass between her fingers. She'd sneak up behind me to do it. So then I'd chase her down and give her a pummelling. It seemed to be what she wanted. We didn't know how to play without scaring or hitting each other.

The waitress brings me the wine. "Your party not show up yet?"

Duh.

I'm taking my second gulp from the new glass when I'm aware of someone standing beside my booth. It's a big man, overweight, in a long beige trenchcoat, and for some reason I think he will ask if he can share my table. I look up at his face, ready to make some surly reply.

It's Hale.

"Jesus." The word plops moronically out of my mouth.

Hale had been, everyone agreed, an unusually handsome man, but now he is heavy with extra flesh, with the doughy anonymity of the fat man. His black hair is still long and thick, but it looks out of place on him, an unearned vanity.

"I guess you mean ... I've changed," Hale says.

Wonderful. The first thing I say makes him think I am the same tactless, self-absorbed ass I was in 1995. I probably am, but I was hoping to hide that fact for at least five minutes.

It takes all the strength in my jaws to hoist something like a smile onto my face. I gesture at the seat across from me. "Sit down," I say.

He does. "You look the same," he says.

Great. He's going to be the classy one. I want to drain the whole glass of wine, but I make myself take only a restrained sip.

"Want a glass?" I lift my hand for the waitress.

"I'm hungry," he says. "I thought ... since this is a restaurant —"

"Sure. Of course. We can have something. My treat."

My treat. Could I possibly sound more sycophantic? I feel like pulling myself to my feet by my hair and giving myself a shake.

"The special was fettucine," he says. "Maybe I'll have the fettucine."

"Sure. Sounds good. Me, too."

We place our orders, looking at each other with only brief, rather furtive glances. I'm reassured to sense his nervousness. He isn't enjoying this meeting, either. He shrugs, with some difficulty, out of his coat. I see he's wearing a navy suit jacket with a white shirt, a rather formal look, making me wish I'd worn something other than a pullover and vest.

"I suppose you're wondering why I wanted to see you," he says.

"Well, yeah." My voice sounds croaky. I clear my throat, but it doesn't dislodge the lump of dread stuck there.

"My sister Kani — you remember her? She worked at the JAC?"

"Yes, sure, I remember."

"She lives in Seattle now, and I went to visit her ... and I thought, well, it's not far to Vancouver from there. I always wanted to see Vancouver."

A little hope bubbles up in me. He's here because he wanted to see Vancouver. He's doing what people sometimes do in strange cities, look up someone they know.

"It's a nice place," I say. "Not as nice as Hilo in the winter, but still."

"But mostly I wanted to talk to you."

The bubble of hope shrinks. "Well, I'm here." I try to sound jovial, agreeable.

"It's about what ... we ... did to Bruno's computer that time. You remember?"

The smile on my face probably looks hideous. Do I *remember?* Fucking sadist.

"I suppose so," I say.

"Well, I've been thinking about that a lot lately."

"It's a long time ago, Hale. Twelve years. Ancient history."

"There's something that still seems ..." He holds the next word in his mouth so long he could be making a pearl out of a grain of sand. "Unfinished."

Unfinished. Not a pearl. Not even a grain of sand.

"Nothing's unfinished," I say. "It's over with. A done deal."

"The problem is ..." Again he makes me wait. "The problem is Bruno."

That surprises me. "Bruno."

"He came to Hilo two months ago, to sell his father's house. He had a party there again. As he did when ... you were there. A reunion, in some ways. And a farewell."

"I remember the house."

The waitress brings our orders, and I writhe with impatience as she offers more water, more wine, ground pepper on our salads. Hale has some inane questions for her about all of these, then asks for everything.

"Anyway," he says, when she has finally gone, "he wanted to talk to me about what happened that day. The day ... his computer was unplugged."

"What did you tell him?"

"I said I didn't really remember."

My bubble of hope begins to inflate again. *Didn't remember:* a puff of pure helium.

"Why was he asking about it now? After all these years?"

"He said it had just been on his mind lately. After the ... incident ... he was quite upset. That was why I almost lost my job —"

"And you didn't, remember, because I went to bat for you." I'm exaggerating my role in it, though Hale wouldn't know that.

"But what I learned at the reunion ... was that the reason Bruno became most upset was that he had one of the techs do a search on his hard drive ... and he found the missing data."

"Oh. I didn't know that. He didn't say anything to me."

"I assumed he hadn't."

"So, like, what? You think finding the data made him suspicious? You think he blamed me?"

Hale begins to eat his fettucine with careful, delicate movements, small bites. "Maybe."

"Well, so what did he say after you told him you didn't remember? Was that the end of it?"

Hales chews, taking so long to swallow I want to Heimlich the answer out of him.

"It could be," he says at last.

"What does that mean?"

"I've been thinking about this," Hale says.

The waitress brings his wine. Recklessly, I order another glass, too. I have no idea where Hale is heading, what to expect.

"And what have you decided?"

"Bruno has ... AIDS."

"What? Are you sure?"

"Yes. Kani told me."

I can see Bruno's cheerful face. Ah, Jeez. Poor bastard. He doesn't deserve this.

"Well," I say, "it's not the death sentence it once was. There are treatments now. You can live with it."

"The treatments don't work for everyone. They aren't working for him. You could see that."

"Well, that's rotten. I am truly sorry about this. But I don't see what it has to do with me."

"Don't you?" Hale asks.

And suddenly I know what he wants me to do. I lean back in my seat, as though he has whacked me physically in the chest. My left hand even goes to my heart, some instinctive movement I know confuses people because when they clutch their hearts it's with the right hand.

"No." My voice is too loud.

The waitress brings me my third glass of wine and I take a big gulp, feel a drop spill out of the corner of my mouth and run down my chin. I can feel Hale's gaze drizzling down my chin, too. I wipe them both away with my napkin.

"I want you to admit to him what you did."

I stare at my fettucine. It's inedible, a pile of white worms.

"And if I don't?"

"Then I will."

"We had a deal, Hale."

"Now Bruno is sick. I think he deserves to know the truth."

"Why?" I demand. "What good would it do him now? Just make him more bitter, maybe. He's had a good career. I don't think he has regrets."

"But he still thinks about what happened. He hasn't forgotten about it. If he has suspicions it would be ... a relief for him to know for sure."

"Maybe not. What will it help him to know someone he trusted was a thieving shit? And if he finds out what I did he'll find out what you did, too, remember."

"He already blames me," Hale says. "Now he'll blame me less."

"He thought it was an accident. Now he'll find out it was deliberate."

Hale scratches at his right eyebrow, stares off across the room. Damn, I think I got to him. He hasn't thought this all through. And is this what it's all about, some attempt to clear his name?

I lean forward. "You see? An accident is unintentional. It's easy to forgive someone for an accident. But if he learns the truth he'll know you did this on purpose."

He thinks about it for a while. I try not to fidget.

Finally he says, "The truth will only reflect better on me. Poor simple Hale: he was talked into taking the blame for Avey Fleming, a much ... smarter man. Hale thought he was doing something ... kind for Dr.

Fleming. He didn't understand how important this was ... or how Dr. Fleming would benefit. To Hale it was just an unplugged computer."

I stare at him. The odious slug. Poor simple Hale, all right.

"So who do you think you are, God?"

"I know this is upsetting for you. I know I'm not being ... entirely fair with you."

"Oh, well, that's all right then. So long as you know." I throw down my fork so hard it bounces, rattles against my water glass loudly enough for the people across from us to glance over.

Hale doesn't answer.

"It didn't even turn out to be a planet. You know that, don't you?"

"That might make it easier to tell Bruno the truth."

"Jesus, Hale. I don't understand you. This isn't going to help Bruno. I don't see the point. If he's as sick as you say he might not live that much longer anyway. Let him die in peace."

That came out sounding so coarse and cruel that even I wince.

Hale raises his eyes to me. "I guess," he says, "the point is ... that I want him to die in peace, too."

If I'd had any chance to argue him out of this I've blown it. Damn it, damn it, damn it.

"Okay. So what will it take for you to forget about this? To just let Bruno alone?"

I have no idea what I will say if he asks for Kate again.

"I'm not trying to negotiate. You just have to tell him. He's in Hilo now, for ... another week, maybe, finishing up the house sale. I want you to go there and talk to him before he leaves."

"I can't drop everything and fly off to Hawaii."

Hale shrugs. "It would just be for a day or two. You can make arrangements."

"I might send him an email, all right? Or write him a letter. Phone him, even."

"That's not the way he should be told. It should be in person. Face to face. And it's better that ... you are the one to tell him, don't you think? Instead of me?"

Bastard.

For Hale this is some whim. For me it's the end of everything. If Bruno is still brooding about what happened after all this time he's going to want justice, want the credit due him. Oh, I can see the headlines already. If he weren't son of the famous Orlovski, weren't the princeling usurped by the hunchhearted commoner Fleming, it wouldn't make such a tasty scandal. But he is, and it will.

Hale gets up, reaches for his coat. "All right?" he says. "So you'll go to Hilo before the end of the week." He drapes his coat over his arm, smoothing it down.

I don't answer. He bends over, picks up my napkin which has fallen on the floor, places it on the table. It's the kind of detail my mother told me to notice in people, that it spoke to a quality of character. I resist hurling the damned thing back on the floor. *That* would speak to character.

"Well, then." Hale pulls a scarf from his coat sleeve and slides it around his neck. "Thanks for lunch."

When he's gone the waitress comes over and asks if I want dessert. I laugh and say, "Yes, just desserts."

She gives me a confused look and sidles the bill onto the table before she backs away. I have to pay for his meal, of course. I said I would. We had a deal.

Back at work, I'm just unlocking the door to the outer office when Louisa comes down the hall, gives me a big smile. She's wearing some kind of huge blue flower on her lapel. It looks ridiculous.

"Hi," she says. "Nice to have some sunshine, isn't it?"

"Louisa. Have you ever done something so colossally stupid you have to spend the rest of your life regretting it?"

I hadn't planned to say that. The words seemed to speak themselves. God knows I can't possibly be intending to blurt out my sordid story to Louisa. But maybe some part of my brain is ahead of me, is doing preemptive damage control. When my disgrace is served up for the gossip entrée at the Faculty Club, Louisa might remember this, might say I had been feeling remorse and guilt all along, that I'm not the amoral thief they claim.

Louisa stares at me. "Has something happened?"

"It's all right. Nothing I can bother you with."

But she is excited now, curious, wants to be helpful. But I can smell the sour perfume of *Schadenfreude* in the air. I shake my head stoically, tell her it's okay, it'll be okay, I'm just having a bad day. But then, as I'm turning away, I think, well, maybe I can take advantage of her offer to be helpful after all, and I ask if she could take my Thursday afternoon 102 class.

"Of course," she says.

"I'll return the favour," I say. "Schedule me for a guest lecture for your 303s sometime."

"Not necessary, really."

"You're a sweetheart, Louisa." I dredge up a smile that fakes only some of its gratitude. "Just do the chapter on the Planck mass, give them the questions at the end."

"All right. Of course." She touches my arm. "Take care."

When at last I'm in my office I try to navigate my way through the online airline ticketing maze, where flight times and prices seem to change from one click to the next. I almost give up and make Joan do it as usual, but I don't want her to know where I'm going.

At last I'm done, I'm going somewhere. I'll have to wait for the confirmatory email to see if I haven't booked myself to Afghanistan.

I phone Kate. "Sorry for the short notice," I say, "but something's come up. I just found out I have to make a trip to Hilo."

KATE

"A trip to Hilo!"

"Yeah. Leaves tomorrow. Not thrilled to be going, but there it is."

"Well, it might be nice. You can look up some of your old colleagues."

Avey grunts. "Doubt I'll have time for socializing. And, uh, don't tell anyone where I've gone, okay? There's an emergency with one of the telescopes, and they don't want to advertise it."

"All right."

We hang up before I give in to the impulse to say, "Hilo. What a coincidence. I'm just going out to meet someone else we knew at Hilo."

I should have told him. He probably wouldn't have cared — it had been his idea, after all, for me to go up the mountain with Hale that awful day. But now I have made our meeting some secret.

So I feel furtive, deceitful, as I pull my jacket and runners on, and it annoys me, as it does that Hale has insisted we meet. I'd hoped I would never have to see him again after I walked away from him at the Visitors' Center on Mauna Kea. It took me a long time to convince myself that what happened to me on the mountain must have been the result of altitude sickness and not Hale's malevolence. I felt ashamed then of the wild things I said to him, and I suppose that's really why I've agreed to see him now.

But of course I also can't forget that I had fallen into bed with him practically the first time I ever saw him. Last night I had vivid and frantic dreams about David, making love with him in dangerous places, and I know they came from talking again to Hale, who had reminded me so unfortunately of David that day at the condo. That day is a hold Hale has over me, though now, surely, not one of erotic power but one that comes from knowing a discrediting secret. What does he want? Has he come to blackmail me somehow? Will he threaten to tell Avey? Will he resume his childish demands that I continue to see him, to sleep with him? I am filled with dread.

Before I leave I check my email, and there is one from Sandy, responding to my question about the legal status of the Bosnian couple:

Hi, Mom,
    Frantically busy here. Sorry I can't offer you any advice about the tenants. Doesn't seem as though they have any legal recourse to eviction. But, hey, it's nice that you care about them. Maybe philanthropy is your thing. I'm proud of you.
                                                            love ya, Sandy

I'm proud of you? A bit patronizing, maybe, but it's also probably one of the nicest things she has ever said to me. I stare at the message for several minutes, imagine her writing it, my diamond-edged daughter, telling me she appreciates my softness.

Since the day was sunny I had decided to walk to the MacMillan Planetarium where Hale suggested we meet, but I may have left it a bit late. It's a good twenty blocks. I set off briskly, waving to my neighbour Jenny in her living room sitting at her loom, and head down Broadway, then veer off to Fourth Avenue with its more interesting shops and vestigial remains of its Sixties culture. I find myself going down one more street, to Third, to the big white house, and I stop and look helplessly at the curtained basement window where the Bosnians are waiting for the next misery to befall them in this country where they were promised refuge. A few days ago I took down the "Sold" sign from the front lawn, but that only makes the grimness of their futures seem more inevitable.

I walk on, follow Point Grey Road to Cornwall, past Kitsilano Beach Park which is busy with teenagers ricocheting away from school, and then there is Vanier Park and the planetarium, where I have often been because Avey is a consultant there. The building's roof reminds me of the conical hats flaring out at the top that I've seen in pictures of the Nootka.

I'm only a few minutes late, but I can see someone in a long beige trenchcoat standing in front of the big metal crab sculpture and fountain by the front door. It must be Hale.

In spite of myself, I run my hand through my hair, brush the perspiration from my forehead, glance down at myself to make sure I haven't omitted some part of my wardrobe. My body has apparently not forgotten that this is a man I once desired and slept with, has not forgotten its small vanities. I remind it not to forget the unease I felt all along with Hale's moody expectations, not to forget the terror I felt on the mountain, even though I know it's not fair to blame him for that and it's I who owe him the apology. But I am talking to my body, which remembers but doesn't think, which might need something like fear to outmuscle sex.

When I get closer I see that he has gained weight. His face has a pudgier look. It's still attractive, but no longer one people would stare at. Perhaps that's a relief to him. Perhaps it's a relief to me.

He smiles when he sees me, lifts his hand in a wave.

"Hello," I say.

"You're paler than I remember," he says.

I make a face. "That's how we look up here in winter."

I hold out my hand so that he won't think we should give each other a hug, and he takes it, gives it a somewhat limp shake. His hand is cold. He must find this climate unpleasant.

"Well," I say. "Shall we go for a walk on the beach? Or are you too cold? We could go inside somewhere, have a coffee."

"A walk ... would be fine. I'm wearing almost all the clothes I brought."

We head off along the beach, past the Maritime Museum, following the gravel path. There are many walkers, and it's hard to walk side-by-side. Our little attempts at conversation keep snapping off in mid-sentence.

At last Hale gestures to a bench, says, "Let's sit," and we do, look out at the sailboats and the huge tankers anchored at the mouth of False Creek. Across English Bay we can see Stanley Park and the glistening high-rises of Vancouver's West End. A breeze from the water has an icy slice.

"You'll be glad to get home," I say, "where it's warm."

"Where it's home," he says and smiles a little. He looks off across the water to the west. "When I was young, a geologist stayed with our family for a few months. He was studying what he called 'land memory.' It had to do with ... water levels and rain, how water wants to return to the same place. Something like that. And I thought ... maybe people have land memory, too. I suppose the idea ... influenced me."

"I'm not surprised."

"Why? Do you think it ... explains me?"

I laugh. "You're too complicated to be explained by only one thing."

He's pleased, of course.

"This is my first trip to Canada," he says. "It's not really as cold as I'd thought it would be."

"This isn't really Canada. This isn't really winter. I come from Edmonton. They have a real winter there."

"Edmonton. You said it was beyond the mountains. Where you felt safe."

"Safe? I said that?"

"The day we went up to Kilauea."

"Funny I don't remember. Not that I didn't say it. But of course memories aren't always trustworthy."

I give an apologetic little laugh, as though I might be wanting to prepare him for my denial of other things that happened in Hilo. But really I'm just thinking of my mother warning me about the unreliability of memories, how, the older they get, the less faithful and honest they become. They're tricky and sticky, she said, streams that gather silt and twigs, pebbles, the bones of the dead and the lies of the living. So maybe, I said, having just seen the first Star Trek movie, they're like V'ger, who goes out to learn, to collect knowledge, but on the way loses itself. That made my mother sigh and say something about how if I could make such analogies why couldn't I make more of an effort in my English classes. I would have been about twelve then, I guess. If I can trust that memory. It's a lot older than the one about my trip to the volcanoes with Hale.

"But now you live on the same dangerous ocean as I do." Hale gestures at the grey sea in front of us.

"I guess I do."

"Why did you move here? Because of the winter?"

"Not really. I'd still be in Edmonton if Avey hadn't taken the job here."

"Are you happy with him?"

He asks the question so casually that it takes me a moment to realize how inappropriate it is. I was thinking, this is going to be all right, he's grown up, he's no longer an impetuous boy.

But when I try to answer with what I know I must say — *yes, of course I'm happy with him* — the words are reluctant to form.

I think about it, for too long, probably, and then I say, "It's not really something you have the right to ask, Hale."

"I know. I'm sorry. That was rude of me."

I glance over at him. His response is more mature than the one he would have given me twelve years ago. He looks out at the bay, his eyes crinkling a little in the sun.

"So, you're still at the JAC?"

He nods. "It's a good place to work." He pushes his scarf, which is too light to provide much warmth, higher up his neck. "Just before you left I made a serious ... error there. They could have fired me, but they didn't."

"I remember you mentioning it. Didn't you say Avey interceded on your behalf?" I'm glad he has given me a chance to mention Avey in this context, a man who has done him a kindness, not a man whose wife he could still want to pursue.

He smiles. "Yes." We're silent for a moment, and then he says, "And your work. Tell me about it."

So I do, trying to make it seem interesting, which it is, sometimes; and then I find myself telling him about the Bosnians.

"It's obvious what should be done," Hale says. "It's obvious what they want."

"Is it? Well, tell me."

"They want to go home."

I look at him, surprised. *They want to go home.* "Yes," I say. "Of course they would."

"They don't belong here."

I laugh. Hale's old way of seeing everything.

"I think you're right," I say. "But what if home is no longer there? What if the war has destroyed it? What if they no longer belong there, either?"

"They would probably still choose to go. Besides, the war is over now, isn't it?"

"I guess so. Thank you for the suggestion, Hale. Really. It's something I'm going to investigate."

"Maybe your agency can hire me. As a consultant. I would send everyone back to where they came from."

My laugh must sound a little indecisive. I'm almost certain he was joking, but, as always with Hale, there is that ambiguity.

"Oh. I almost forgot," I say. "I brought something for you. To take back home." I dig in my purse until I find it.

Hale looks at it, puzzled.

"Don't you remember?" I prompt. "I picked it up the day you took me to Kilauea. You said it would be bad luck to keep it. You said Pele would be angry."

He turns the piece of lava around in his fingers, runs his thumb down the smooth ropey sides, the way I had done when I first found it and then again when I picked it up after it fell from my jacket pocket last year.

"I don't remember," he says.

I'm annoyed to feel disappointment. Did I think that every foolish thing I ever said or did with him would stay enshrined in his memory? He'd just reminded me of something I'd apparently said about Edmonton that I'd completely forgotten. The tricky, sticky stream is often not sticky enough.

"So," he says, "did it bring you bad luck?"

"Not yet. And surely after twelve years the statute of limitations on bad luck has run out."

"All right. I'll take it back with me."

"You don't have to. It was just this, well, this silly thing I remembered I had."

Hale's thumb strokes the piece of lava. I make myself take my eyes from it, look at a sailboat with striped orange sails yawing at dangerous angles too close to shore.

We talk about Hilo then for a while, about his life there. He mentions casually that he was married once, briefly, but that it was "a mistake." He tells me little bits of gossip about people I remember, about his sister Kani, about Karen. Karen: I wonder if Hale knew she had brought him to me like a present. Karen and Joe live in Japan now, he says, where they both have jobs at a university.

"What about Bruno?" I ask. "Do you know where he is? I think he and Avey lost touch with each other."

"Bruno's in England now. He's just sold his father's house in Hilo. Do you remember it?"

"Yes, of course." I wish I hadn't added the "of course." Bruno's house is where I met Hale.

"It was a beautiful place," he says.

We lapse into a rather amiable silence. Two young women walk by wearing blue windbreakers and very tight jeans and what I remember are called yashmaks: veils worn by Muslim women that cover both the top and bottom parts of the face leaving only the eyes visible. The eyes look at us, perhaps challenging, perhaps amused. I wonder if Hale will say something about the incongruities in their dress, but though he watches them until they turn a corner he doesn't comment.

Finally he says, "I had a ... special reason for wanting to see you."

I keep my expression neutral. "And what was that?"

"I wanted to thank you."

"Thank me! What for?"

"For telling me the truth back then. That day on Mauna Kea. You said I was selfish and ... arrogant. You said all my talk about outside things coming in and destroying Hawaii ... was just an excuse. You said

I blamed that for everything I didn't like about my life."

I recognize my own words, flung at him as we stood outside the Visitors' Center.

"I was very harsh," I say. "It wasn't fair."

"Nobody had ever dared say such things to me. Maybe I'd been waiting for someone to say them."

"But I had no right. My brain was probably still oxygen-deprived."

"You were telling me what you thought. You were telling me the truth."

"I was ranting. I was delusional. Paranoid. I thought you had deliberately hidden and then locked me out of the observatory." I laugh apologetically.

He doesn't answer. I look over at him. Even then, seeing his face, it takes me a while to understand. A cold cramp in my gut stops my breath.

"I *didn't* imagine it, did I?"

"I'm very sorry. That's the other thing I needed to say to you."

I didn't imagine it. I sit absolutely still, as though my body is a vaseful of memory I mustn't spill: my mounting panic in the observatory as I ran through it searching for Hale, my heart flailing, and then outside, the terrible cold, the disorientating and hopeless climb over the jagged cinders towards the Keck, the growing terror that I would die there.

Hale had wanted it all to happen. It was exactly as I'd first believed. I hadn't imagined any of it.

I stand up, stare down at him. He doesn't look at me, fixes his eyes on his running shoe which he is kicking lightly against the side of the bench.

"How could you do that? My God, I was terrified. And I could have frozen to death out there."

"I always knew where you were. I wouldn't have let you freeze."

"So, so you hid, and then when I went outside you locked the door —"

"I'm sorry. It was a terrible thing to do. I was upset because you … you didn't want to continue our … relationship. I hadn't planned to go so far. Maybe I was suffering from altitude sickness, too."

"But you'd planned some of it."

He shifts on his seat. "Some. Just a little. I didn't think you'd go outside. I'm not sure whether I wanted to ... punish you or rescue you. Both, I suppose."

"It was so cruel! Sadistic! First to terrify me like that and then to make me doubt most of it even happened, to make me think I'd gone crazy. I had nightmares about it for months."

"It was ... a horrible thing to do. I was very ashamed. I'm still ashamed. I'm asking you to forgive me."

I stand there looking down at him. People walking in groups on the path jostle me as they go by, annoyed that someone is there not moving and with her back to the view.

Hale sits slumped, his head bent. I could let myself be impressed with the way he refuses to break his penitentially downcast gaze with a glance at me to see if abjectness is still required.

Has he really felt guilt all these years? Well ... well, *good.* As a punishment guilt is better than forgiveness.

But I can feel my anger easing. It has taken some courage for him to confess, after all. I would like to make him wait a bit longer for my response, to make him doubt what it will be, but I suppose he knows as well as I do by now what I will say.

"All right. I forgive you."

"Thank you."

I sit back down, and we stay there for some time, looking out at the water, watching people pass by. Many of them are wearing short sleeves, some of them in shorts, and it makes me shiver to see them. My Scottish grandmother would say, *Cast nae thy cloot 'til May be oot.* I pull the zipper on my cloot up a bit more. I watch the little ferry docking at the Maritime Museum. It disgorges a field-trip-size pod of children and heads away again down False Creek.

"Can I see you again before I go back to Hilo?"

"I don't think that's a good idea, Hale."

"Perhaps the three of us. Avey, too."

It's a surprising suggestion. But I realize I don't have to make up any excuses when I have a legitimate one. "He's going to be away now, actually. Out of town."

"Maybe he has to go to Hilo."

I give him a sideways glance. Is he just speculating? He still works at the JAC — he may well know why Avey has suddenly had to go there.

"Why do you say that?" I ask.

He shrugs. "No reason."

Ten

There are infinite worlds
both like and unlike this world.

— EPICURUS

AVEY

Hilo. My flight was delayed so I got in late, and then my room wasn't exactly a pleasant surprise. It's small and noisy and not clean. There are spots where the texture of the wallpaper makes me doubt it was flocked that way to start with. The whole place has that musty, moist smell that reminds me of the house Kate and I rented, and the advertised ocean view is visible only over a parking lot and construction site. There's no air conditioning, of course, and the room seems to swell and bulge with heat. The ceiling fan grunts as it churns through the air like a mixer through dough. When the construction noise woke me up at six a.m., I felt like Dorothy Parker opening her eyes in the mornings and saying, "What fresh hell is this?"

I walk out along Banyan Drive, find a small place selling coffee. When I pay with a handful of change into which a Canadian quarter has shuffled, the woman pushes it back at me with such distaste it's as though I'd offered her a turd. I take the coffee to a park bench in Lili'uokalani Gardens and sit there staring out at the palm trees, at the Pacific grinding away at the beach. The coffee is foul. Kona coffee is grown on the other side of this island and is supposed to be among the best in the world, but if this is Kona coffee it's made from grounds that have sat in compost for a few weeks. I drink it anyway. It goes with this whole horrible trip.

I can see the place on Banyan Drive where Bruno and I sat parked the day of the power failure. We talked about what would become of us. Is this it, this misery on a park bench, what I have become? And have I become what I'm going to be for the rest of my life? I'm only halfway through the damn thing. Bruno told me about how his father had asked his retired colleagues what the most important discovery of their careers was. Well, I might be at the end of my career, too: what would I write down on my questionnaire? One guy, Bruno said, wrote that his biggest discovery was his "true self." Huh. Of course, he might just have discovered his true self was a mean, greedy, rat bastard.

My good luck was Bruno's bad luck, I told Kate all those years ago. The inexorableness of the Exclusion Principle, I told her. Well, I've lost my spin, my seat on the bus now. In this configuration I'm Antoine Duquennoy, not Didier Queloz. Duquennoy was the first partner of Michel Mayor and should have gotten the co-credit for the first exoplanet discovery, except that he got killed in an accident in the Alps, and Didier Queloz walked into the best luck of his life.

It's late in the morning. I should phone Bruno, but I can't make myself do it. Maybe he's away, and I'll have come all this way for nothing. But when I drove in last night from the airport I went past his place and there were lights on, someone moving around inside. I know I should have called before I came, to set up some kind of appointment. I checked the phone listings on the Internet, and there's still a number under his name for the house. Maybe I was thinking that somehow I could go back and tell Hale, well, I went all that way, see, here's my ticket, and he wasn't there, you said he'd be there and you were wrong.

I tilt my head back, squint up at the sky that has only a few smears of cloud left from the overnight rain. Out there is the star system that has the star that has the planet that isn't a planet that Avey found and didn't find. Maybe there's some single cell on it right now struggling to grow up to discover us someday. Forget it, that's my advice. Growth is nausea, Sartre said. Life is just nature's way of dealing with the toxicity of oxygen. Life is just rust on a few unlucky planets. Dr. Ferrous Oxide, that's me. How are you today, Ferrous? Nauseous. Skysick.

I drop my eyes back to the horizon, back to land, the way one is supposed to. A backhoe is digging up something in the Gardens, and I watch it for a while, the driver apparently confusing his gears and repeatedly backing up and surprising himself, running finally right into a big palm tree. When he gets out to look, the tree throws a coconut onto his cab roof. It rolls off and hits him on the shoulder. I laugh, a cackly, bitter noise.

"Nobody walks under palm trees unpunished," I say, out loud, apparently.

My voice attracts a mangy, yellow dog that comes slowly at me with his head and tail lowered, and I try to remember, from my days of delivering papers in Edmonton, if that is supposed to be a posture of threat or subservience.

"No," I say loudly to whatever his intentions are.

He seems to believe me and slinks off to my left, sniffs at a purple-leafed bush. He lifts a rear leg, stretches up on his other three, aiming higher, higher, so he can show that next dog what a big stud he is — oh, I know all about that, you pathetic little pisser. But when he does let fly what he lacks in height he makes up for in velocity. Some of the spray goes past the bush and hits my pants.

"Stop that!" I jump up, and the dog gallops away.

Damn it. My pant leg is speckled with dog piss. Oh, the omens get better and better. If I were poncey Yardley from the English Department now I'd pull out my little notebook and jot this down for some poem, which I'd work on conspicuously during faculty meetings and then publish in a thin and boring book which I'd expect everyone to buy. I'd call this poem "Pathetic Fallacy." I'd be both the pathetic and the fallacy.

I limp back to my hotel room, trying unsuccessfully to stop my leg from brushing the peed-on pant leg, and take a shower. The water pressure is so poor I have to stand right under the shower head. I change into shorts, the only other pants I brought. The telephone beside the bed looks blackly at me. I more or less run out of the room.

When I finally remember which rented Honda in the parking lot is mine, I drive up Kamehameha Avenue and get lost somehow, which shouldn't surprise me, since I went practically nowhere when I was here except from the house to the JAC. Eventually I find Kamana Street, find our house. The Pupuka. It looks even more squalid than I remember, the front steps broken right through. There are the usual signs of habitation, though, probably by some version of myself, driven enough by excitement and ambition and overwork not to notice what a sty he has to live in. I'll have to tell Kate that the front window is boarded up again. Maybe the owner took the glass out after we left.

I remember, suddenly, something that happened on our last day. Kate was carrying a suitcase through the kitchen and stepped on the soft spot on the floor. It broke under her. She shrieked, managed to stumble away. We stood there staring at the collapsed boards, then began laughing wildly, in that jubilant and celebratory way of people whose accomplishment is the life they are losing as much as the life they are gaining.

It's just another memory that will turn sour once I am exposed. I've been trying hard not to think of how Kate is going to react. What did I ever have to offer her except my success or my potential for it? Who could blame her if she left me?

I sit there in the idling car long enough that a woman waddling out of a neighbouring house says as she passes my window, "Hey, man, you can turn the car off. *Mai maka'u.* We ain't gonna steal it."

I give her a stiff smile. Yeah, I know: I'm just a tight-assed *haole*.

When I drive away I notice at the end of the street a single battered red carpet slipper sitting at the edge of the sidewalk. It makes the back of my neck tingle. How long have I been gone? Twelve years or twelve minutes? I turn the corner, and then suddenly I'm pulling over, getting out of the car and walking back and picking up the damn thing. It feels, surely, too soft, too unrotted, to be one of the pair I remember, but, still, picking it up feels creepy, as though I might be rupturing the time-space continuum or something. I throw the stupid thing onto the passenger seat and drive on.

It's a route I remember well now, up Komohana Road, turning at Nowelo. At first I think I've made a mistake, because there are more buildings on the left than my memory assigned there, but of course these are centres for the newer telescopes built on Mauna Kea. There's Caltech just as I remember it, but the JAC is flanked now by the Gemini on one side and the fancy Subaru centre on the other. I remember all the buzz about the Subaru, how it would have the largest single-piece mirror in the world. Now the buzz is about how it's going to be remotely controlled from Japan. Remote-viewing is getting more remote all the time. On the downslope of the street I can see the green roof of the new

Smithsonian Astrophysical Observatory, and a big information centre has been built beside it. The Keck centre, of course, the one that would have been the brightest star in this constellation, is up north on the other side of Mauna Kea, in Waimea, on a site probably as big as this whole Astronomy Row.

I don't know why I came here. Did I intend to go inside, to be greeted by people as the celebrity I was when I left? Did I want some final memory to take with me before I become their big disgrace, before I get downgraded, plutoed, the way my planet was? Maybe I wanted to go and find my old self, plug Bruno's computer back in, have the other life I was supposed to have.

My mind is full of such confusions of memory and regret that I feel myself panicking, afraid of being discovered here, and I back the car sharply into the driveway of the Subaru centre and speed away so fast the tires squeal on the turn onto Nowelo. The slipper slides off the seat, and I grab it and throw it back.

"Sit still," I say.

Back at the hotel, I carry the slipper with me up to the room and lie down on the bed, listen to the headache beating its drum on my forehead.

I should phone Bruno. Bruno, Bruno, Bruno: I say his name over and over to myself until it loses all meaning, a kind of anti-memnonic.

I have to phone him.

What I do instead is break the seal on the bottle of duty-free Jack Daniels and have two long swallows, right from the bottle. They burn their way down, burn the headache right out of my head. Captain Jack will get you high tonight: oh, yeah. And take you to your special island. It wouldn't be *this* island, that's for damned sure. The slipper sits on the armchair and watches me drink.

For some reason what ratchets itself up into my mind then is a TV image from my childhood, of John Dean during the Watergate hearings, how in answer to one of the prosecutor's questions about why he apparently decided finally to confess, he said something like, "My father told me that if I ever got deeply into trouble to just tell the truth." My mother nodded, turned to me and said, "That's a lesson for you, Avey." I remember thinking: lesson? What lesson? That I was supposed to trust my *father?* That it's okay to lie and cheat until you're caught?

Yeah, right, it's all my mother's fault. Hers and Nixon's.

Once I phone Bruno that will be it. The path of no return. Heading for the town-without-mercy of Blowback, home of the equal and opposite reaction.

But if I run away from Bruno there's only Hale at the other end. *It's better that you are the one to tell him, don't you think? Instead of me?* That soft, sly, executioner's voice.

I pour one of the bathroom glasses half full of whiskey, cut it with water this time before I drink. I can already feel the alcohol, the antiseptic, the bloodthinner, its clever unclotting.

I pick up the phone, punch in the numbers. It rings only once before someone picks it up.

"Hello?"

"Hi, Mom. It's Avey."

"Avey! How nice to hear your voice. Are you in Edmonton? Will we get to see you?"

"I'm in Hawaii, actually."

"Oh! Oh, well." She pauses, probably wondering as much as I am why I'm calling. "It must be nice there. Nice weather."

"It's Hawaii. There's always nice weather." My voice sounds cranky. I can almost hear her wince. It's the tone of my voice that tells me why I must have called, whom I must be wanting to speak to. "Is Dad there?"

"Yes, yes. He just got home. I'll go get him."

When she puts the phone down I reach for the whiskey again, take another big swallow. It doesn't burn. It feels cool.

"Avey?"

"Hi, Dad."

"You're, what, in Hawaii?"

"Apparently."

I can hear him chewing on something, swallowing. There's a crackle of paper.

"So? You just calling to say hello or what?"

"I'm not sure exactly why I'm calling."

"Yeah, well, take a guess."

"I think I called to tell you you'd be proud of me."

"I would, huh. And why would that be?"

I think about it for a minute. I want to say it properly. "Well, I've become like my old man. I'm sitting here getting drunk."

"I beg your pardon?"

I beg your pardon. It's what he would say to any answer, including silence, that displeased him, what he would say with that inevitable step toward you, and how it's impossible for me to ever hear those words free of their threat and ugly irony, and how that's not something you can explain to people at a noisy cocktail party as you flinch and take a step back.

"I said, I've become like my old man. I'm sitting here getting drunk and I'm a fucking piece of shit."

There's a long silence. This is more than I have ever dared with him. I feel a flood of perspiration that is pure fear, fear that somehow I am still not far enough away from him.

There's a clatter as he puts the phone down. But he hasn't hung up. I take another swallow from my glass. It's almost empty. After a minute Mom comes back on.

"Avey?" Her voice is barely a whisper. "Did you say something? He looks upset."

"Good."

"Oh, you shouldn't have. You know how he gets ..."

"Of course I do. I'm sorry."

But I don't sound sorry. I sound as angry at her as I did at him, angry at this shushing voice that kept us both cowed and afraid of him all of our bloody lives. But, yes, of course I am sorry, too, because I know that she'll be the one to pay for what I said, and that's how it's always worked, his retribution falling on her to punish me and on me to punish her.

"I have to go," I say, and I really do. I'm feeling dizzy. The room looks speckled with yellow dots.

"Thank you for calling," she says. Ah, Jesus.

I drop the phone into its cradle and finish what's in my glass, jamming my palm over the bottom to shove those last drops down, homage to the man I saw do this about ten thousand times. I let myself fall back onto the bed, close my eyes.

Close my eyes: I wish. I close my eye*lids*. Behind them my eyes keep on staring. Just because you pull the drapes shut doesn't mean the house goes to sleep. It just makes the rooms more claustrophobic.

I pull the pillow out from under the bedspread and press it over my eyes. I put it over my nose, too, see how long it takes before I have to open my mouth to breathe. I guess smothering oneself isn't one of the options for suicide.

And I think about that for a while. Suicide.

But I haven't the courage, I guess. I'm calibrated for self-loathing but not for self-termination. It feels as though some detached part of me is just too ... I try to find the right word. Curious. That's it. Curious about what the hell will happen next.

Imagine that. Saved by curiosity. The astronomer's best friend.

I throw the pillow to the foot of the bed, get up, head to the toilet. I stumble against the bedside table. Ah, the staggers. They're only funny when someone else has them. Everything about my body feels stupid. My brain is stupid, my feet are stupid, my eyes are stupid. Even my dick is stupid, dribbling onto the outside of the bowl.

I scratch at my right ear, forgetting that for some reason it can bring on the hiccups, so now here they come, the bastards, jerking up into my mouth foul spasms of gas obviously intended for a different exit. I hold my breath and drink a glass of water, but it doesn't help. A good scare is supposed to work: I make myself look into the big mirror above the sink, at the haunted, red-eyed, police-lineup, Kafka face, its cheeks sunken, rugose. *Rugose.* Another one of those damned eccentric words of my mother's, still using up a neuron in my brain. It takes a moment before the commoner word comes. Wrinkled: there we go. I stare and stare at that face.

Avey Inversus. His father's backwards boy. His toy that he took apart too many times and put together not just backwards but with pieces missing. Like the Devil, my mother's priest said. In the mirror, though, he's normal, not dextrocardiac but levocardiac, like everyone else. But even with his heart over there on the left he still looks like a fucked-up mess.

Though by God he's cured my hiccups.

I lurch back to the bed, pick up the TV remote, flip through the usual network programming, pause on a news channel with a crawl of headlines along the bottom: it's a loop, the same items repeating. I suppose I should be cheered that the station hasn't found enough new miseries in the world today and has to recycle. I keep clicking, finally up through channel after channel of static. Some of it is good old CMB: the cosmic microwave background, leftover radiation from the Big Bang. Fifteen billion years later and we can sit in hotel rooms and watch those photons cooling.

It reminds me of hunting for the planet. Somewhere in the crackle there's that magic cluster of atoms, that something that isn't nothing. I keep looking. I'm up over 100 now. Still no planet. Then suddenly I'm back at Channel Two. Back on Earth. The universe is closed, not open, after all. The static is supposed to make sense again. The pixels turn themselves into news, a sitcom, advertising, a movie, the sweet syringe of sleep.

*

When the phone rings I squint open one eye, confused about where I am. I seem to have drooled onto my hand. I wipe it onto the bedspread. My body feels thick and heavy and hard to move, as though someone sewed me to the bed while I was sleeping.

"Hello?"

"Avey?" It's Kate. "Are you all right?"

"Yeah, sure, never better."

"It's just, well, your mother phoned. She said you called and sounded upset. She thought maybe I should call to see if you were all right."

I run my hand hard over my face. "Yeah, I'm fine. I shouldn't have called them. I was a little ... intemperate." *Intemperate.* I didn't even know I had such a prissy word in my vocabulary. Must be another one of Mom's.

"Oh. Well, she was just worried, I guess."

"That's her trouble. She worries but never does anything about it." I don't want to get into discussing my parents. "So what else is new there?"

"It's raining. You won't be missing that. But, oh, I have to tell you, I ran into that Dr. Kilbride at the grocery store, and we had a nice little chat. He said something about someone retiring, Schneider, maybe, and about how in his mind you were his best choice for the deanship."

I start to laugh. The whole room is filling up with my laughing. It sounds more than a little crazy.

"That's great," I tell Kate. "Oh, that's just perfect."

K A T E

"Oh, that's just perfect."

His laughing doesn't sound right. It's not that of someone hearing welcome news.

"Is that ha-ha happy or ha-ha ironic?" I try to make my own voice sound ha-ha happy.

"Oh, both. Neither. I'm a little drunk, as you may have gathered. Or maybe hungover. It depends on how long I was asleep. I have to go pee now."

"All right."

The line goes dead, and I frown at the receiver in my hand. Something's wrong. His mother said he "used a curse word" when he talked to his father, which in itself might be a healthy thing, but I don't think it's something he's ever done before. Even more surprising is his reaction to my news about seeing Dr. Kilbride. I'd have thought he'd have been delighted, would have wanted me to repeat to him every word of our conversation.

Nevertheless, I'm a bit relieved that he hung up when he did, because I was about to tell him I had seen Hale, and I don't know quite what I would have said. Something about my visit with him, about the way it ended, made me feel he was playing some game with me, withholding something. It seems too coincidental that he apparently knew Avey had gone to Hilo. He must have heard that from the JAC people. But why not just say so? I'm annoyed at Avey, too, for making me promise not to tell anyone where he's gone, so I, too, had to be evasive. It felt as though all three of us were at a costume party peeking out from behind masks.

Still, I'm not sorry I saw Hale. There was, after all, that unfinished business between us about what really happened on the mountain that day, and that is done with now, surely. Wasn't it the whole point of his seeing me?

I push the cat from my lap, exclaiming as I always do at the veil of hair he leaves behind, get my jacket and drive down to the white house on Third Avenue.

The interpreter I'd arranged for is already there, standing frowning at the back door. She says nothing to me as I get out of the car, just holds her hand out.

"Of course," I say. "Just a minute."

I take the forty dollars from my wallet, hand it to her. She crunches it up, slides it into her jeans pocket. Her name is Anna. She seems young, barely out of her teens, short and very thin, with a pretty, large-featured face but the sour and cynical expression of someone who expects the worst. I don't know where the agency found her in the first place, and my boss doesn't know I've contacted her again, but she will be someone the Bosnians at least have met before. Perhaps I should be referring to them as Bosniaks now, a new term, I have heard, for their ethnic group that has apparently replaced the religiosity of "Muslim."

"Say to them, '*Dobar Dan*,'" Anna says. "It means 'hello.'"

"*Dobar Dan*. All right."

I knock at the door. I'm steeling myself to have the son jerk it open, but there is no answer. I'm sure they are home. I have a key I haven't yet surrendered to the new owners, but I will use it only as a last resort.

The interpreter shouts something so loud and apparently angry that I step back, alarmed. She gives me a grin. One of her bottom teeth has been replaced with something grey and metallic.

"Don't worry," she says. "I just told them we're not the police."

That this reassurance is what makes the Karolyis open the door gives me a sad little shiver. Anna goes in first, and the three of them begin immediately to talk in low and urgent tones, casting ambiguous looks at me. It is not, I think, the way an interpreter is supposed to work. The suite is small, just one room with a hotplate; the bathroom down the hall was shared with other tenants who moved out a month ago. The furniture — a plaid couch with a pullout bed, a kitchen table with two chairs, a large TV, a wardrobe and bookcase in one corner — is surprisingly new, probably not things the old owners had merely demoted from their own use. But the room is almost empty of personal possessions.

"*Dobar Dan*," I say, rather loudly, as much to the interpreter as to the Karolyis, who turn their faces to me.

They are very small people, even shorter than Anna, making me feel, unusually, too large and clumsy. They are probably not yet sixty, but they seem older, slightly stooped, their faces sun-weathered. They look amazingly alike, their brown eyes heavily lidded, their noses small but with wide nostrils, their greying hair cut the same, and they are both wearing black pants shiny either by fabric or by overuse and blue shirts with the sleeves too long. The hands that protrude from the tight cuffs are large, labourers' hands. I try not to look at the man's, to notice the missing fingers.

"*Dobar Dan*," he says to me and follows this with a long elaboration which I finally hold my hand up to interrupt, smiling and shaking my head helplessly.

"What did he say?" I ask Anna.

"Just the same as before," Anna says. "They have no place to go. They have no money. Their son is —" she frowns, snapping her fingers soundlessly as she searches for the right words "— gone over to the dark side." She gives a little snuffle of laughter.

"I really just want to ask them one thing," I say. "Do they want to go home?"

"Home?" Anna inflects the word with a kind of hostility.

"Yes. Just ask them."

She does. I watch their faces. It's clear even before they answer what they're saying.

"They are excited. They want to know what you mean."

I dig into my purse for the map. They look alarmed, as though I might be pulling out a gun.

I spread the map on the table. It's of Europe; Hungary and the new countries carved out of Yugoslavia are included somewhat theoretically and incompletely at the right edge. "Tell them to show me where home is."

She tells them, and they peer eagerly at the map, point at the letters that say Bosnia and Herzegovina. "Tell them to show me more exactly," I say.

She does, and their broad-tipped fingers press hard at the map. I have to nudge them out of the way to see they have pointed to a town about a hundred kilometres from Sarajevo.

"Gornja-Grabovica?" I say.

They nod excitedly, say the name again and again, make me say it again and again until my pronunciation is better. They prod at the spot on the paper as though there were something alive there they want to make move.

"They actually come from a smaller village, too small to show on this map. Gornja-Grabovica is just the closest town."

Then Anna points to a large city on the map, this one closer than Sarajevo.

"Mostar," she says. "You have heard of Mostar."

And because she is not making it a question I realize that I must have. Mostar: ethnic cleansing, mass murders, rapes, genocide.

I point back to Gornja-Grabovica. "Ask them if ... their home, their house, is still there."

"Of course it's still there," Anna says. "Someone else took it. The same people who killed their daughter and their grandchildren."

I feel such shame, standing here in my incomprehension, my easy history. Losing David seems altogether different from the kind of devastation they have endured.

"I thought ... people can now legally reclaim the homes they were evicted from."

Anna snorts. "Why would they want to go back to a place where such horrible things happened? Would *you* want to?"

"I don't know. Maybe. I think the Karolyis do."

Anna shrugs.

"Ask them if ... if there is anyone else there, any family, any friend, they could contact if they went back. Perhaps someone in Sarajevo. Someone to help them. If they went back."

Anna asks them, translates the man's reply: there is still a sister in the village and a cousin in Sarajevo; the Karolyis have had a few letters from them. Then she adds, perhaps her words, perhaps his, I'm not sure: "But what difference does it make? The flights are far too expensive."

"Tell them —" And I take a deep breath, because I know once I say this I will not be able to take back the words. "Tell them I will get them the tickets. Tell them they must be ready to go on very short notice."

Anna looks at me for a while before answering. "You know what you're promising? The church people want nothing more to do with them, I told you. Who's going to pay for this?"

"I am."

She laughs. "You're crazy. There's easier ways to get them out of the house."

"Just tell them, please. Say I'll provide them tickets to Sarajevo. There'll be a transfer in Frankfurt, but I'll make it as simple as possible. And I'll give them six hundred Euros to help them when they get there.

But the offer isn't for the son. He's on his own. And they had better not tell him anything about this."

She shrugs, but it belies the obvious level of interest in her now. Her conversation with the Karolyis is long and animated, but at last she turns to me and says, "They think there is ... something fishy. A string attached. They think maybe your company is doing something illegal with this house and so you want to get them out of the way. Maybe this is a bribe."

I laugh. Given what they have endured I suppose their distrust is only logical. I can't help feeling annoyed, though. Perhaps I expected them to fall to their knees and kiss my feet and weep with joy. But I can't change my mind because they are not properly grateful.

"But they did say they wanted to go?"

"Yes."

"Well ... good. I'll make the reservations. Tell them as soon as I know the day I'll come by and give them the time I'll pick them up. I hope they'll be able to understand."

"I can write a sentence down for you. You can fill in the time. We have to make sure there's nothing fishy." She gives me a smile that could mean anything.

When I drive home I'm surprised that I am not feeling better about this. I suppose I *had* expected gratitude, but if that were my only motive it serves me right that I didn't get it. Maybe I'm worrying that I am simply sending the Karolyis back to a worse place. I admit I'm also nervous about what Avey will say when I tell him what happened to my commission for selling the house. It will just cover the cost of the tickets.

At home I send an email to Sandy telling her what I've done. I suspect she will abruptly cease being proud of me and will be horrified, will think that I will soon be easy prey for televangelists, that this is the onset of Alzheimer's. I have read how the sufferers from that disease, when asked where they are going on their endless, restless walks, answer "home." Perhaps I have a variation; I want to send others home. Alzheimer's-by-proxy.

Hale, I realize, might be the only one to understand. The thought isn't a comfortable one. It would probably never have occurred to me to send the Karolyis home if it hadn't been for Hale and his way of wanting everything to stay where it belonged.

I'm heading into the kitchen to replenish my coffee when the phone rings.

"Hello, Kate?"

I catch my breath, feel a prickling in my neck. It's as though my thoughts have conjured him.

"Hello, Hale."

"I want to see you one more time. I'm leaving tomorrow. But I have something to give you."

"Oh, Hale. We've said our goodbyes. This isn't a good idea."

"Somewhere public. I don't want you to be afraid."

And I suppose it's the challenge in those words that makes me sigh and say, "All right. But I'm quite busy now. It can't be for long."

"Perhaps at the same bench, then? By the planetarium? In half an hour?"

I have something to give you. As I reach for my jacket I begin, in spite of myself, to speculate on what that could be.

I decide to drive instead of walk to the planetarium because the day has turned cold and blustery, rain coming down in unpleasant, thick spasms. I think of the rain in Hilo, which I learned to like and which might have been unexpected but was always warm. Here it is expected but rarely warm, and I have never learned to like it. A few days ago, leafing through an astronomy magazine of Avey's, I paused on an item about how some brown dwarfs have dust clouds that settle in the atmosphere around alkali metals, a process called "iron rain." It's a good term for Vancouver's winter.

One of the prerequisites for being a realtor is finding parking in impossible places, and I am able to squeeze into one so small a man on the sidewalk actually congratulates me. I'm early, but Hale is already standing at the park bench, hunched and shivering, without an umbrella. So of course I have to suggest we go somewhere inside.

We find a small Indian restaurant on Fourth Avenue and I order some chai for both of us. Hale has never tried it, and I can tell he doesn't find it pleasant, but he smiles and says it's interesting. I remember the kava he gave me to drink when we went up to see the volcano: "interesting" was probably the euphemism I used, too.

He seems so miserable, still shaking with cold and damp, that I am barely able to resist suggesting we go to my house where he can dry off.

Looking at him I can feel a tolerant fondness for him, affection even.

He laces his fingers around his cup: I remember those hands on me when we made love. My body quickens with the adrenaline pulse of desire. It frightens me so much I want to jump up and run. I close my eyes, make myself think about the trip to Mauna Kea and what he did to me there. That puts a chill on the pulse of desire. In fact, when I open my eyes I think crabbily, yes, he deserves to sit here for a while shivering with cold.

"So," I say, "you're going home tomorrow."

"Yes. My holiday is over."

"I hope you got to see some of the city. The weather wasn't the best."

"I took a bus tour. I saw some friends." He gives me a smile that seems a little coy.

"I should thank you — or blame you — for your advice about the Bosnian couple. I decided to send them home. Now of course I'm wondering if that was a mistake."

"Your company is paying for the tickets?"

"No. I am."

He raises an eyebrow. "That's very generous. Perhaps you can buy me a ticket to come out here again."

I laugh, tell myself he wasn't serious. But just to be sure he doesn't misunderstand my laughter I say, "The point was to send them home, not on a holiday."

He shrugs. I don't know what that means.

I've almost finished my chai. Hale has hardly touched his. I'm wondering how long I have to wait to find out what it is he has to give me. It's not something large, not something he can't carry in a pocket.

Two young, small Asian men come into the restaurant and take the table beside us. They're laden with books and notepads, and they don't say a word to each other before they spread their books and papers onto the table and begin to work. The one closest to me is ambidextrous, writing with one hand and using a yellow highlighter with the other. The waiter, without asking, brings them coffee. There is something embarrassing about such focused and private labour in a public place, and I feel like a voyeur. But they are a distraction from waiting for Hale to speak.

"What I have to give you," he says at last, "is information."
My eyes snap back to him. "Yes?"
"Twelve years ago, in Hilo, Avey and I made a ... bargain."
"Bargain? What bargain?"
And he tells me.

He tells me Avey stole his discovery from Bruno's computer. He tells
me why Avey insisted I go up to the observatory.

Hale's words hit me like a succession of blows. I feel a lurch of nausea,
that struggle of mind with body to make sense of what is happening. I
stare dumbly at Hale. He is lying. He must be. What he's told me is too
bizarre. Avey is ambitious, but he has his limits. He wouldn't have stolen
Bruno's work. He wouldn't have ... *sold* me like that. It's ridiculous.

"You may think you don't believe me," Hale says. "But deep down
you do."

I swallow. I can taste the chai coming back up from my stomach.
Under the table I clench the fingers of my left hand, hard, so that the
nails cut into my palm, and I concentrate on that pain. But the longer I
wait the more the pain does the opposite of what I want. It sends itself
slowly up along my nerves, jumps easily across synapses, and whispers
that it could be the truth.

I can't let Hale see how he's shaken me.

"That's an incredible story." I try to keep my voice cool, calm. "But
it, well, it doesn't really make sense to me. I don't mean just about Avey.
Why would you have deceived Bruno like that, risking your job? After
I'd told you several times there could be nothing more between us."

"I suppose I was still hoping this bargain would make something
possible. You kept telling me it ... was only because Avey would be hurt
that you couldn't continue. So if you could see that it didn't really matter
to him ..." He lifts one shoulder, gestures with an open hand, a shrug.

I *did* use being married as my excuse. I shudder.

"I don't mean to blame you," Hale says. "This was all my own ...
scheme. Of course it was about you, but it was also because ... Avey
interested me. For himself, not just because he was your husband. He
had such ... need. Maybe I wanted to see how far he would go."

"That's very puppetmaster of you."

He smiles, as though I've complimented him. "Maybe I also wanted
to see ... how far *I* would go."

I think of us on the mountain, feel the cold trickle down my neck. *See how far* I *would go.* With me as well as with Avey, I assume he means.

"If this is all true, why are you telling me now?" I release my finger-nails from my palm, which has gone numb as wax.

"I wanted to prepare you. Avey went to Hilo because I made him go. To confess to Bruno. There will likely be ... repercussions."

Eleven

*The fate of human civilization will depend on
whether the rockets of the future carry the
astronomer's telescope or a hydrogen bomb.*
— BERNARD LOVELL, *British astronomer*

AVEY

As I head up the walk to Bruno's house my feet feel as though they're
plodding through freshly poured concrete. I'm dead man walking. Behind that door is the end of my life.

I can feel my lips moving, some whimpery prayer to whatever cosmic chef has cooked up my particular postmordial soup today: *Save me,
save me, save me, and I'll be good, I swear from now on I'll be good.* Yeah,
sure. I can still hear Bruno quoting Ambrose Bierce to Louisa about
how prayer is a request that the laws of the universe be annulled for one
petitioner confessedly unworthy.

I slow down, look at the tangled thicket of hibiscus in the front garden. It's bigger than I remember and dense with yellow blossoms. The
flowers last only one day, opening yellow and slowly withering into a
dark orange by the evening. *Sic transit gloria.* I stare at them as though
they will be the last natural thing I see before I'm blindfolded and
strapped into the chair.

I run my hand hard back and forth across my face as if I'm holding soap and a washcloth, which, now that I think of it, I forgot to use
this morning. I didn't shave, either, and when my hand rubs over the
stubble it drags the skin around. I might be growing quills. I drop my
hand, hope my face will settle back into place. Even my teeth feel loose.

I shuttle my jaw back and forth a few times, trying to match up the tops and bottoms again. Something gastric burps up into my mouth.

The purple bougainvillea along the walk is heavily overgrown, and when I trudge up the steps its thorns scratch at my legs. I can see a thin line of blood on my knee. It's right on the darkened patch of skin that seems to have been permanently tattooed with the ground-in dirt from my bicycle accident outside the JAC. For a long time whenever I looked at my knee I had to remember everything that happened that day. Now it's bleeding again. Some kind of stigmata.

Bruno opens the door before I can knock.

His old baggy body is a lot more trim now, and he looks good. I remember only at the last second not to comment on it because of course the weight loss would be because of his AIDS. He's wearing floppy khakis and a faded Toronto Blue Jays T-shirt I think I recognize from the old days.

"Avey," he says, grinning. He holds out his hand and then turns the gesture into a hug. One of us smells bad. Probably me. I stand there in his embrace like some rotting log, and by the time I realize I should return his hug, that he'll think my stiffness is because I'm afraid of his disease, it's too late; he's drawn back.

"Bruno," I say, trying to make up for it in my voice. I almost succeed. I almost *am* glad to see him.

"So, it was great to hear you were in town," he says, standing aside and ushering me in. "You been up to the JAC yet?"

"Not yet."

The house is a snarl of half-packed boxes and furniture pushed into corners. The floor is littered with papers, and the dust balls are so big and dense we could take them outside and play catch. A sandy grit crunches under my sandals. But it's not just the usual chaos of moving; the whole place is dirty and rundown and smells of neglect and mildew. The pale grey living room carpet has two large stains in the middle and dark spatter-pattern spills at the entrance to the kitchen. The wall behind the sofa has a similar spray of stains, in varying shades of yellow, as though the previous resident had used it for target practice with fluids about which I'd rather not speculate. A railing is broken from the elegant spiral staircase where I remember cornering Dr. Schultz from U of C to suck up for a job. In the wall beside it is a fist-sized hole.

"It's a mess, isn't it?" Bruno looks sadly around. "It was such a beautiful house. But the last renters were pigs. I should have done a cleanup before I put it up for sale. But you know how it is, just not enough time."

"Yeah."

"So, sit down. Thank God the new owners bought most of the furniture, too. Don't know what I'd have done with it otherwise. There's actually not a whole lot I've got to ship home." He nudges aside a pillow on which someone has scribbled with a blue felt marker. "I've got some iced tea in the fridge. Want a glass?"

"Sure, that'd be great."

I sit down in one of the armchairs, which swivels so I can look out at Puhio Bay. The big sliding door open onto the lanai has a crack running diagonally all the way through it. Looking at it, I can feel tears pushing at my eyes, goddamned tears, because of a crack in the glass.

Bruno hands me the tea in a mug with a chip out of the rim. "Sorry," he says. "Couldn't find any glasses."

"Thanks." I take a sip. There's no sugar in it. I set it down on an end table that has had circles bitten into it right through the varnish. There's a saucer there with a stub of cigarette, and I recognize then the faint odour in the air: not tobacco, but marijuana. Oh, right: AIDS. Grass is supposed to help with the nausea and loss of appetite.

"So you heard the news?" Bruno asks.

"What news?"

"The new planet. You haven't heard? It was announced this morning. The first Earth-like planet. Small, rocky, and in that magical habitable zone."

"No kidding." In spite of myself, I feel that lurch of excitement. The first new Earth. Another one of us. "Which system?"

"In Libra. Gliese 581."

"That's among the hundred closest to the Earth."

"Yeah," Bruno says. "They'll be selling real estate there in a few months."

"Marcy and Butler found it, I assume."

"Nope. Another Swiss team."

"The *Swiss?* Again? The Americans must be pissed off."

"Well, I'm just glad I'm not running around after all that anymore,"

Bruno says.

I'm eager to agree. "For sure. A moment of glory and then it's on to find the next new thing — the first biological markers, the first life, the first intelligent life, the first blue-eyed Aryans, whatever."

"Yeah, well. Our reach should exceed our grasp and all that."

"Still, after 51 Pegasi B you'd have thought it would really *mean* something to the world, in some long-term way, wow, another planet out there, but except for astronomers and a few theologians who really cared? Kate showed me an article in *Time* called '80 Days That Changed the World,' choosing events from the last eight decades, and the first exoplanet discoveries didn't make the list."

"What kind of things did?"

"You won't believe it. These are things that changed the *world*, remember. Only three events in the 1995-1998 period did make the cut: first, the O.J. Simpson verdict; second, the death of Princess Diana; and, third, the FDA approval for Viagra."

"The first planets outside our solar system not as profound as Viagra." Bruno laughs, shakes his head.

"Puts things into perspective, I guess."

The *Time* anecdote is true, but I shouldn't have gone on about it. I've been too obvious. Now my confession will be even worse because it'll seem I've tried to manipulate him into thinking how unimportant it all is.

Bruno stretches his arms up over his head. "So. Twelve years since we were the big planet hunters. Seems like yesterday. And here we are. All grown up now."

"Bruno." I clear my throat. *Tell* him. I cross my legs, lace my fingers over the top knee, pull it a little towards me. I probably look as though I'm in pain.

He sits down opposite me. "Avey." He raises his cup in a toast. His mug has only half a handle.

There's a thud in the kitchen. We both jump. Then a tall orange and white cat walks out past us, casually, its tail straight up and with a curl at the end as though it might have just fallen from a hook in the cupboard. It strolls out onto the lanai and trots down the steps into the garden.

Bruno looks after it, his eyebrows raised. "I guess that's where my second fried egg went this morning."

"At least it was more willing to leave than the mongoose. Remember the mongoose?"

Bruno hoots. "God, yes. That was one determined weasel."

Then there's someone at the door.

"Ah, hell," Bruno says, getting up. "It's probably the guys I'm giving the dining room set to. They were supposed to have come hours ago."

He lets them in, two big native Hawaiians he seems to know. They joke about a trip in a van they all took to Kailua-Kona on the other side of the island. I don't want to have to meet them, to be introduced as an old friend whose name Bruno doesn't yet know is Judas, so I go out onto the lanai, stare past the mango tree into the huge ocean. There's a warm breeze off the water, and the air smells of plumeria. This is paradise, of course.

One of my professors at U of A told me once, after I'd aced a particularly vicious exam, "You'll go far, Fleming."

Yeah. All the way to hell.

I should have done something else with my life. I shouldn't have gone to university at all, let alone become a prof at one. The truth is that half of us there are crazy and the other half are afraid they soon will be. The hallways of every university I've ever been at smell of paranoia and thwarted ambition and unfinished term papers. I'm always after Kate about how she's squandered her intelligence, but maybe that's why she's a better person than I am. I should have become a realtor like her, selling something concrete, something where the stakes and the moral dilemmas would be smaller. But then her Bosnians were a moral dilemma for her. I remember how unsympathetic I must have sounded. How unsympathetic I *was*. The poor buggers, out on the street. Unlike me, they did nothing to deserve that.

Ah. Was that a moment of actual empathy? Now that I'm about to lose everything, too, am I going to learn humility and charity and compassion? Is this an epiphany?

I think about that for a moment. It's the way it's supposed to happen, the way it happens in the movies. I suffer, I learn, I become a better person. Or does it need the *deus ex machina*? I close my eyes, squint up at the mango tree, look for divine intervention. Ah, yes, there's God, sitting in one of the upper branches, looking a lot like Patrick Stewart on the starship Enterprise, and he leans his aristocratic Sistine-Chapel forefinger my way and says, "Make it so."

I glance across from the mango tree to the window above me, where Louisa and I had stood having our stiff little talk about religion. She was saying something about how quantum mechanics was strengthening her faith. But now her sister is dead and the face God has turned to her is too cruel or indifferent so she's turned her own face away. It seems so damned sad suddenly, all of it, God, too, of course. Even if he *could* look like Patrick Stewart. Even if he *could* make small, rocky planets in the habitable zone, the Goldilocks zone, not too hot, not too cold, just right.

The thudding and banging in the house seem to be over, and then I hear Bruno say, "*Mahalo*, guys," and shut the door.

I give the mango tree one last prelapsarian look and go back inside.

"Sorry about that," Bruno says. "But they said when I next come to town they'll serve me a dinner at my old table. They saw you on the lanai and said I could bring my friend." He grins, drops himself onto the sofa.

I'd rather not sit down again, but since Bruno has I pretty well have to. I swivel my chair to face him.

"When you hear what I have to tell you, you're not going to ever call me that again."

"Call you what?"

"A friend." I lick my lips. The saliva on my tongue feels like glue.

"Uh-oh. Sounds serious." He doesn't seem worried. He leans back, props his bare feet up onto one of the boxes. I can see farther up the legs of his shorts than I want to.

"It's about ... the planet. You know. Finding the planet. The brown dwarf."

"Yeah?"

I swallow. *Spit it out, boy.* My father standing over me, slapping the back of one hand into the palm of the other, crack, crack, extorting whatever confession from me that day that he wanted.

"I ... did something so shitty. Unbelievably shitty. It was your computer, your program, that found the curve. I walked in and saw it. And then I just, I just panicked. I didn't know what I was doing. I saw it and, like some greedy kid, I grabbed it. I didn't think. Suddenly I was down there on the floor unplugging your computer. I talked Hale into taking the blame. The discovery was yours. I stole it."

And then I'm crying. I sit there with my face scrunching up and going wet and stupid, blubbery noises coming out of it. It's over, my whole screwed-up life is over, and I can't blame anybody but myself. This is what grief is. And shame. Shame, shame, shame.

It takes me a while to hear the other sound in the room. It takes me a while longer to identify it.

It's laughter.

I squint an eye open, shove the back of my hand across it to wipe away the wetness and bring Bruno into focus. He's sitting there with his head back and these roaring bursts of laughter coming out of him. It shocks the crying right out of me. How can he be sitting there laughing? He should be in the kitchen finding a knife to stab me.

Finally he gasps, "Well, of course I suspected as much."

"I'm sorry, I'm so damned sorry, Bruno —"

He's still laughing. He wipes at his eyes with a paper towel he picks up off the floor.

"Did you ever wonder," he says, "how my fucked-up program was able to produce such a perfect data display?"

I stare at him.

Jesus Christ.

"You used my program modifications."

Bruno takes his feet down from the box, one heel catching it and tipping it onto its side. There's a rattle of cutlery.

"I knew I wasn't keeping up with you," Bruno says. "There was some kind of hiccup in the program and when I tried to fix it I just made it worse. So I went in one night and downloaded your program and began to use it. Worked like a dream."

"So — shit — let me get this straight. I've lived with this dark secret on my conscience all these years, and you're telling me that basically I just stole back what you stole from me in the first place?"

"I suppose so, more or less."

"Jesus. Jesus." I leap up, stride around the room. My feelings are all over the place: confusion, anger, relief, and complicated compounds of all of these that make me want to start crying again, or screaming, or punching something. I pick up a half-burned round candle from the bookcase and toss the thing back and forth in my hands, hard enough that it hurts.

"Except, of course," Bruno points out, "you were the one to get all the benefit."

"But if you'd walked in before me that day and seen the curve first, you'd have been the one to get all the benefit, right?"

Bruno pulls his mouth over to one side, squints an eye half-closed. "I suppose so."

I stop my pacing, lean against the wall with the fist-hole in it. There's a kind of denouement silence in the room. Bruno and I can't quite look at each other; our gazes when they meet skid quickly off each other.

But something has been precipitating out from my muddle of emotions, and it makes my knees literally go weak. I press my back harder against the wall. What I'm realizing is that Bruno's not going to expose me.

I've been given my life back. Just like that.

Finally Bruno says, "Remember what Kruschev said to his son about the space program in 1961? He said, 'We have nothing to hide. We have nothing, and we must hide it.'"

"Except you and I did have something. We had the planet."

"The brown dwarf, you mean," Bruno says.

"Well, for a little while it was a planet."

"Yeah."

"We could have agreed right at the beginning to work together, you know," I say.

"I didn't think you'd want that."

"I suppose I didn't."

Bruno crumples up the paper towel he wiped his face with and throws it toward the garbage can by the entrance to the kitchen. He misses by a good two feet.

"You can see why I'd never win a pissing contest," he says.

"If the pressure's great enough maybe you would."

"Yeah, well. It would still just be piss in a garbage can." He gets up, retrieves the paper towel, drops it into the can, comes back and sits down. "By the way. Just curious, but why now? I mean, why come to tell me all this stuff now, twelve years after the fact?"

I consider several evasive answers, but since the truth has served me well enough today I decide to trust it some more. "Hale came to see me.

He said I had to tell you or he would."

"Hale? Interesting."

"He said that at some reunion party you asked him about what had happened. He said it was obviously something you were still brooding about."

"Ah." Bruno taps a finger on his chin. "I was just trying to needle him. I'd always thought his story about accidentally unplugging the computer was more than a little suspect. That's why I was so annoyed with him then. Though I might have exaggerated that a bit."

"Exaggerated? Why?"

Bruno uses the finger at his chin to push his jaw first one way, then the other, as though he's trying to decide which side has the answer he will give me. Finally he says, "Well, I had to look upset, right? Especially after you made your big announcement. If not for Hale's bungling it would probably have been me to make the discovery, right? The truth is that I was relieved."

"Relieved." I had tried telling myself at the time that was what he might actually feel, but I could never convince myself of something so conveniently exculpatory. "You were that sick of looking?"

"Well, that, too, but what I mean is that I was relieved it wasn't *me* who made the discovery."

"Huh?"

"Think about it. If it had been me, how could I have explained my program modifications? *Your* modifications. I hadn't a clue how they worked. But they were brilliant."

"Thank you."

"Plus, well, I'd have felt too guilty. Aforementioned dark secret and all that."

"So I'm the one who got to push that rock up the hill all these years."

Bruno shrugs. "Maybe we both got what we wanted."

"I could have done without the guilt part. I could have done without the Hale part."

"How did you get him to take the rap for you, anyway?"

Should I tell him? But maybe Bruno's just playing with me. Maybe he knows exactly what happened. "It's ... a tad sordid. He sort of had this thing for Kate. He said that if I ... encouraged her to see him he'd take the blame for what I did."

"'Encouraged her to see him?'" Bruno's eyebrows twitch up. "That sounds euphemistic for, you know. For pimping her."

I wince. *Pimping.* Nervy of him.

"I know it sounds horrible," I say. "But I don't think he was intending anything, well, coercive. He just wanted to see her. I wasn't selling her into sexual bondage or something."

"Still."

"I was desperate. I mean, he comes in and sees me crouching under your desk with the cord in my hand and panic sweating out of every pore. I'd have hacked off a testicle if he'd asked me to."

"Just one?"

"The bigger one," I say.

"So what happened with him and Kate?"

"I don't know, really. He took her up to the observatory, and she was upset when she came back. I guess I was afraid to ask what happened."

Bruno shakes his head. "You don't deserve her, man."

"I know." .

"So why is Hale coming after you after all these years?"

"Some attack of conscience of his own, I guess," I say. "He thinks I've cheated you out of your rightful fame and glory. And now that you're, you know, sick, he wants me to make it right."

"Sick?"

"Yeah. You know."

"I don't, actually. I'm not sick."

"Yeah, but ... you know. The HIV. The AIDS."

Bruno gapes at me. "What the hell is he playing at? Does he think I have AIDS? I don't have AIDS."

"You don't?"

"No. I don't."

"Well, Jeez, that's a relief." I hope he knows I'm sincere when I say that. I gesture at the joint in the saucer. "So this is just ..."

It takes him a moment. "Oh. Just housecleaning. Found it, smoked it. So your confession wasn't exactly to someone on his deathbed. Sorry about that."

I suppose I deserved that. "I'd have told you regardless. Hale didn't leave me any choice. The AIDS thing, hell, I don't know why he had to add that. You'd have to pry open his warped brain to ask him."

"Maybe he thinks all gay people have AIDS."

"I don't think he's that dumb."

"Probably not. I always thought he was smarter than he wanted people to think." Bruno smiles. "Wasn't he beautiful, though? My God."

"He's not anymore. He wouldn't turn any heads now. Though you might. You look pretty good." That sounded sucky, but what the hell, it's the truth. I'll have to hope Bruno feels good about himself these days — flattery is supposed to work when it agrees with the person's self-assessment. Maybe that's why I was flattered when Bruno called my program modifications brilliant.

He grins. "I've dropped a few pounds."

I pat my stomach. "I've dropped a few, too. Just not far enough."

It feels good, this bantering. Like the old days.

"So if Hale's in Vancouver now," Bruno says, "and he's sent you off here — do you think that might have been some convoluted scheme to get you out of the way so he could see Kate again?"

"That's too Byzantine even for him."

"I dunno. Two birds with one stone."

"You really think so? You think he could be there hitting on Kate?"

"Well, it does seem to have motivated him before. Maybe you should call her, give her a heads-up."

"I suppose. Shit. Who knows what he's told her. You don't think she could be in any kind of, you know, danger?"

"Unlikely, but ..." Bruno nods toward the phone sitting on the arm of the sofa. "Call her. I think it's still working."

I sit down, pick it up, punch in the numbers. My hands are sweating; I wipe them on my shorts. Just when I think it's over there's something else to worry about.

I'm hoping to get the machine, to leave a message where I won't have to explain anything, but Kate answers on the first ring.

"Hi," I say. "It's me."

"Hi, Avey."

"I shouldn't talk long, I'm using Bruno's phone, but I thought I should tell you that Hale's in Vancouver, and, I dunno, it just dawned on me that he might try to get in touch so I thought I should, well, warn you."

"Warn me?"

"Well, yeah. I forgot to tell you before I left that he dropped by the office. Sorry. I was rushing around so much. Just, well, you know how he liked you, and now that Bruno and I got talking I thought, hey, it's possible he'll try to contact you so I should tell you he's there ..."

I sit listening for longer than I expect to the static crackle of the Pacific in my ear. I suppose she's wondering what the hell I'm going on about, but at least that means she hasn't heard from Hale.

"Oh," she says at last. "Well, thanks for the warning." She pauses. "How was the telescope?"

"The telescope." My mind is blank.

"The emergency with the telescope. The reason you went to Hilo."

"Oh, that, that. Of course. It's fine. Turned out to be nothing, really."

"I see." She pauses again, and I'm just thinking I'd better embellish my lie when she says, "So what else is new?"

"New. Well, Bruno just told me the Swiss have found the first Earth-like exoplanet. The Swiss again, can you believe it? So that's rather exciting."

"I guess." She doesn't sound too excited. "So you're at Bruno's. How's he?"

"Great, couldn't be better."

Bruno is heading to the kitchen carrying his empty glass. "Hiya, Kate," he shouts at the phone as he walks by.

"Hear that?"

"Yes. Tell him hello back."

"Hello back," I tell Bruno. He makes a kissing sound toward the phone. "All rightie," I say to her. "Gotta go. See you tomorrow."

KATE

"See you tomorrow."

I sit there so long holding the receiver that the beeps come on, and even then it takes a lot of energy for me to hang up.

Twelve years ago, in Hilo, Avey and I made a bargain.

Maybe I should have told Avey that I'd seen Hale, should have told him what Hale said. But all I did was listen to Avey's voice, waiting to hear in it some implicit denials, some reason to make me think Hale had been lying. Instead I heard Avey say he had seen Hale in Vancouver and had somehow forgotten to tell me; I heard him sound puzzled when I asked about the emergency with the telescope, allegedly the whole purpose of his trip. And he'd gone to see Bruno. Both of them sounded cheerful, though: probably Avey hadn't yet confessed. Maybe the call to me was just procrastination, or a way of reminding Bruno he has a wife Bruno had liked, or a way of making Hale sound dangerous and unstable.

I kept telling myself that Hale was wrong, that he had, at best, misunderstood. I kept telling myself, yes, Avey is thoughtless and greedy sometimes, but basically he is honest, and he loves me, of course he wouldn't trade me to Hale for some advantage at work, no matter how important.

But now I have to face it.

I believe Hale. What he told me is a stone thrown into the pool of the past, the ripples changing everything, the reflections broken and twisted. Avey comes home with his jubilant discovery: but he has stolen it from Bruno. Avey insists I go see the telescope with Hale: but this is nothing generous, nothing thoughtful, this is me being sold.

Twelve years ago, in Hilo, Avey and I made a bargain.

I sit there for a long time, staring dully at a long-legged spider moving slowly across the carpet. The cat sees it, too, goes into an intent crouch, springs. The spider is gone.

Avey's cat. I look at him with loathing.

I walk around and around the house, and everything my eyes land on fills me with loathing, too. What Hale told me is everywhere, triumphing like vision over blindness. All Avey and I have was stolen from Bruno. It was never my house. I'm just another bit of the furniture. I can be traded for something better. To Avey I am weak and passive and disposable, useful only the way a pencil is to his hand.

I thought I had known Avey at his worst and still managed to love him. Perhaps that was because I was sure he loved me, needed me, would be lost without me. Serves me right, then.

I don't know how to be this angry. All my life I have flattened out what would have been such anger, have worn the smoother personality people would like.

The cat comes and presses himself against my leg, gives an ingenuous little meow. It has nothing to do with affection, I tell myself; that's a conceit people allow themselves. I am just property that has gone outside and must be repatriated. I push him away, hard enough that he topples over, and he stares at me. I am not like that, he remembers.

I see myself in the small hall mirror and my face is strange, my hair at odd angles, my eyes large and saying something loud and shrill because my lips are pressed too tightly together for speech. I lean my face against the mirror. My breath fogs it up. I disappear.

I have an urge to phone Hale, to tell him ... I don't know what. To thank him for the truth? To say, let's sleep together before you leave, let's give Avey what he wanted, what he paid for, what you paid for? It's a good thing Hale would have checked out of his hotel by now. Besides, it's hardly gratitude I owe him. I don't understand any of what he's done, really, but then I never expected to understand Hale. With Avey, on the other hand, I thought I had held the fabric of his nature up to the light and seen him clearly: not just the strong weave of him but the worn places, the patched and frayed places, the blunt and chafing corners. I remember how, before we were married, I had thought: how honest he is, this man who will not even pay me a compliment because a compliment is flattery instead of truth. I suppose it's my own misjudgement that makes me feel so betrayed now.

Of course this is my fault, too. If I hadn't slept with Hale in the first place he wouldn't have wanted to make his absurd bargain. If I blame Avey for treachery and deceit I also have to blame myself. Neither of us has been honest.

I sit down at the computer and load a word game I play to relax, but the game gives me too many words with a C in them, and it's a game where you have to make as many two-letter words as possible, and there are no two-letter words with C. *No more moves*, the game says, *no more moves*.

I realize suddenly that I'm late picking up the Karolyis. After all my elaborate planning the last thing I need is to have them miss their flight. Anna had written down a message for me in Bosnian, leaving me only to fill in the time I would pick them up, and when I left the note for them last night they seemed to understand. Mrs. Karolyi even laughed, nodding and exclaiming eagerly, when I made flying motions with my arms and pointed at Sarajevo on the map.

When I get to the house they are ready and waiting, standing on the back doorstep with two ancient, brown suitcases wrapped around with duct tape because the clasps have broken off. I will have to hope any security checks inside the bags will involve replacing the tape. I'm relieved not to see the son anywhere.

"*Dobar Dan,*" I say.

They answer me at much greater length, and I have to put my hands up and smile and shake my head.

We're just putting the suitcases into the trunk when I hear another voice, words in Bosnian, and I jump, banging my head on the trunk lid. The son, I think in a panic. He's found us and will refuse to let us leave —

But when I whirl around it's Anna I see. I put my hand on my heart, say, "Oh! You scared me."

"Sorry."

"You didn't have to come," I say. She must have been in touch with the Karolyis to find out when they were leaving. I'm wondering if she's expecting to be paid for this visit.

She shrugs. "I thought I'd see them through the airport mess. It gets confusing."

"Well," I say. "Thanks." If she were expecting payment surely she would have said something about a fee. Her generosity perks up my spirits a bit.

There is some confusion about who will sit where in the car, Anna trying with surprising vehemence to put Mrs. Karolyi in the front seat, but the woman keeps shaking her head and gets in the back with Anna so her husband can sit in the front. As I drive, the three of them carry on a loud and excited conversation. Twice Mr. Karolyi hits me on the shoulder as he gestures ardently through the space between our front seats. He pats my shoulder, says something lengthy that Anna translates as, "He apologizes."

The lineup to check in is long and slow, but the Karolyis seem not to mind; they point at things around them and talk to Anna, who has stopped bothering to translate anything for me. Only when we are heading to the boarding gates does she turn to me and say, "They're worried because both their bags have been taken."

"Oh. When we checked in, you mean. But you explained to them —"

"Yes, yes, of course. But I guess they expected to have one of them on the plane. They brought Aspirins, apparently, since someone told them it helps with blood pressure or something on flights, and now they've lost them."

"That's a shame. Too bad we didn't know." We are passing through the food court, and I point to a stand selling toiletries. "I'll pick up some for them. Go ahead — I'll meet you at the security gates."

Anna leads the Karolyis off down the corridor as I buy the packets of Aspirin. It takes me only a minute, but by then they are almost out of sight. I run to catch up.

And it's then I understand why Anna has really come.

She is holding out her hand and Mr. Karolyi is putting into it the six hundred Euros I gave him last night. From the tightness of the paper band I put around the bundle I can tell none of the bills have been removed.

We are near the security check now, beyond which only passengers can go, and people are crowding together, jostling and hugging and saying goodbye.

I grab Anna's arm. "Give it back," I say.

She whirls and stares, startled to see me right behind her, but it takes her only a moment to recover. The hand with the money shoots into her pocket.

"This is none of your business," she hisses.

"Of course it's my business. You're stealing their money!" I make no effort to lower my voice. Making a scene is the only chance I've got.

"I made a deal with them. My brother in Sarajevo is going to drive them to their village."

"Karolyi has a cousin there who's going to look after them. They don't need your so-called help. It's extortion. Give the money back."

"This is none of your business. You don't know how things are done there. My brother will protect them."

"Give the money back."

She says something then to the Karolyis and they look at me with frightened eyes. What has she said? I am powerless to contradict, to reassure.

"It's all right," I tell them helplessly. My words seem only to alarm them more. They press against each other, clutch each other's arms in that terrible, frightened way they did when I first saw them.

"It's all right," I tell them again, but my voice falters; my voice sounds anything but all right.

When I turn to Anna, to make some final appeal, she is gone. I look frantically around but she has disappeared into the crowd.

People are jostling us impatiently closer and closer to the security gates, and all I can do is thrust the packets of Aspirin at the Karolyis. They look at them suspiciously.

"You were right," I say. "It helps the blood, it helps stop blood clots."

I realize even as I say it that not only don't they understand me but that the whole question of the Aspirins was likely just invented by Anna to get me out of the way. She had probably planned to collect the money in the car but was thwarted by being seated beside the one who wasn't carrying it. I smile at the Karolyis, but they don't trust me, I can see it in their faces, Anna has told them not to trust me. They don't take the Aspirins. And then they are pushed forward to the front of the line; someone is examining their boarding passes and someone else is pointing them toward the security check. They don't look back.

Miserably, I watch until they are out of sight. There is nothing I can do but walk away.

I find myself heading not toward the exit doors but down the long concourse of the international terminal. I go past the food court and the huge green Bill Reid sculpture, past the US airline counters at the end. When I reach the wall I stare at it for a few minutes, then press my fingertips against it in a way that probably looks stuporously jet-lagged.

I know I should start home before the rush hour starts, but the thought of being in the house fills me with such aversion that I sit down instead in one of the hard plastic chairs and close my eyes, listen to the confusion of sounds around me. Someone behind me is playing a video game that makes harsh, repetitive noises, and I try to focus on it, as though I can make it be music.

Finally I make myself get up and start walking back down the corridor. A JAL flight is boarding. A few of the passengers are wearing white surgical masks that cover their mouths and noses. A man pushing a luggage cart into the long lineup hits me in the ankle with it. I stumble against his suitcase. He says something to me in a language I don't know, and it could be apology or it could be accusation. Even when I look at his face, his expression tells me nothing. He says something else. I still don't understand.

Twelve

*The distinction between past, present and future is
only an illusion, however persistent.*

— ALBERT EINSTEIN

AVEY

"You're in a good mood today, Fleming."

It's Cheswick, from Mathematics. Not my favourite mad scientist, but I give him a collegial nod as I hold the door for him at the Faculty Club.

"I am, rather," I say. "Feeling expansive. Like the universe."

"I hear the Swiss have found that Earth-like planet you lot have been looking for."

"It appears so."

"Maybe it will just turn out to be a brown dwarf. Remember your brown dwarf?"

It probably surprises me as much as it does him that I chuckle instead of trying to slam the door on his stupid face.

I've been trying hard all day to remember that feeling I had at Bruno's. Not the one of colossal relief, which I don't have to work at remembering, but the one just before that, as I stood on the lanai. When I saw Patrick Stewart in the mango tree. Okay, I can laugh; it wasn't exactly a classic Damascene conversion. But something happened to me there, just for a moment. Something serious. Something important. I had a glimpse of a better self somehow. A healthier self. Why shouldn't my self be able to improve, to get better the way a cold does, a bruise, a cut? Why should my elbow be smarter than my brain?

So I'm taking it for a test drive, this better self. Just to see how it runs so far. I'm not expecting a whole new personality overnight.

So at work this morning, the day after I got back from Hilo, I surprised Louisa with a dozen roses and a thank you note for taking my class, and I left another dozen in a vase for Joan on her desk before she came in.

"Who are these for?" Joan asked suspiciously.

"For you."

"Who are they from?"

"From me."

She stared. "Why?"

I kept smiling. "Just to thank you for holding the fort while I was away. I don't thank you enough for keeping the office running."

It was likely the last thing she thought she'd ever hear me say. That I wasn't completely sincere, I thought, shouldn't matter. I'd work up to sincere. I hoped it would be one of those behaviour modification things: change the behaviour and the attitude changes, the way you're supposed to be able to make yourself happy by smiling. When I thought about how to go about becoming a better person, I concluded that one way, surely, was just by being nicer to people, especially those you didn't have to be nice to.

When I get to my classroom I make myself walk in grinning, aiming for a nice, easy smile, not my usual stiff, ironic one. I tell them about the new Earth-like planet around Gliese 581, try to get them to feel its significance. It's there, maybe, on one or two faces, but the rest have that same exhausted will-this-be-on-the-exam look, and a part of me feels sad and even a little guilty about that. Then I hand out photocopies of the Walt Whitman poem. I have to remember to thank Kate for the idea.

"I came across this poem on my desk," I say casually. "It's a reminder to all of us that astronomy isn't just about the math and the science. It's about getting out into the country some clear night and looking up and letting yourself be completely awed."

I ask one of the students to read the poem aloud, and he does, stumbling over so many words I have to stop myself from putting my hand over his mouth. I watch the other faces, tell myself not to look for one that seems sneering or sly, tell myself that's not why I brought in the poem. So what if I won't know who left it for me? This is a good test of my negative capability.

"So what do you think?" I ask. "Isn't that a great poem?"

A desk creaks, there's a cough, nobody making eye contact, nobody answering.

"Well, it is," I say. "Read it again sometime. Okay." I clap my hands together, more heartily than I intended, making some of them jump. "So, how many of you would like an open-book final?"

There's some shuffling of feet, whispers, wary glances, and then one after the other the hands go up.

"All right, then. Open-book it is. You're a smart bunch. You'll ace it."

The wary glances tip over into incredulous, but there are also tentative smiles, relieved murmurs. Fleming's losing his mind, they might be saying; and I don't care.

They don't know, of course, that one of the reasons I don't care is that I had lunch with Kilbride and told him I was applying for the deanship. With him in my corner I can't see myself losing it. So this might be the last class I ever teach. Maybe I'll miss it. I don't know. But I think I'd make a better administrator than a teacher.

Besides, in my department I'm very obviously no longer the hotshot of the year. The new technology is beyond me. And I can't bring in the big grants any more. I haven't published anything for a year, and my last research project on neutrinos was an embarrassing washout. I don't want to become the old guy dining out on past glories who can't learn anything new. I don't want to be reading theses by young geniuses like Peterson when I no longer really understand them.

Well. That last one was hard to admit. But there it is. The scientific brain burns out early. The administrative brain, on the other hand, can take you right into senility. Examples abound. You can have the power and the salary and you don't have to keep proving you deserve them.

Before I go home I check my email. There's an address I recognize, though it's been a while since I've seen it. Or used it. It's from the JAC in Hilo.

I skip to the signature. Bruno. My breathing goes shallow. Now what?

Avey —

Thought you'd like to know what Perry here just told me. Seems our friend Hale is off on sick leave. Something serious, I gather. Something terminal. To do with his liver. His meds are screwing up his metabolism, so that's why he's gained weight. Anyway. Poor bastard. Thought you'd like to know.

Bruno

I lean back in my chair, stare at the screen. *Something terminal.* Hale's dying.

To my surprise I realize I'm feeling the same way Bruno does: poor bastard. Beautiful Hale, still so young. Maybe there's always some immediate lurch of identification there, even when it's someone you don't like, even when it's someone you wanted to kill a few days ago.

If he's dying that might explain his obsession with my confessing to Bruno. Hale just transferred his own illness to him. A psychiatrist would love it. Well, hadn't Bruno and I said Hale wasn't as simple as he seemed?

I sit here for a while just looking at the screen. The terminal. The place things end.

I suppose I'm still waiting for some relief, even satisfaction, to hit me. I wonder why it doesn't. After all, if Hale dies I'm not going to have to be looking over my shoulder the rest of my life, wondering if he'll pop up again. Is this my better self responding? Maybe it's because in a surely unintended way Hale did me a favour by making me confess: not only is that burden off my conscience but I realize it could have been fifty pounds lighter all along.

Joan is standing at the door. It gives me a start. She's wearing her faded green cardigan with at least two missing buttons, and she pulls it across her chest now with both hands as though she's cold.

"Yes?"

"Dr. Fleming. About the flowers." She looks down at her feet, then back up at me, or rather at some point above my right ear. "I really appreciated that. I've been feeling ... as though you thought I was doing an awful job. I've been feeling ..." Her eyes drop again. "I've gone home crying some nights."

"Ah, Joan." She's gone home *crying?* I stand up, make some kind of gesture at her. I'm glad the desk is between us, because I don't know what kind of physical contact I should offer. "I'm sorry," I say. "I'm truly sorry."

And I am. She's about the last secretary I would have chosen from the secretary store, but she has the right not to go home crying.

"I feel as though you think I'm too old and stupid to do the job. I know you've made jokes about how I'm in the Witless Protection Program."

Shit. Who would have told her that?

I give a little wincing laugh. "That was just — it wasn't a joke about *you*. It was a joke about a *typo*."

"Well, that's the point. It was just a typo. It wasn't because I can't spell."

"Of course not. Your spelling is fine."

"I was going to quit," she says. "Take early retirement. I was just feeling so bad here."

"I didn't know." I start to explain that it never occurred to me she would be that sensitive, but that hardly seems appropriate. So I say instead, "I get so tied up in my own problems I guess I don't realize I can be kind of, well, impatient sometimes."

Her big eyes are glistening. "Thank you," she says. "So — and please be honest — do you want me to quit? Or I could apply for a transfer. I will if you want me to."

This is my chance: I could say, gently, that maybe it's a good idea, that maybe we need to be free of each other. But I can see on her face that isn't what she wants to hear. I swallow.

"I don't, Joan. You know the job. You know me." I give an embarrassed laugh that might imply nobody else could stand me.

"Okay." She smiles, nods, turns to go, then turns back. "I have to leave half an hour early today," she says. "I hope that's all right." My own smile must have turned sardonic because she adds, "I'm not taking advantage. I'll make it up tomorrow."

"It's fine. Go."

I sink back down in my chair, watch the door close behind her. I had my chance to get rid of her, and I let it go. If I did the right thing, the thing my better self expected, then why do I feel less than happy? It occurs to me that since I now seem like a human being to her there's a possibility that if I get the dean's job she might want to come with me, the way the current dean's old secretary did.

I sigh. Doing the right thing comes back to bite you in the ass as much as doing the wrong thing does.

By the time I'm ready to leave the office I'm feeling better, though. Surely what happened with Joan is okay, is a positive thing for both of us. All in all, I decide, it hasn't been a bad day. I remind myself that tomorrow I have a meeting with Peterson to discuss the state of his dissertation, which is not good. He is way behind schedule and has hopelessly over-researched. Now he's fretting not one but two foot-notes into two whole new chapters. I suppose I'll have to cave and give him his three-month extension, though it will mean I'll have to slog through the damned thing in the summer. As I found out with Joan, it costs one something, this being a better person.

I drive home slowly, down Marine Drive, the windows open, breath-ing in the cool, damp, briny air. There's a faint smell of sap, too, sleep-ing things stirring back to life. It's hard to believe yesterday at this time I was in Hilo, talking to Bruno. It seems like weeks have passed since then. CBC is playing something symphonic from Bach that sounds as though it's been recorded in an emphysema ward, but I don't change the station.

I sneak in through the side basement door and pick up the package for Kate I've given a quick wrap in red foil paper and trot up the stairs with it. Last night I took a cab back from the airport, and Kate was al-ready in bed, so we only mumbled a few words of greeting at each other, and she had left for work when I got up this morning, so this is my first chance to give her her present.

She's sitting on the loveseat in the den flipping through a real estate catalogue. She's wearing one of her ugly old oversized shirts, this one with a bleach stain on the arm, and she has her hair pulled into a lop-sided ponytail at the back of her neck. On the end table beside her is not just a glass of red wine but the bottle as well. Something's not right. I'm wishing I'd brought her something nicer, a real present.

"Hiya," I say. "Brought you a prezzie from Hilo." I hand her the package.

"Thank you," she says. She doesn't look at me.

Definitely something wrong. There's this weird tension in the room, pitched just above the range of hearing. Kate picks at the tape which now seems to me to be strangling the package like a thick noose. Finally she gets a finger under it, tearing the paper.

"Remember?" I ask. "It can't be the same one, I mean, surely it can't, but it looks the same, and it was sitting there in exactly the same place. I don't know why I picked it up. Anyway. Thought you'd get a kick out of it."

She stares at the slipper. Finally she says, "It's supposed to be glass, isn't it?"

"Gla — Oh, right. Good one. Good one." She made a joke. That's got to be a good sign.

Without actually touching the slipper, she picks it up in its red wrapping and sets it carefully, as though it's a pile of razor-sharp shards, onto the end table, and then she looks up at me.

"Hey," I say as though I'm only just noticing. "What's wrong?" I sit down opposite her. The cat jumps up into my lap. "Go see Kate," I tell him. "She's got such a preeeeetty lap."

Both the cat and Kate pretend I haven't said anything.

"Kate. Come on."

"I don't know how to do this. So I'll just tell you. Hale came to see me while you were away. He told me about you stealing your discovery from Bruno. He told me about your bargain. About how he wouldn't say anything about it if you ... gave me to him. I didn't want to believe him, but I think I do."

Jesus *Christ*. I should have seen this coming, but I so completely did not.

God *damn* that bastard. Why is he so determined to ruin my life?

I can feel myself getting mad at Kate, too, of all irrational things, simply because she *knows*, because no matter how much I apologize now she's never going to stop knowing this about me. It's not as though I don't think she'll eventually forgive me — it's that I'm going to be forever diminished in her eyes. And why? Why the hell is that necessary, Hale, you fucking son-of-a-bitch?

My hand on the cat's head must have been imagining it was closing around Hale's throat because the cat gives a moan and jumps off my lap. I lean forward.

"Ah, Kate." Where do I start? "Look, the whole thing was this huge, stupid mistake. Bruno and I actually had a good laugh about it yesterday. As it turns out, he had in fact stolen some of *my* work so I just stole it back. But it was my bad luck that Hale saw me."

"Bruno stole something from you?"

"Yes, yes. His program was screwed up so he took mine. I'd spent weeks writing code and getting it to run properly. Without it he'd never have made the discovery."

"But you didn't know he'd done that, did you, when you claimed it was your discovery?"

"Well, no, but ... now we're even, I guess."

"And to buy Hale's silence you essentially sold me off to him?"

"It wasn't like that. Hale just said he wanted to spend more time with you. I thought, what's the harm? I wasn't your owner, I didn't have the right to say yes or no." I reach over and try to take her hand but she pulls it away, shoves it under her thigh.

"You knew how he would take it. He thought you were stepping aside so he could ... have me. You sent me up to Mauna Kea with him. When I told him nothing more could happen between us he locked me out of the observatory. I was absolutely terrified. I don't think he intended it to go so far, but I thought I'd freeze to death. I didn't tell you about it because I didn't want you to be angry with him."

"Jesus. I'm sorry. Really. I had no idea he'd do something like that."

"Well. He did."

"He's dying, you know. Hale."

"What?" Her hand goes to her throat. The real estate catalogue falls to the floor. She ignores it.

"Hale's dying. Bruno told me. Some fatal illness. That's why he looks so bad now."

She's more upset by the news than I'd have expected. "Poor Hale," she says. "He was ... interesting. Complicated."

"Complicated. That's a nice word for it."

She starts picking at a thread on her shirt cuff, both pulling it loose and then trying to tuck it back into the seam. I'm wondering if it's over, if we've talked this through enough to satisfy her, when she says, "So, was it worth it? What you did, to Bruno, to me, to Hale, to yourself, was it worth it?"

What kind of answer can I make to that? I shift on my seat.

"I ... thought it was at the time," I say.

"And now?"

"Now? Well, I mean, it gave me all this —" I gesture vaguely around, raising my hand high above my head to show I mean more than just the house. "It gave me this life, the life I wanted. But it gave me guilt, too. A great whacking truckload. All this time thinking I'd cheated Bruno out of something. And he called me a pimp. That's not exactly the kind of career path I'd imagined for myself." I laugh. She doesn't. Shit. Why did I have to give her that word?

She drains her glass of wine. She looks flushed, feverish.

"I know —" She pauses. "I know you think I'm angry with you. And I was. But I'm not anymore. Because I'm to blame, too, for what happened."

"Yeah?" I raise an eyebrow.

"I didn't want to tell you. I didn't think it would serve any purpose. But you've the right to know. To know the guilt isn't all yours. If I'd told you at the time you probably wouldn't have made your bargain with Hale."

"What are you talking about?" I'm not liking this, not liking this at all.

"The second time I saw Hale in Hilo I slept with him."

I gape at her. "What?"

"It was —"

I leap to my feet. "You *slept* with *Hale?*"

"It was ... this impulse. It was just the one time. It was a horrible mistake. I made it clear we could never do it again."

I'm having a hard time breathing. My arms are pumping up and down as though they want to make me airborne. Jesus. Jesus.

"So that's why Hale wanted that stupid bargain! No wonder he did! No wonder he thought that if I just stepped out of the way you'd be free for the picking."

"If you hadn't had me as a bargaining chip Hale might not have agreed to take the blame for you."

I can tell from her voice even she knows that doesn't work as an excuse. She *slept* with the guy. With Hale. With my worst enemy.

"You tell me he did this creepy thing to you on Mauna Kea and make me think it's *my* fault! Well, who knows what I can believe? Who knows what you two really did up there?"

"That was the truth. I —"

"This is so fucking *cheap*. You had an *affair*. Jesus Christ. All these years, there were women I could have had with a snap of my fingers, but, no, hey, I'm tempted but I know where to draw the line. I have a wife. I don't cheat on my wife."

"I can't justify what I did. I've been ashamed of it ever since."

"So why? Just tell me why."

"I was ... lonely, I guess, missing Edmonton, missing my life there, missing David. Hale reminded me of David."

"Oh, that makes me feel so much better. Knowing he reminded you of David. I've never been able to compete with David. Nobody can compete with the dead first husband. Life with him was perfect. Life with him would still be perfect. No need for affairs when one has a perfect husband."

She winces, won't look at me. "That's not fair," she murmurs.

"Sleeping with Hale wasn't fair, either."

The more I think about her with him the more furious I get. I can see them together, naked, naked. I feel my hand turning into a fist. And I want to hit her, oh dear God don't let me don't let me, want to hit her right under her left eye, knowing how to do it in a way I have feared all my life might be hard-wired into my brain because it's what I saw again and again for over half of my life.

I turn and slam the fist toward the wall. At the last minute I open my hand so it's just my flat palm that hits. Even so, it rattles the picture on the wall a foot to my left. It's the one the Astronomical Society gave me.

I grab hold of it, jerk it down. The nail pops from the wall.

"Avey! Don't!"

I sail the picture across the room. It clips the CD stand, and jewel cases spill out across the floor. The glass in the frame doesn't shatter, but I can hear a crack as the picture lands. Something has broken.

"It didn't belong to me in the first place," I say.

The cat tiptoes in from the kitchen, his tail bristled, assessing the damage.

"I'm so sorry, Avey. It was just that one time." She's staring at the picture on the floor. Her face has gone pale.

She's afraid of me. Contempt for both of us lurches in my gut, a hard spasm, nausea. I take deep breaths, try to imagine them cooling the hot rage. Okay. Be calm. You're okay. You didn't hit Kate. You're not your old man.

I go into the kitchen, prop my hands onto the sides of the sink and stare out at the yard, the cedar hedge trimmed to a degree of precision that suddenly seems contemptible.

I don't know how long I stand there. Twenty minutes, maybe. At some point my legs get too tired to support me and I sink down to the floor, sit with my knees pulled up and my back against the cupboard doors. One of the knobs digs into my spine. They are new and expensive, those knobs, forty dollars each.

Slowly my breathing comes back to normal. The rage ebbs, and then there's just this ... dullness, this *sadness*. The one person I trusted completely: that she'd sleep with someone else is the last thing, the absolutely last thing, I thought she could do. And with *Hale*. With that goddamned piece of shit Hale. The only thing worse than sleeping with your husband's best friend is sleeping with his worst enemy.

But there it is. I have to deal with it.

I think of the good day I've had. *Hubris*. Isn't that the word? It's only in retrospect, of course, only when something bad happens later, that you'd call feeling good *hubris*. I thought I had turned toward some better direction for my life, but apparently the real test of my better self was yet to come. Here it is. Right here.

Just that one time, she said.

All right. I can survive this. We can survive this.

Forgiving her will be hard, but I can do it if I put my mind to it. I can make myself believe she just used the same thermometer of poor judgement as I did. I can make myself believe she won't do it again.

I go back to the den. Kate doesn't seem to have moved. I sit down again opposite her. For a long time we don't say anything. The cat bats at one of the jewel cases on the floor. We watch him until, disappointed at our silence, he walks away.

"I'm sorry about the picture thing," I say. "There's no excuse for that."

"It's okay."

The phone rings. The answering machine picks up, and we listen to a voice from Kate's office about some cancelled meeting.

"Lucky you," I say. "You didn't want to go to that meeting, anyway." I've no idea if she did or not.

"Not particularly."

"Well. Good. Here we are. Just normal again. Having a normal domestic conversation."

"Avey —"

"Well, isn't that what we should do? Just get on with it? Pretend it never happened?" I expect to hear a sour bite of irony in my voice, but I don't. I suppose that's how I know I really want just-getting-on-with-it to be the solution.

"It's not that easy."

"So what do you want us to do? Talking isn't going to change anything. Women always think if they talk for hours they'll understand something better. But what more is there to understand? We can keep on pouting and sulking and blaming each other, but it's a waste of time. I did something bad, you did something bad. Let's just try to forgive each other and get on with our lives."

"I think ... I want to go home," Kate says. "Back to Edmonton."

"What? Edmonton? You were just there a month ago."

"I mean to live. To move back there."

I stare at her. "You're kidding, right? Why would we want to move back to *Edmonton?*"

"I never wanted to leave in the first place. It's always felt like home. And Vancouver hasn't. I'm lonely here."

"*Lonely?* You know tons of people here. You even know the neighbours. How can you be lonely?"

"I want to go back, that's all."

And then it hits me, what she's really saying. "You want to go back whether I go with you or not."

She doesn't answer, doesn't look at me.

I swallow. The room is looking fuzzy, the edges of things blurring. "So ... look, I'm reeling here. I'm just getting my head around the fact you slept with that snake Hale, and now you want to *leave* me. Jesus Christ, Kate. Jesus Christ. Is this about Hale? Did he put you up to this?"

"No, no, of course not. But maybe what he told me was, well, the catalyst."

"The catalyst. I don't understand you. What happened in Hawaii was twelve years ago. Haven't we been okay together? I thought we were doing okay together."

"We betrayed each other —"

"Twelve *years* ago!"

"We're still the same people. We — Oh, I don't know, we don't care enough, we let each other get away with things. We did then and we do now."

"Things, what things? You're not making sense. You think I don't love you? I love you. You *know* that." My panic is the same I felt when I saw the curve on Bruno's computer, my mind flailing about desperately looking for a solution. Now I can't even think of a lunatic one, a computer to unplug, a janitor to bribe. It's not up to me. How did we get from me deciding to forgive her to *this?*

"I'm not trying to punish you. It's not about that. I want to move back to Edmonton." She pauses. "There's nothing to stop you from doing that, too."

"Edmonton. That's just — I can't do that. I can't leave my position at the university. That would be crazy. I'm on the verge of getting the deanship. I'm not going to go begging for some little lecture job at U of A. How could you ask that of me? Look, we can work this out. We can get beyond this. Can't we?"

And then I wish I could take back the question, because there are only two answers, and one of them I can't bear to hear.

The clock in the kitchen chimes. Seven o'clock.

KATE

Seven o'clock. Seven small pings of sound. In the silence they sound loud as tolling churchbells. It's getting dark, the first of the three stages of twilight. The furnace clicks on, a sighing in the house.

My eyes drop to the slipper in its clumsy wrappings. Poor Avey: he thought he was bringing me something to make me laugh, but instead I just sat thinking it was something I should mail back to Pele. Though it doesn't really belong to her, either. Poor shoe, that nobody wants.

"I'm sorry," I say. "I've made up my mind."

"So what have I done all this for?" Avey waves his hand in the air. "Worked my ass off. Why, if not for you?"

"I'm just a small part of it, Avey. I always was."

"For Pete's sake. Kate."

I can see how alarmed he is. I hate seeing him like that, knowing I am the cause.

"You'll be fine without me."

"I *won't* be fine without you."

"Maybe you'll be better than fine. I was never ... well-suited to you. Maybe my, my casualness about things just made you more driven, made you think you had to pick up the slack." What I don't add is that probably the personality that made David happy with me only irritated Avey.

"Driven. I like the way you almost take responsibility for something and then turn it around to make it an accusation about me."

"I didn't mean —"

"Okay, okay. Driven. Maybe I was. Maybe I am. You want me to change. Well, I can change. I know I can be an asshole sometimes. There. I admit it. But today was — I was going to tell you about it, today was — I mean, before I got home. After I got home you have to admit everything got nuts. But before that, at work, I tried to be a better person. Yeah, yeah, it sounds hokey, it sounds phoney, it sounds superficial, but I made a promise to myself in Hilo that I would try to be a better person. All day at work I tried to be a better person, a nicer person. You can ask people, they'll say, hey, maybe Fleming's turned over a new leaf."

"For one day anybody can be nice."

"You don't believe me. You don't think I want to change."

"It's not that easy to change," I say.

"Of course it's not *easy*. But I'm making a *start*. It's not as though today I took a bullet for somebody, or quit my job to run an orphanage in China or something, but, I mean, it doesn't work like in the movies, some big cinemascope sacrifice. It's little things. It's *trying*. It's hearing Cheswick needling me and not slamming the door in his face. It's — there was this thing with Joan. I was, well, just *decent* to her. Maybe

I can look back on this day twenty years from now and say, *this* was my biggest discovery, the beginning of my true self, my better self. Why couldn't it happen that way?"

I know Avey is sincere, is not just loosely tethered to the truth to get what he wants. It takes all the will I have not to relent, to go to him, to say it will all be okay, that I won't leave.

"You could move back to Edmonton, too."

"Stop saying that. I've told you I can't. I hate that fucking city. You're making it sound as though you're giving me a choice, but you're not. This is just selfish of you. Selfish."

"That's probably true. Maybe it just feels like ... my turn."

"*Your turn?* It's been your turn your whole easy, lazy life."

I think about it. "I guess that can be true, too."

"I hate when you do that, pretend to agree just to avoid an argument."

"But we're not avoiding it, are we?"

The furnace clicks off with a gentle shudder. Then the house is utterly quiet, the way it is the few seconds after a power failure, before you quite understand, before you get up and fumble for candles, before you have to improvise.

*

I've driven without stopping, over the Coquihalla, which still has snow at the elevation where the toll booths are, and through Kamloops. I'll have to get gas soon, but I'm reluctant to stop.

Mostly I have just felt numb. There was a brief time when, at Hope, starting up the hill of Highway 5, I felt a kind of excitement, exhilaration, as though, yes, this was the beginning of a new adventure. But now I seem to have gone back into a sluggishness that simply directs me to press my foot on the gas pedal and stare at the oncoming road.

I was cowardly about leaving, waiting until Avey was at work and then packing my bags and leaving him only a cryptic note. I told myself he would be expecting to find me gone, but I couldn't convince myself. I had never, after all, opposed his wishes in anything really important. My turn, I'd said. I think suddenly of my grandmother, how when she was old she'd want us to play board games with her but didn't care about the rules. No matter whose play it was, she'd shout, "My turn! My turn!" All I understood then was that she was cheating. I don't know how I understand it now. It's not a comforting memory.

I have tried not to think about when Avey comes home. If I let myself feel what he feels I would turn around and go back. This is not a tidy parting.

Last year my cousin in Quebec told me that when she and her husband divorced they had one last romantic rendezvous — wine, a catered meal, sex — because they wanted, as the French would say, *finir en beauté*. Well, I'm not doing that, obviously. But it is hard to think of endings as anything but sad, burdened with regret and loss and fear of what comes next.

I stop at Heffley Creek for gas. A middle-aged man at the adjoining pump says loudly to his wife coming out of the washroom, "Hurry up! I'm freezing my unmentionables off!"

I smile. An eavesdroplet for my mother.

The man is right, though — the air is cold, raising goosebumps on my bare arms. The sun which has kept my Honda warm all day has lost its strength and is slicing in low from the west now. Once Avey and I did the drive to Edmonton all in one day, but I don't think I can manage it; I'll have to look for a motel soon.

I have never in my life stayed alone in a motel room.

"Well, then it's time you did," I say to the rearview mirror as I turn back onto the road. My eyes look back dubiously. But there are many things I will have to learn to do alone now.

A curve turns me northwest into the sun, and I fumble for my sunglasses in my purse on the seat beside me. I find the case, but as I pull it out my fingers touch something unfamiliar. I grope at it, puzzled. It's something hard and has a paper wrapped around it with a thin rubber band. It feels like a rock, the kind you would see in movies thrown through windows, the note saying something threatening like, "You're next." I'm disconcerted enough that I pull to the side of the road, stop.

I stare at the object blankly. Surely I would remember, even in the dazed state I was in as I packed, putting something like this in my purse. Carefully I pull at the rubber band. It snaps off, shoots itself against the windshield, making me jump. The paper unfolds.

And inside I see the piece of lava I gave to Hale when we met at the planetarium. The next day he must have slipped it into my purse as it sat under the table at the restaurant.

I smooth the paper out on the dashboard. It's a photocopy of a page from a book, and I recognize the Walt Whitman poem about astronomers, the one Avey said had been left for him anonymously by one of his students. But it must have been Hale who left it. And now he's given me a copy. Maybe it's some kind of test, to see if I know the implications of the poem, to see if Avey shared it with me and if I will now share this with him. And will I? I can send it to him from Edmonton, I suppose; he has the right to know he shouldn't accuse any students, though it might upset him even more to think of Hale's intrusion into yet another part of his life.

I turn the paper over. Written in the middle, in a careful script more printed than cursive, it says,

> *Sometimes the bad luck*
> *is the truth.*
> *I'm sorry.*

I look at it so long the words stop making sense. Hale has arranged them on the page like another poem, a kind of haiku, or a koan, whose purpose is to make the reader supply some of the meaning. What was he thinking as he wrote this? He says he is sorry, but he returns to me the piece of lava which allegedly carries the bad luck.

Finally I just shake my head. It is all so deliberately enigmatic and melodramatic.

"Oh, Hale," I say out loud.

I rewrap the lava and return the package to my purse. I can't think of what else to do with it.

I pull back onto the road. But I keep thinking about Hale. He's dying, Avey said. It's hard to believe. He's still so young. I think of him in the restaurant, his hands around his cup of chai, his face, his mouth, his lips that I have kissed, and I blink at the sudden, blurring tears.

Twelve years ago, in Hilo, Avey and I made a bargain.

Is this what he wished for me, this leaving? If he is dying, his revelations about Avey could have produced no personal benefit for him. Was it still some revenge for my rejection of him all those years ago? I called him a puppetmaster, and he seemed more pleased than insulted.

I'll never know his reasons for sure. He doesn't want me to. Con-
fessions by the dying are supposed to be free of worldly motive, the
truth some final pure thing we hold out in our unclenching fingers, but
it can just as easily be some last grenade we hurl back as the portal closes.
I have heard that when people think about death and dying, they want
to punish their enemies and reward their friends. Am I Hale's friend or
enemy? Is the truth a reward or a punishment?

I think of the truth I hurled at Avey, about sleeping with Hale. I
told myself it was something he had a right to know, and I told Avey it
was something that would lessen his own guilt, that would make him
see how incomplete our relationship was if we could do such things to
each other. But perhaps I simply wanted him to feel as betrayed as I did.
Maybe I shouldn't have told him. What purpose did it serve? Will it help
either of us to accept my leaving?

I drive on, following the Thompson, north, north, back to Alberta.
I think of my future there, the people I can be with again: my parents,
Sandy, my aunts and uncle and cousins, David's parents, my old friends
Ingrid and Laura and Melanie, my co-workers at the office where I used
to work and where I have kept in touch, have referred clients a few
times: I know working there again will be possible. It is the life and place
I unwillingly gave up to follow Avey. Land memory.

The one radio station I can get is thick with static, but I don't turn it
off. Right now it's playing John Denver's "Rocky Mountain High." The
lyrics penetrate the static in odd little bursts, and I try to hum along in
between, but I'm always a few notes behind.

In Clearwater I check into a motel, a room that smells of Lysol and
cigarettes but that has the reassurance of a firm mattress, a toilet that
flushes, familiar laugh tracks on the TV.

I remember I promised to call Carol at work. She had, of course,
been more than willing to assume my listings. "Take all the time you
need," she said, when I told her, guiltily, there was a family emergency.

I'm not surprised that she's still in the office.

"Anything new?" I ask.

"Nope. Oh, maybe a strange email. It came in to the general box,
but I think it must be for you. Made no sense to me. The header said
something about Karols? Karolyis?"

"Yes, that would be for me." I assume it's from the new owners, wanting confirmation that the Karolyis are gone.

"Want me to pull it up for you?"

"Please."

The Karolyis: what has happened to them, I wonder.

"Here it is. The English is a hoot. Okay. *'Dearly Kate, I am brother to Anna. Yuri Karolyi have this business card has your name. He say Anna took money for me to help. So I help. But Anna is too much. I pay back half to Karolyi. So now you know.'* That's it. There's no signature. Does it make sense?"

"Yes. I guess it does." I can tell she wants me to explain, but I only say I will get in touch with her again when my plans are more definite.

I fall back on the bed, smiling. Surely the message is good news. The Karolyis have arrived safely. Anna actually has a brother and he doesn't sound as though he is in some mafia. A door has cracked open and it's the face of human decency peeking through. My attempt at philanthropy, then, has not been a total failure. I might try it again. If people tell me I'm crazy I can tell them that giving money away to the homeless is not just ethical in these rabid real estate markets but for a realtor is entirely logical, a kind of self-interest.

I smile at the thought, but, as I head to the diner across the highway, the idea accumulates enough gravity to actually slow my steps. Why not, I think. Really, why not? I might be motivated to make money if I didn't have to keep it.

The diner is small, smells slightly of gasoline, and has paintings of horses for sale on the walls. I'm the only customer. I'm ravenous, I realize: I haven't had anything but coffee for ten hours. I order something with no meat but lots of fat french fries, which arrive on the barely edible side of burned. I ketchup them into flexibility. For dessert I have the huge cinnamon bun I saw in the display case. It's the best cinnamon bun I ever ate.

As I head back to the motel my eyes are drawn to the pleats of the Aurora Borealis in the north. They are low in the sky, crepe-paper streamers caught in the tree branches.

"Hello," I say, because I haven't seen them for years. In the southern hemisphere the aurora are now appearing simultaneously and symmetrically, a mirror-image of what I'm seeing here.

I walk down to the river and sit on the bank, listen to the rattle of the water on the rocks. I can no longer see the horizon: the last stage of twilight is over. Above me the night sky is rich with stars, the moon only a thin slice.

Just twelve years ago I would have looked up at the sky and not known for sure there were other planets beyond our solar system. Now it's impossible not to think of them there. At least one is a planet like ours.

I remember the night in Hilo when Avey and I walked down to the park. He showed me where his star was. I might be able to see it from here if I knew where to look. He said he would name his planet after me. Though I wound up being only a brown dwarf.

Oh, Avey. Already I miss him, miss his need of me, I suppose. But I have always made things too easy for him, allowed him to do everything he wanted. But I was the one who slept with someone else. Of all such betrayals in a marriage isn't that the worst? *I did something bad. You did something bad.* But just balancing our transgressions against each other is a childish answer, means that nobody has to admit fault or responsibility. *Now we're even,* Avey said of Bruno. Surely it's not that simple.

We are not stones, though; we can try to soften our natures. When Avey said he had tried yesterday to be a better person I was dismissive. But how else do we change, except by simply starting one day? It's not impossible. Maybe he will even decide to move back to Edmonton. But I don't think he will. He would hate it too much there, hate me for making him do it. Maybe he was right when he said I wasn't really offering him a choice. Maybe it was a test I was giving him knowing he would fail.

A shooting star. It falls into the northern forest.

My father taking me along on a business trip to the Peace River country once: we stood out at night beside a field of rustling barley, him pointing at the falling stars, so many of them, a meteor shower, him telling me it's where we all came from, ancient collisions of matter. He pointed out the faint, round glow of Gegenschein in the southeast, said it was the sunlight reflecting from tiny particles of asteroidal dust, that it was related to a daylight phenomenon called "the glory" he'd seen from airplanes. I'd loved the words: Gegenschein, the glory. Names for ghosts of light.

My father and I stood there for a long time, staring up at the sky, the uncountable stars. He told me we were really looking into the past, that the light from the stars set out on its brave voyage to us centuries ago, that all those suns might be gone now, long dead.

So our own light travels out, too, into space, telling the story of what we once were. Somewhere out there in the light our past is still alive.

Somewhere in that light David is still alive.

Tears blur my eyes: remembering, remembering. That terrible sadness, that yearning for what is gone.

Am I here now, heading back to Edmonton, because I am still looking for what is gone? Looking for David, for a ghost of light, looking for that happiness again?

Nobody can compete with the dead first husband. Life with him was perfect. Life with him would still be perfect. Avey's cruel words. Perhaps I deserve such mockery. Is there something unhealthy, neurotic, in what I am doing?

Maybe so. But I have just told myself that I am not a stone, that I can change. The brain, that small clever planet, is capable of more than history. Every day, whether I want it to or not, it grows new neurons, learns new things, invents itself. Surely someday it will learn how to let David go.

I stare up at the wonderful sky. There is the swirl of the Milky Way, looking so distant I have to remind myself that we belong to it, too, that we are part of it, that we have named as other what is only our own arm.

How crowded the darkness is with stars. But of course there is almost unimaginable distance between them, unimaginable emptiness. Though apparently it's not emptiness: space is filled with invisible dark matter and dark energy. The dark energy is making the universe expand, but for now the dark matter is still exerting enough gravity to hold galaxies together. Scientists say that they don't know what the dark matter is but that it's not like us, the ordinary atoms and molecules. But how can they be sure? It was born of that same great burst of beginning as we were. And now there is another bewildering force, the "dark flow," that is drawing galaxy clusters at millions of miles an hour to a point beyond the cosmological horizon, beyond the knowable universe, beyond our point of origin, calling us not just home but beyond home, before home.

Oh, don't anthropomorphize, Avey would say, don't be silly. Yes, yes.

In the northern part of the Andromeda constellation right above me is the fuzzy splotch that is a whole other galaxy. I said something to Avey that night in the park about how from far enough away there are no individuals, how everything becomes a kind of great collective, a forest of light.

Is that a comfort, to think that from far enough away Vancouver, Edmonton, Hilo, the small village where I hope the Karolyis now are, and everywhere else on this planet are the same place? To think that every person is the same person? I suppose to me it might be, a comfort: to escape from the lonely self, to be welcome during even our most difficult journeys. Home can be what we carry inside us. I should be able to believe, then, that I belong to where I am right now, here beside this river. And tomorrow I will belong wherever I am then. Besides, didn't I say to Avey that whether something is an anomaly or not depends also on the point of view of the anomaly?

No, that wasn't to Avey. It was to Hale. It doesn't bother me as much as perhaps it should that I have conflated two memories. It's what happens when you look at something from far enough away.

I think of the piece of lava in my purse. It's a foolish bit of sentiment, I know, but I dig it out, unwrap it, rub my thumb one last time on the smooth striations, and then I set it here among its cousin stones. It is absorbed by the darkness.

My eyes start to follow a star that seems to be moving slowly and evenly across the sky: a man-made satellite. There are many up there now. From here they are as big as stars. As big as galaxies. I track it to the west, through the constellation of Ursa Major.

I find some of the other constellations, then — Cassiopeia, Taurus, Gemini, Pegasus — drawn there so long ago by the ancient Greeks and Arabs and not abandoned by modern astronomers, who are no different from them or from the rest of us, I suppose. They look for mysteries and answers to them, look for our origins, our destinies, our kindred ships of atoms who began the same voyage.

Tomorrow I will go to Edmonton. That will be the right answer for me, for now. Perhaps happy people are those who can believe the answer becomes right because they choose it. Around me the sky is filled with light.

Acknowledgements

My thanks to my nephew Brad Gom, who took me to see the James Clerk Maxwell Telescope and answered many questions; to Douglas Pierce-Price, the JAC's Science Outreach Specialist, for his invaluable advice and answers to many more questions; to Jane Greaves, who allowed me to interview her at her office; and to Wendy Light for permission to use the JAC as my setting.

For the factual information in the novel I am grateful in particular to three excellent books on the search for the first exoplanets: *Looking for Earths*, by Alan Boss; *Planet Quest*, by Ken Croswell; and *Other Worlds*, by Michael Lemonick. Any errors in my explanations are without doubt my own. Other books on astronomy that have been useful include *The Whole Shebang* and *Life Beyond Earth*, by Timothy Ferris; *The Astronomers*, by Donald Goldsmith; *The Sky at Night*, by Patrick Moore; *Space Odyssey*, by William Harwood; and *The Cold Light of Dawn: A History of Canadian Astronomy*, by Richard A. Jarrell. Also helpful have been the websites for NASA, the JCMT, the University of Hawaii, and UBC.

The quotations that begin each chapter are readily found in dictionaries of quotations, though the books by Alan Boss and Timothy Ferris introduced me to several of these. The quotation from Robert Kirschner is from his 1991 article in the *Quarterly Journal of the Royal Astronomical Society* and is cited by Timothy Ferris.

Books about Hawaii I have consulted include *Saddle Sojourn*, by Faith Roelofs; *Hawaii The Big Island Revealed*, by Andrew Doughty and Harriett Friedman; *A Concise History of the Hawaiian Islands*, by Dr. Phil Barnes; *Hawaii's Volcanoes*, by Joe Mullins; *Hawaii's Invasive Species*, edited by George W. Staples and Robert H. Cowie; and issues of the *Hawaii Tribune-Herald*, especially the special edition called "Stars Over Mauna Kea."

Walt Whitman's "When I Heard the Learn'd Astronomer" is from *The Comprehensive Reader's Edition of Leaves of Grass* (New York University Press).

Thanks also to Canada Council and the British Columbia Arts Council for their financial assistance; to Rita Patel, George Clulow, and Chris Olson for their help in research; and to the good people at Sumach Press for their continuing support. And most thanks, as always, go to Dale Evoy.

More Fine Fiction from Sumach Press ...